Backstory

Skirmish Cove Mysteries
Book Three

AWARD-WINNING AUTHOR

SUSAN PAGE DAVIS

Scrivenings
PRESS
Quench your thirst for story.
www.ScriveningsPress.com

Published by Scrivenings Press LLC
15 Lucky Lane
Morrilton, Arkansas 72110
https://ScriveningsPress.com

Printed in the United States of America

Paperback ISBN 978-1-64917-297-6

eBook ISBN 978-1-64917-298-3

Editors: Elena Hill and Linda Fulkerson

Cover by www.bookmarketinggraphics.com.

FIRST STORY - NOVEL INN

TO BLUFFS OVERLOOKING BEACH ⇧

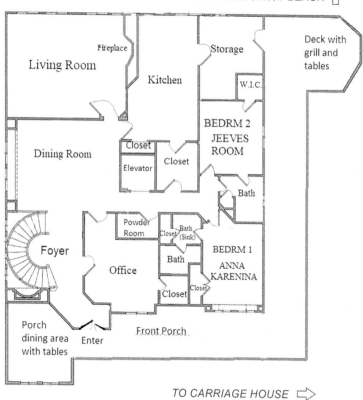

SECOND STORY - NOVEL INN

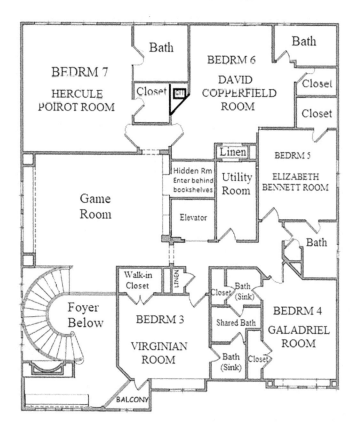

THIRD STORY STORY - NOVEL INN

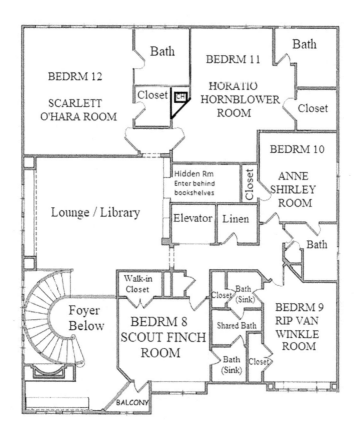

1

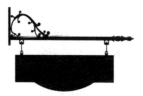

"**Y**ou got some drain cleaner?" Rick Gage looked up at his sister Jillian from where he was hunched over the side of the bathtub.

"Yes, but I've tried that. Twice."

Rick sighed and glared at the inch of water in the bottom of the tub. "What kind was it?"

"Heavy duty." Jillian could see the skepticism on his face. "Hold on. I'll go get it."

"Might as well get me a plunger while you're at it."

Jillian dashed out through the Rip Van Winkle bedroom and across the hall to the third-floor linen closet. She and her sister kept a plunger on each story, in case they or the maids needed it in a hurry. Minor plumbing problems weren't common at the Novel Inn, but once in a while, they cropped up.

She ran back to the bathroom that was shared between two guest rooms. Each side had its own vanity section with a sink and toilet, but the middle section with the tub-shower was shared, with a door on each side. They usually tried to put families, or at least acquaintances traveling together, in Rip Van Winkle and Scout Finch. Two guest rooms on the floor below had the same arrangement, but the rest had private baths.

"Here." She shoved the plunger into her brother's hands. "I've got to run downstairs to get the cleaner. Be right back."

Before he could speak, she was out the door again. The utility room on the second floor was larger than the closet she'd just visited, and it held a washer and dryer as well as cleaning supplies and tools. She ran down the stairs because that was quicker than using the elevator. By the time she got to the utility room and unlocked the door, she was panting.

When she came out with the bottle of drain cleaner in her hands, her sister Kate stood on the stair landing. Jillian made sure the door was locked behind her and walked swiftly to where her sister waited.

"Is that you running around up here?" Kate asked softly.

Jillian nodded. "Getting this for Rick." She held up the bottle.

"Oh. Does he think he can fix it?"

"We don't know yet."

"I sure hope he can."

Jillian blew her bangs off her forehead. "Me too. But don't reserve those two rooms for anyone until we're sure."

"Got it." Below, the desk phone rang. Kate turned and hurried lightly down the curving stairs.

Jillian hauled in a deep breath and climbed to the third story. She was glad none of the guests passed her as she walked briskly by the lounge and down the hall.

Rick was where she'd left him. His sleeves were rolled up, and he was vigorously attacking the tub drain with the plunger.

"This is what I used." She set the bottle of cleaner on the edge of the tub.

He glanced at it and grunted. "And none of the other drains are stopped up?"

"No, just this one. We checked the rooms below, and they seem to be fine."

Rick scrunched up his face and renewed his efforts. After a moment, he stopped and leaned on the side of the tub, staring at the drain.

"I thought it was going to move. Let's see ..." He fumbled with the knob that would turn the water on.

"Wait!" Even as Jillian spoke, water gushed out of the showerhead and soaked Rick's head and shoulders. They both jumped back.

"You coulda warned me!" Rick fumbled for the towel rack.

"I didn't notice it until you turned on the water. Apparently, somebody left the lever up to make it come out of the shower, not the faucet."

Rick muttered as he rubbed a towel over his sopping hair and blotted his wet shirt.

Jillian winced. "So, what do you think?"

"I think you need a plumber."

"But the storm's coming. I don't know if we can get someone here before that."

"Well, it's beyond me."

"But—"

"I'm sorry. I know it will cost money and all that, but I can't fix this. Now, I need to go home and sleep. I'm on day shift tomorrow." Rick dropped the damp towel on the tiled floor. He grabbed his jacket from the second towel rack and headed out. "Let me know what happens," he called over his shoulder.

"Sure," Jillian said bitterly. She stooped for the towel and used it to mop up water that had spilled out onto the floor. The bathmat was wet, too, and she scooped it up to take downstairs.

When she reached the lobby, their night clerk, Don Reece, sat behind the desk. Kate leaned against it, talking to him.

"So, Rick just left," Kate said. "He didn't look happy."

"He was sopping wet," Don said. "What happened?"

"He couldn't fix the tub. We'll have to call a plumber."

Kate frowned. "It's too late tonight."

"I know." Jillian sighed. "I've got to put these in the laundry room. Can you make me a note to make the call first thing in the morning, so I don't forget?"

"Sure." Kate reached for a memo pad and pen.

"I hope you can get someone before Hurricane Cloris gets here," Don said.

Jillian clenched her teeth.

"Do you want to go up and look at it?" Kate asked with a note of hope in her voice.

Don raised both hands. "Not me. I'm not a plumber. Rick's a handy guy. If he can't fix it, I'm sure I can't either."

———

"That hurricane will be here tonight," Kate said the next morning. She grimaced as she turned her back on the radio and pulled three packages of sliced bacon from the refrigerator.

"Right," Jillian said absently as she chopped onions and peppers for the individual omelets. "We'll have to put up the storm shutters. Maybe Rick can get over here and help."

Kate eyed her doubtfully. "After last night? He's not going to want to come back today. At least we only have ten guests this morning." She plunked the bacon on the counter and cut open the first package.

4

Jillian laughed. "*Only* ten guests. Never thought I'd hear you say that."

"I know. It is kind of weird. Last year at this time, we hesitated to reopen the inn, scared to death nobody would come here. And look at us now."

"Nearly full to capacity most of the winter, which is supposed to be the slow season in coastal Maine." Jillian poured egg mixture onto the griddle to begin the first omelet for the inn's guests.

"You mean the dead zone," Kate muttered, immediately feeling a little guilty since they'd been touched by death that winter as well as by success.

Jillian glanced at the clock. "Is the coffee ready? I know at least three people are checking out this morning, and some might want to just grab coffee and go."

"I made sure the hot drinks and cups are all set, and the pastries and muffins. It's too bad we have to cook everything for so few people."

Jillian shook her tongs at Kate. "Hey, we get great marks for our breakfast spread, and I don't want to stop now. I'd cook eggs and bacon if we only had one guest."

Kate frowned but got out the sausage links and started warming a pan for them. While both sisters were good at preparing the breakfast buffet items every morning, Jillian was the omelet expert, no denying that.

A shadow flickered over the glass in the swinging doors between the kitchen and the inn's dining room.

"Oh, there's somebody." Kate hurried out to greet the early rising guests and assure them that hot dishes would be out momentarily.

When she returned to the kitchen, she said, "Mr. Blake's starting with coffee and a bagel, but he would like an omelet."

"Coming right up." Jillian reached for the shredded cheese.

The radio announcer's crisp voice detailed the forecast for Hurricane Cloris, the early tropical storm making its way up the Atlantic coast. "I have a feeling some people will want to leave early to get ahead of that storm."

Kate frowned. "Do you think everyone will leave because of the hurricane?"

"I hope not. At least three rooms are booked for the whole week, and it's only Tuesday. I guess I wouldn't blame them, though. It's not much fun around here when it's pouring rain and the wind is howling at fifty miles an hour." They worked in silence for a couple of minutes, then Jillian handed her a tray. "Here are four omelets. Take them out, along with the bacon. I'll do a few more."

"I guess we'll be eating leftover breakfast for lunch again if the guests don't eat them all." Kate took the tray and pushed through the dining room door, surprised to see half a dozen guests now slowly choosing their meals. It seemed Jillian was right. Their breakfast buffet was both necessary and popular.

"Heading out early, Mr. Blake?" she said to a man filling a cup with orange juice.

"Yeah, it sounds like the driving could be tricky later."

"Well, here's your omelet." Kate fitted the warming tray in place and smiled at him. "Don't forget to take a travel cup of hot coffee with you."

Within an hour, four guests had checked out and left the inn. Later risers straggled in from the elevator or the curved stairway, assuring the sisters they were staying on for at least another night. Kate carried a tray of dirty dishes into the kitchen right behind Jillian, who had just refilled the coffee and hot water urns.

"It's only eight o'clock, and I've checked out four people," Kate moaned.

"It's okay. It might be better to have fewer people here

when the storm hits." Jillian peered out the kitchen window. "It's already overcast, and the trees are blowing like crazy."

Kate went to stand beside her and gazed out toward the whitecaps dotting the bay. "It's not supposed to hit until tonight." The few trees she could see from this vantage point weren't leafed out yet, but their late April buds waved frantically in the blustery air. "Isn't it early in the season for a hurricane?"

"Yes, a little. I guess the main storm is still down the coast, but we're getting the fringe, that's for sure." Jillian's face tightened, and she turned away to start loading the dishwasher.

The radio's newscaster moved on to a report of a jewelry store robbery in Bangor. "... and the clerk did not survive his wounds—"

Kate snapped the broadcast off. "Why don't they just say he died?"

"I think that's the latest euphemism," Jillian said. "At least for news people."

"More proof our language is deteriorating," Kate muttered. Her sister was a former English teacher. The fact that English was fluid and grew from the bottom up was a topic she could expound on for hours.

This time, Jillian didn't answer. The door flew open, and their brother plowed into the kitchen in his full police officer's uniform.

"Morning, ladies."

They greeted him, and Kate said, "Have you eaten?"

"Yeah, but I wouldn't say no to coffee, and maybe a Danish."

"You know where we keep them," Kate replied.

"And maybe a couple slices of bacon." Rick arched his eyebrows at Jillian.

"Go ahead," she said, pouring another omelet. "There's plenty today."

"Great. Thanks."

He ducked back into the dining room.

"Did you check the butter and cream cheese?"

"Yeah, everything's fine," Kate said. "Nobody's eating cereal, so the milk is fine too."

"Comfort food today." Jillian hesitated with the pitcher of egg mixture in her hand. "Okay. I've got six more omelets here. I guess I won't make any more. We'll probably end up eating a couple of them ourselves as it is."

"Let's go sit down with Rick." Kate untied her apron.

"Okay. I'm surprised he came back here so early."

"Me too," Kate said. "He doesn't seem to be upset about last night."

Jillian pushed the plate of fresh omelets into her hands. "Can you take this in? I'm going to see if Zeb's got his flags up."

"In this weather?" Kate said, but she took the plate. Zeb Wilding, their nearest neighbor, was a special friend of Jillian. The retired naval officer used the flagstaff beside his front porch to send messages sailor-style or simply to assure them he was all right.

Only three guests were in the dining room when Kate entered—vacationers Charles and Marie Simon, and Roger Cowper, a salesman who was making the inn his base for a few days while he visited businesses in the surrounding area. Kate transferred the omelets to the buffet table, poured herself a cup of coffee, and joined Rick.

"So, yeah, it's going to hit hard around suppertime, I think," Rick said. He took a bite of his pastry and picked up his coffee mug.

Jillian slid into the chair across from him.

"Did you call the plumber?" Rick asked.

8

"Yeah, just a few minutes ago." Jillian's gaze followed a guest making her way along the buffet counter.

"Great omelet, sis," Rick said. "Even better than Mom's, if it's not a crime to say that."

"If it were a crime, you couldn't take it back," Jillian pointed out. "You have witnesses." She winked at Kate.

Kate flashed her a quick smile. "I was just asking if he could help us get the shutters up."

"I'll try," Rick said. "I've got to check in at the station this morning, and I may be on the front desk a while. I know the sergeant wants us all available to help people with storm prepping, and later to help anyone with trouble. If he doesn't stick me on the desk, I might be able to give you some time while I'm on patrol."

"That would be a big help," Jillian said. "It's the first time we've felt those shutters were needed since we took over, and they're awkward. But we'd understand if you can't help us."

"Tell you what ..." Rick took a big gulp of coffee. "If I can't come, I'll send Dave or Geordie."

His sisters nodded. They knew Skirmish Cove's small police contingent well, and any of the patrol officers would be welcome at the inn, lending a hand with the heavy work. The inn had once been the home of a well-to-do sailing family, and the storm shutters were a bulky holdover from the era before triple-glazed windows.

"We'd probably be okay without them, but the weatherman was saying scary things about flying debris." Kate sipped her coffee and noticed Jillian hadn't fixed any for herself. "Is Zeb okay?" she asked.

Jillian's lips twisted. "His flags aren't flying, as you predicted. But I admit, I'm a little concerned. Is it just because of the weather, or is he ill? I mean, it's eight thirty now ... He's usually up before this. Maybe I should run over."

"You want me to do a wellness check when I leave here?" Rick asked.

"Do you mind?"

"No, I've got my SUV. I'll drive over. That'll be better than you running across the bridge. It's really windy out there already."

"Thanks."

"Aren't you late reporting to work?" Kate asked, glancing at her phone's screen.

"They expect we'll have to work late tonight, so the chief told some of us to come in later."

The Simons had risen and were placing their dirty dishes on the counter by the trashcan. Jillian stood. "Guess it's time to finish loading the dishwasher."

"Yeah, you don't know if you'll have power to run it later," Rick said.

"Don't say that!" Kate glared at him.

Her brother shrugged. "I'm just sayin'—be prepared."

"Thanks, Boy Scout. Maybe we should get the generator set up when you come to do the shutters." Jillian gave him a wry smile and started to turn away.

"Hey, wait a sec, Jill. I, uh, wanted to tell you both something."

Jillian sat back down, and Kate leaned in, curious. Rick usually spoke his mind, but he sounded a little cryptic now.

"What?" Kate prompted.

"Uh, well, I might as well just say it. Diana's pregnant."

Kate leaned back, staring at him. Rick and Diana's youngest, Joel, was twelve years old, and Ashley was fifteen. Had they planned on more children? Or was this a real surprise?

Jillian grinned widely. "Wow! Fantastic! Congratulations."

"Thanks," Rick said, smiling sheepishly.

"I'll call Diana later," Jillian said.

"Yeah, do that."

"Is she happy about it?" Kate asked.

Jillian tossed her a glare as a warning to be quiet, but Rick nodded affably.

"Yeah, we're both pleased. Didn't expect it, really, but hey, the more the merrier."

"Right." Kate sipped her coffee.

Rick shoved back his chair. "Well, I'd better get moving. I'll stop at Zeb's, and someone will be over later to help with your shutters."

He grabbed a take-out cup, filled it with coffee, and left. Kate looked around the room. "So, has everyone eaten now?"

"Uh, Don checked someone in last night. I don't think—"

Jillian broke off, and Kate swiveled her head to see what she was staring at. The man in the lobby doorway glanced toward the coffee station, but then his gaze flicked to them, and his eyes locked on Kate's. His huge brown eyes.

The last person Kate expected—or wanted—to see.

Luke Brantley.

2

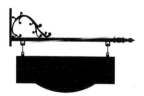

K ate dragged Jillian into the kitchen and yanked her around to face her.

"Did you know?" Kate's face was white and taut.

"No, I promise. Don said last night he'd checked someone in, but I didn't look at the name."

"I want him out of here!"

Jillian laid a hand on her shoulder. "Settle down. Don't you think you should find out why he came?"

"No. I don't want to speak to him. Just ... just get rid of him. Please." Tears glistened in Kate's eyes.

Jillian let out a slow breath. It had been ten years since Luke Brantley walked out on her sister. As far as she knew, Kate hadn't seen him or spoken to him since he'd turned his back on their engagement and gone off with Tara Wright. Kate was upbeat and fun. She dated occasionally, but she hadn't had a serious relationship since Luke's devastating exit from her life.

"Okay, leave it to me."

Jillian pushed through the swinging doors. Luke was alone, diffidently grasping a sheaf of bacon with the tongs and laying it beside his omelet. She walked toward him and spoke as he reached for a banana.

"Luke, I'm guessing you're the guest who checked in late last night. Our night clerk mentioned it, but I didn't realize it was you."

He turned toward her, holding the plate and the banana, a hesitant smile on his lips.

"Jillian. Is Kate upset?"

"She asked me to speak to you. Are you here for any particular reason?"

"Well, sure. To see Kate." He moved to the nearest table and set down his food, then turned to the coffeemaker.

She stood waiting. No way would she make this easy for him, after what he'd done to her younger sister.

Luke returned with a steaming mug and sat down. He blinked at her as if surprised. "Have a seat, Jillian."

"No, thanks. This is a busy time of day for us."

He shrugged and began to eat. He seemed unconcerned, his attention on the food.

"Why are you here?" Her voice had a sharp edge.

"I told you—I wanted to see Kate."

"After ten years?"

He sipped his coffee and set down the mug. "Maybe I've begun to realize what an idiot I was to throw her over for Tara."

Jillian processed that while he peeled his banana. "Where's Tara now?"

His handsome face squeezed into an unbecoming frown. "Back at our house in Brewer. Or should I say at *her* house?"

"You're separated, then."

"Nearly divorced. Should happen any day now."

Jillian frowned. "That takes at least sixty days."

"Like I said, it should be final soon. It's over."

She waited while he finished the banana. The wind tore at the trees outside the large windows. When he reached for his fork, Jillian said, "Kate doesn't want to see you. She doesn't want you here at all."

Luke paused and gazed past her toward the tossing trees and the broody sky. "It's getting nasty outside. I thought I'd stay another night. Wait until this storm passes."

"You can get home before it breaks."

He chuckled without mirth. "I don't have a home anymore."

She studied his face for a moment. "You must have been staying somewhere."

Luke picked up his napkin and wiped his mouth. "One can't impose forever on the kindness of friends."

Something hardened inside her. Friends, not family? It would take quite a lot of freeloading and bitterness for a friend of hers in a similar situation to wear out his welcome. On the other hand, if he truly had nowhere to go ... She gave herself a mental shake. There were other hotels in town.

"What about your job? Don't you have to work?"

"I'm taking a couple of personal days." Luke's expression softened. "Look, I promise I'll leave tomorrow. Just ... let me stay here one more night, okay? I really like my Phileas Fogg room, and it will give me time to make other arrangements."

Oh, did Don have to put him in that room? It was the one Jillian had just redecorated, with the *Around the World in Eighty Days* theme. She loved it too. Ordinarily, if a guest said something like that, she'd immediately ask if he'd read the book, and did he like the movie posters and other creative touches she'd collected for the room. But this was Luke. With Kate hurting in the next room, she would not offer him the slightest scrap of friendliness.

Still, she felt her barriers crumble just a little. Luke was still charming, and that smile ... To tell the truth, she'd always thought he was terrific for Kate. The whole family had liked him. Until he smashed Kate's heart to smithereens.

"I'll speak to my sister." She whirled and strode into the kitchen before he could reply.

Kate was fitting a few more cups into the dishwasher, her lips in a grim line.

"He says he wants to talk to you," Jillian said. "Apparently, he and Tara are splitting up, and he says he realizes what an idiot he was."

Her sister barked a disdainful laugh.

"I don't know what happened between them," Jillian said.

Kate grimaced. "We don't need to. We know who's out of the house, don't we?"

"Well, yeah. He said Tara's got the house."

"That says a lot."

"He wants to stay one more night because of the storm."

Kate glanced toward the windows on the back of the house, facing the bay. "It's not even raining yet."

"I know. I told him he could get home before the hurricane hits, and he says he's homeless."

"Oh, great." Kate scowled and reached for the box of soap pods. "He's not staying here indefinitely, if that's what he has in mind."

"I agree." Jillian watched her close the dishwasher and start it.

Finally, Kate turned and faced her, every muscle tight. "I don't want to talk to him. At all. And I want him out of here. I don't care where he goes. I don't want to know a thing about it or his situation with Tara. Just make him go away."

That made sense. Kate had held on to the hurt for a long time. Jillian had watched anxiously as Kate finally started allowing male friends into her life. In fact, she'd accepted a date from persistent but shy admirer Geordie Kraus, one of Rick's fellow officers, for Friday night.

"Luke did say if we gave him a day's reprieve, he'd try to make other arrangements for someplace to go."

Kate let out a big sigh and leaned on the counter as if she would crumple without its support. A blast of wind made the windows shudder, and something flew across the back patio.

"Oh," Jillian cried. "There goes a deck chair. We need to get those in."

She ran through the storage room and out onto the side porch, then around to the back of the house. While she chased the chair, Kate grabbed another that the wind had trapped against the porch railing. They wrestled the two chairs, a small table, and two potted plants into the storage room, and Jillian slammed the door. They stood gazing at each other.

"That's pretty fierce." Kate scrubbed a clump of wild hair back from her face.

"Yeah. I wouldn't want to be driving in it right now."

After a moment's silence, Kate said, "One night, and that's it. I'll just stay out of sight when I can. I can start making fresh muffins now for tomorrow. Maybe he can help you make sure there's nothing else outside that we should put away. But even if he helps, he pays the full regular rate."

"Understood." Jillian brushed a hand through her hair and resolutely turned toward the door.

Luke still sat where she'd left him, working on what she guessed was a second omelet. When she broke the news to him, he nodded soberly.

"Okay, then. I appreciate it."

"Someone's coming later to help put up storm shutters," Jillian said. "Are you willing to help with that?"

"Sure. Just let me know when." Luke polished off the last bite of omelet and took his dishes to the stand in the corner.

Then he headed up the stairs that wound from the lobby up to the game room landing on the second floor, which was close to his room.

An hour later, Rick was back, holding his hat on as he pushed across the parking area to the front porch. Together, he and Jillian worked to shut the door.

"You okay?" Jillian asked.

"Yeah. I've got an hour, then I've got to check on other people close to the bay. Oh, by the way, Zeb's not feeling well. I told him not to even consider putting up his flags today."

"Right. Do you think I should go over? I could drive."

"No, don't do it."

"Okay. Maybe I'll give his nephew a call."

"That sounds better. Tell him not to try to come until the hurricane's past. Now, what needs doing most? The shutters?"

"Yeah, I think so. And Luke said he'd help with that."

"Luke?"

Jillian winced. "Luke Brantley's here. We didn't realize it until breakfast. Don checked him in last night, not knowing he was Kate's ex."

"Oh, brother."

"He wants to ride out the storm here. Then he says he'll leave. But he did offer to help with storm prep." She raised her eyebrows. "Our generator's down in the garage. I thought maybe we ought to get it up here."

"Get him down here." Rick's scowl was plainer than Zeb's warning flags would be.

"Don't you start in on him, Rick. Kate's not going to talk to him, and he knows that. She's going to stay in the background, and he seems to have accepted our terms. Don't get him riled."

He held up both hands in surrender. "I'll play nice. I don't suppose his wife's with him?"

"Uh ..."

"I'll take that as a no."

"They've split up."

Rick rolled his eyes heavenward. "I'll keep him busy for the next hour. You make sure Kate stays out of sight."

"That's the plan."

"Good. We do *not* want him hitting on her." Rick went to get out the shutters and tools, and Kate called Luke's room.

"Luke, my brother's here, and he could use your help."

"Sure," Luke said. "Where is Rick? In the lobby?"

"No, I think he's in the storage room right now, or maybe out on the side porch."

When Luke came down the elevator wearing his jacket, she directed him around the porch and in through the side door if he didn't find Rick outside. Then she flipped through her address book, where she kept Lee Wilding's number for just such cases as this. She'd consciously avoided adding him to her contacts on her cell.

She picked up the desk phone and punched in his number. She was mildly surprised when he answered promptly.

"Hi, Lee, this is Jillian Tunney."

"Well, hi, Jillian. Good to hear from you. Wait. Is Uncle Zeb okay?"

"That's why I'm calling. The hurricane is coming—"

"Tell me about it," Lee said. "I spent yesterday afternoon securing my boat."

"Yeah, well, it's really windy here already, and Zeb didn't run up any flags this morning. My brother went over, and Zeb's not feeling well. I just thought I'd tell you."

"Should I come up there?"

"Not today, certainly. We'll keep an eye on him. He'll probably be fine. But you might want to call him."

"Of course. And if it's at all serious, I'll drive up as soon as Cloris has done her worst. Or I could take the boat up."

"I don't think that's a good idea right now."

"Yeah, you're right. It's pouring buckets here now."

"Really?" Lee was only a couple of hours down the coast. "They said it would hit here around suppertime, but it wouldn't surprise me if we saw rain before that. The wind's really howling."

"You're right on the water too," he said.

"Not *right* on. We're a little farther back than your uncle's house, but our bank is shallower, and the carriage house where Kate and I live is closer to the bay than the inn."

"Hmm. Well, I wish you the best. Have you got guests?"

"A few. One of them's out there now with Rick, putting up our storm shutters."

"Good. You don't want broken glass when those hundred-mile-an-hour gusts start flinging stuff around."

"Right. Well, I'm sure you have things to do too," Jillian said. "I'll let you go."

"Okay. And if I come up, we can touch base."

"Sure. 'Bye." Her stomach clenched as she put down the receiver.

Lee liked her—she knew that. But if he had ideas about asking her out, he'd be disappointed. She had settled on Craig Watkins, Rick's sergeant. They hadn't talked about making their relationship exclusive, but she considered it that way. She hadn't dated anyone else in the five years since her husband died, and right now, she had no desire to look around. She'd tried to make that clear to Zeb—but had he passed the news on to Lee?

The phone rang as she headed toward the kitchen, and she turned back to the lobby.

"Novel Inn."

A repeat guest was calling to cancel the booking he'd made for the next night. No surprise. Jillian made the necessary changes on the computer and went to check on Rick and Luke's efforts.

They'd already shuttered the storage room, kitchen, and living room windows, which faced the bay. Now they'd gone around the side of the house and were working on the large dining room windows.

"You guys are doing great," she yelled, hugging herself against the icy wind.

"These are the last ground-floor rooms where there's no porch," Rick noted. "Do you want us to do the rest on this level or start doing the upstairs windows?" The upstairs windows had regular, decorative shutters, not the more solid storm shutters. They could be closed from inside the rooms, which meant the guys wouldn't have to climb ladders in the gale.

"Well, the wind's coming from the east. We should probably do as many as we can."

"Okay. Make me a list of the rooms that are occupied. We'll get as many as we can, but my time's more than half gone."

"I can take care of the ones that close from inside, if you show me how to do one," Luke said.

"Great, buddy. Thanks." Rick clapped him on the shoulder.

Jillian hurried back inside. The quiet haven of the inn greeted her. As she made her short list, she pondered Rick's attitude pivot toward Luke. Instead of being still angry with him, Rick was treating him the same way he had ten years ago, when Luke and Kate were engaged—like a friend. And a potential brother-in-law? She certainly hoped not.

She supposed it was hard to work with Luke and not get positive vibes from him. He was likable and a willing helper. Personally, she wasn't ready to drop her resentment and skepticism. She'd be interested to hear Rick's impressions later.

By the time the two men came inside, she'd taken two more cancellations, and Rick's hour was up. Even so, he went up the stairs to Luke's Phileas Fogg Room to give him a quick tutorial on the upstairs shutters.

The phone continued to ring. This time it was Mindy Nelson, the part-time housekeeper, ringing in on Jillian's cell phone.

"Hey," Mindy said. "I tried to come over to clean, but there's a humongous tree down on my street. It took down the power lines, and they're telling everyone to stay put until it's cleared."

"Don't worry," Jillian said. "We've had several cancellations. I don't expect anyone new tonight, and four parties have checked out. Kate and I can handle doing up those rooms."

"Are you sure?"

"Of course. Stay home, Mindy."

3

Kate took the elevator to the third floor, a bundle of fresh towels and sheets in her arms. Jillian had already stripped the bed and emptied the trash in the Horatio Hornblower room and was now cleaning the bathroom.

"Everything okay in here?" Kate asked as she restocked the towels.

Jillian stood and backed away from the shower with a can of disinfectant cleaner in her hand. "Yeah. Just a sec, and I'll help you make the bed."

Kate went back into the bedroom and paused for a moment by the walnut binnacle Zeb had built. It held an old ship's compass they'd discovered in one of the inn's small, windowless chambers they called secret rooms. He'd done a beautiful job. She ran her fingers over the smooth wood that edged the glass in the top of the case.

"Let's do this," Jillian said, flinging back the duvet. They stripped off the sheets and pillowcases and replaced them almost as quickly and neatly as Mindy would have.

"Go ahead down to the desk," Kate told her. "I'll dust and vacuum the lounge."

"It'll probably be okay for another day," Jillian said. "Mindy just did it Friday."

Kate shrugged. "I don't mind." She'd finished her baking for the day, and she was keeping away from the second floor, where Luke's room was. Since he'd finished fastening the shutters over all the upstairs windows, she didn't think he'd venture up here to the third level again.

"Suit yourself," Jillian said. "We don't need to do anything to Scout Finch or Rip Van Winkle." Those were the two rooms with plumbing problems in the connecting bathroom.

Kate frowned. "This storm could delay the plumber."

"I know. And some people are already putting the brakes on their vacations. I doubt we'll need the rooms for a few more days."

"I don't like Mindy's power being knocked out. We could lose ours anytime."

"I know. If it wasn't so nasty out, I'd run to the store for extra supplies."

"We can get by for a day or two with what we have, but not much more than that." Kate scooped up the dirty linens.

"Want me to take those down?" Jillian asked.

"Would you?" Kate was glad she didn't have to take the dirty things down—the elevator opened right opposite the door to the Phileas Fogg Room, where Luke was staying, and the utility room was off the same hallway.

Jillian bundled everything in her arms, and Kate tucked in a stray hand towel.

"I might go over to check on Zeb and take him some soup and a muffin."

"The wind is awful," Kate said.

"Don't worry. I'll drive."

24

"Well, let me know when you're ready, and I'll go down to the office." She could shut the hall door there. If Luke came into the lobby, she supposed she'd have to face him. She clenched her teeth and picked up her cleaning caddy.

———

Just getting out to her Taurus was a struggle. Jillian carefully put the box containing Zeb's treats on the passenger floor. Chicken-vegetable soup, breadsticks, and a half dozen oatmeal cookies. That would at least get him through lunch. When she edged the car out onto the road, no other traffic was in sight, but a big branch from a white pine lay on the shoulder.

Zeb's driveway was only a tenth of a mile past the inn. Smaller limbs littered her short drive. Once in his yard, she picked up a plastic planter that must have been thrown off his porch.

She knocked, and with her ear to the door, she heard his feeble reply. She swung the door open. He should keep it locked, but then, he probably didn't want to have to get up to let in any callers.

"Zeb? You okay?" She quickly scanned his snug living room, but he wasn't there.

"In here." She set down her box of treats and the planter and followed his voice to his bedroom—the captain's cabin at the back of the house, overlooking the bay. She'd never been in there before. Finding Zeb sitting up in his bed, she stopped short in the doorway. "Hi. Sorry to bother you. I brought soup and cookies."

"Bless you." Zeb punched his pillow without much force. "I just didn't feel up to going on deck today."

She smiled. "It's not a crime to stay in your berth one day, Zeb."

His scowl said otherwise.

Beyond the window, the whitecaps swelled on the bay, colliding and merging as they surged toward shore. The wind whistled around the eaves. His little house didn't feel nearly as solid and secure as the inn.

"Have you got storm shutters?" she asked.

"Just for these back windows. But ..." He settled back on his pillows and pulled the quilt over his legs.

"I can send someone over to put them up for you." Who could she send? It would be a chore. But she'd fret about Zeb lying helpless in a bed so close to a large, uncovered window. "Are you sure you're okay here alone?"

"I'll get by." He let out a little moan. "Can you turn the heat up a notch?"

"Actually, it's quite warm in here." She stepped to the bedside and laid a hand on his forehead. "I think you have a fever, Zeb."

"Wouldn't surprise me." He pulled the quilt up higher.

"Do you have a thermometer?"

"Medicine cabinet."

She hurried to the small bathroom and foraged until she found it. Two minutes later, she squinted for the reading. A hundred and one.

Jillian did some quick calculations. She wouldn't sleep well tonight. She'd be worried about him over here alone. He wouldn't like it, but ...

"I'm taking you to the inn."

"Wha—?"

"Come on, I mean it. You can't stay here alone." Large drops of water pelted against the window.

"Look, it's raining already," she said. "If phone lines go out, I won't be able to call you. Have you got a duffel bag? Tell me what to pack."

"I—my seabag's in the closet, but—"

"No buts. We've got a nice, comfy room right near the office."

"Hornblower?" A gleam lit his watery eyes.

"No, that's on the top floor."

"Oh."

"Come on, sit up and I'll help you get your shoes on." She decided not to tell him the room she had in mind was Anna Karenina. Zeb would probably prefer a room representing a masculine character. "When you're feeling better, I'll take you up to see Hornblower. I promise."

She dashed back to the bathroom and grabbed his toothbrush and two prescription bottles, then went back to his room and pulled a few clothes out of the dresser.

"The windows." His voice was so low she barely heard him.

His room had two windows on the back wall. The house was quite close to the cliff, and she saw what she hadn't noticed before. Against the wall below each frame hung a hinged board panel.

"Your shutters are inside," she said.

Zeb nodded. "Just these two. I had Lee fix 'em, so I wouldn't have to climb a ladder. It won't protect the glass, but it'll keep the rain out if the window breaks."

Jillian brought in the chicken soup and ordered him to eat while she worked. She cleared the floor beneath the windows, dragging aside a small table and a few pairs of shoes. Then she hoisted each shutter. Small deadbolts were attached to the top and side edges, and she soon had them secure.

"Any others?"

He shook his head. "The rest of the storm windows go outside, and they're put away in the cellar. Leave them."

She strode to the bedside. "All right, then. Let's get going."

Helping him stand was an effort, but they managed. She

turned off his bedside lamp and guided him to the doorway. As they passed through the living room, she hoped he wouldn't make a plea to bring along his telescope. It was a large one on a tripod, and she wasn't sure she could get it safely out to the car on her own.

He didn't mention it, and somehow she got him bundled up and into the car, along with the hastily packed canvas seabag. He'd eaten the soup she brought and one of the cookies while she raised the shutters, and she left the rest of the food.

She started the car. "Is there anything else, Zeb, before we go?"

"You locked the door."

"Yes, and I got your toothbrush and clothes. Have we got everything you'll need for the night?"

"Aye."

The rain deluged the car, but with the wipers going top speed, she managed to get them back to the inn and pulled up with Zeb's door broadside to the front steps.

"You sit tight while I get someone to help us," she told him. Not waiting for an answer, she hopped out and slammed the door harder than she'd meant to, with the wind's help. All her strength was needed to get around the car and push her way to the front door. Without the railing, she doubted she'd have made it.

Luke Brantley was coming down the stairs as she tumbled inside. He ran down the last few steps into the lobby.

"Jillian! Are you all right?"

"Yes, but I've got our neighbor in my car out front, and I've got to get him inside. He's sick, and I didn't want to leave him alone. Can you help me?"

"Sure. What's his name?"

"Zeb Wilding."

She hated to confront the storm again, but Luke plunged

outside without a coat. Rain pummeled the porch roof and gushed from the downspouts at the corners. Luke ignored the storm and flung Zeb's door open, standing in the downpour.

"Mr. Wilding, let's get you inside." He took the old man's arm and half pulled him from the car and up onto the porch.

"Get him into my office," Jillian said. "I'll get his things."

"Are you—"

She ran down the steps and, with difficulty, opened the back door and pulled the seabag to her. When she got inside, she couldn't close the front door, and wind howled in, choking off her breath.

"What's going on?" Kate yelled from the dining room doorway.

"Help me!"

Both women pushed, and together they shoved the door into place. Jillian locked it and stood panting.

Kate was gazing toward the open office door behind the front desk.

"Luke helped me get Zeb in," Jillian said between puffs of air. "He's got a temp, and I didn't want to leave him over there by himself."

"Where will he sleep?"

"Anna Karenina, so he's nearby."

Kate picked up the seabag. "I'll code a key card."

"Make it two—one for me and one for Zeb."

"Right."

Knowing Kate wouldn't want to come face to face with Luke, Jillian took Zeb's bag from her. "I'll get this. Luke and I can take it from here."

In less than a minute, Kate handed her two cards.

"Thanks," Jillian said.

"Hey," said Luke from the office doorway.

Kate shot Jillian a keen glance and ducked across the hall into the dining room.

Jillian went around the counter with the seabag slung over her shoulder. "I've got keys for the room down the hall on the right. Let's get him dry and into bed, if you don't mind."

"No problem."

Jillian stepped into the office with him. Zeb was sitting in her desk chair, looking a bit bedraggled from his few seconds out in the rain. She smiled as she opened the office's second door, into the hallway.

"There, we've got a nice room for you, Zeb. It's just a short walk down the hall."

"No stairs?"

"Not even one."

She and Luke each took an arm and guided him out of the office, past the elevator on one side and a powder room on the other, to the last door on the right. Zeb eyed the plaque that read ANNA KARENINA, surrounded by chamomile flowers, but he didn't protest. She opened the door and flipped the light switch.

Zeb glanced around the room, decorated with scenes from St. Petersburg and a print of a couple riding in a *troika*, a sleigh pulled by three horses abreast. A display shelf unit held enameled boxes with traditional Russian motifs, a wooden set of brightly painted, nesting dolls, copies of *Anna Karenina,* and other volumes by Tolstoy.

"Let me help you with your jacket and shoes, Zeb," Jillian said.

"I can help him." Luke took the old man's hat and set it on the dresser. "You'd better put your car in the garage if you can."

Jillian dreaded facing the rain again, but he was right. Leaving her vehicle in the parking lot could result in damage on a day like this.

"Thanks. I'll be back in a few minutes with some hot tea, Zeb."

"Thank you," he croaked out as Luke eased his wet jacket off over his shoulders.

Jillian dashed down the hall. Kate was crossing toward the office.

"Hey. Everything okay?" Kate asked.

"Luke's helping Zeb get his wet things off in Anna Karenina."

Kate eyed the car keys Jillian held. "Oh. Okay. Where are you headed now?"

"I'm going to take my car down to the garage. Is your Jeep in there?"

"Yeah, it's all buttoned down tight."

The carriage house didn't have storm shutters, even though it was closer to the bay.

"I'm going to grab a few things from the house and bring them up," Jillian said. "I'll stay in the Jeeves Room tonight, so I can be near Zeb. I think we should both stay here. Do you want me to pick up anything for you?"

Kate glanced uneasily toward the covered windows. The raging wind and the rain drumming on the porch roof hammered in the logic of both sleeping at the inn.

"It's probably a good idea. Don called, and I told him not to even think of trying to get here tonight. So, yeah, I could use pj's and my toiletry bag. Maybe a sweatshirt and a change of clothes for tomorrow, if it's not too much."

"It's not. I'll see you in fifteen or twenty minutes."

Jillian put on a hooded jacket and braved the elements again. She sent up a prayer of thanks for their garage and the automatic opener. Unfortunately, the garage was detached from the little house. After parking her car inside, she took a big breath and stepped out. The overhead door rolled down behind her as she sprinted the few yards to the front of the carriage house.

Years ago, when the inn had been a private home, the carriage house had held their horse-drawn vehicles. At some point, the smaller building had been remodeled into a snug cottage. The Gage siblings' parents had lived there happily for several years after they bought the inn. Now Kate and Jillian shared the cozy space.

The sun hadn't peeked out all morning, but the storm brought true darkness, and it wasn't even noon yet. Jillian hurried to stash a few clothes into a vinyl bag for herself and then for Kate. Plenty of shampoo, soap, and toothpaste was stored at the inn for guests, so she didn't bother with those, but chose other personal items.

Soberly, she tied her hood close and pulled on knit gloves. She'd thought she wouldn't need those again this spring. At last, she shouldered the two bags and was ready to make the run up to the inn.

With the wind hitting her sideways, she raced up the driveway and cut off for the familiar path to the side porch. She burst into the storage room panting and locked the door behind her. She found Kate in the kitchen, piling candles and batteries on the counter.

"Are you all right?"

"Yeah," Jillian gasped, thrusting Kate's damp overnight bag into her arms. "It's really rough out there, though. Sorry that's wet."

"It's okay." Kate grabbed a dish towel and wiped the outside of her bag. "I drew some jugs of water, just in case."

Jillian's heart sank. "So, Rick didn't set up the generator?"

"He brought it up to the side porch, but no. I guess we could ..."

"Let's just wait and see if we need it."

"Okay. What do I do now—pick a room, any room? You said you wanted Jeeves."

"Yeah. I guess you can sleep anywhere you want, as long as it's not occupied or plumbing challenged."

"I've always wanted to sleep in Horatio Hornblower. That couple left this morning."

"Now's your chance."

"Even though it's one of the biggest rooms?"

"Why not? I doubt we'll get any more guests for tonight in *this*." Jillian accentuated her statement with a wave toward the door. "If we do get a guest, you can change the bed as punishment."

Kate laughed. "Thanks. I'll sit on the desk while you go put your things away."

As Jillian lugged her bag down the hallway, the door to Anna Karenina opened, and Luke came out. He smiled when he saw her.

"I think Mr. Wilding's all set. What a character."

"Oh, yeah. Sometimes I think we should dedicate a Zeb Wilding Room, but—oh, wait! He's real."

Luke chuckled. "Anything else I can do for you?"

"Not right now, but thanks, Luke. I'll call on you later if we need to start the generator. And thanks for understanding about—you know."

He nodded and turned away. Jillian lingered in the hall until she saw with relief that he was taking the elevator. No need for him to pass Kate in the lobby.

4

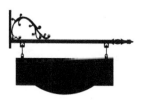

Jillian checked on Zeb to find him sleeping, and at four thirty, she relieved her sister at the front desk. All the guests were in for the night, and no newcomers were expected. They'd made sure everyone had flashlights and bottled water in their rooms. Kate hovered in the doorway.

"I told everyone we'd provide supper, due to the hurricane."

"Looks like we'll have to." Jillian felt a little guilty for not offering their guests lunch, but most of them seemed to have gotten by with food in their rooms or leftover muffins and fruit from the breakfast area. One couple had ventured out but soon returned with a report that the restaurants near the inn were closed. She'd taken Zeb a tray. "What do we have on hand?"

"There's plenty of bacon and salad stuff. BLTs?" Kate asked.

"Let's set out sandwich ingredients, salad, and desserts," Jillian said. "And I think there's some canned chili."

Kate made a wry face. "Not haute cuisine, but there's no time to make something from scratch. I could throw some corn muffins in the oven."

"That'd be great. Take your stuff up to Hornblower first, though."

The elevator had just begun its upward journey when someone hammered on the front door. Jillian rose and hurried to it. She unlocked it and had to jump back out of the way as a dripping man plunged inside, dragging a roller bag behind him.

"Are you open?" he gasped.

"Yes."

"Oh, good. I was afraid you weren't ... I need a room, if you've got one." He pushed damp hair from his eyes, and water drops dribbled down his cheeks.

"We can squeeze you in." Jillian slid back behind the desk and opened the check-in file. "Where are you coming in from?"

"I was down in Castine last night, and I thought I could get to Portland today, but some of the roads are flooded, and there are trees down everywhere."

"That bad?" Jillian shook her head. "Well, you'll be snug here tonight, and by morning the worst of it will be over. What's your name?"

"Alan Dryer."

They continued the sign-in process, and she consulted the list of occupied rooms.

"Looks like we've got two rooms left, and they're both on the second floor. The Hercule Poirot Room, and the Elizabeth Bennet Room."

He blinked at her.

Jillian chuckled. "We're called the Novel Inn. Each room is named for and decorated in the style of a fictional character. Hercule Poirot was Agatha Christie's Belgian detective, and Elizabeth Bennet is the main character of *Pride and Prejudice*."

"Right. I'll take the detective, I guess."

She nodded, not surprised that he'd chosen the only

masculine-themed room available. It was one of the larger rooms, just below Scarlett O'Hara. They usually tried to save those two rooms for couples, like the Simons, who now occupied Scarlett. But this was a hurricane. And anyway, there was room for a couple in Liz Bennet. It just wasn't as spacious as the others, and they usually assigned it to singles.

She coded a key card and handed it back with his credit card. "There you go, Mr. Dryer. Let me show you the elevator. When you get off upstairs, just turn right and go through the game room, toward the back of the inn. You can't miss it."

"Thanks."

She closed the card drawer and walked with him into the hallway. The elevator was humming, and when the door opened, Kate stepped off it.

"All set?" Jillian asked her.

"Yep, ready to cook."

"This is my sister, Kate," Jillian told the guest. "This is Mr. Dryer. He had an adventure getting here from Castine and decided to stop for the night. Oh—that's right. We're providing a light supper for those who want it, since it seems a bit hazardous to go out tonight."

"Great," Dryer said. "I'll look forward to it."

Kate pointed. "Our dining room's right there. And we always serve breakfast. We'll start service at six in the morning. Coffee and a few goodies are there at any time."

"Sounds good." Dryer nodded, pulled his bag into the elevator, and squinted at the control panel.

The door closed, and Kate blew out a breath. "I didn't think we'd get anyone else tonight."

"I hope there aren't any more stragglers. Liz Bennet's the last open room."

"What about—oh yeah, the plumbing. What do you bet the plumber doesn't make it here tomorrow?"

Jillian grimaced. "I sure hope he does. But if more people come in, I guess you and I can share Hornblower. I wanted to be close to Zeb, though."

"I could move down to Jeeves with you."

"Not unless we have to. I want you to have your Horatio Hornblower adventure."

They went into prep mode for the meal, and by the time Kate's corn muffins came out of the oven, Jillian had the buffet ready, where guests could put together sandwiches and take chili and a variety of vegetables she'd found in the freezer. A few choices of soft drinks were available, along with coffee, tea, spring water, and juice.

"I'm glad we don't have any kids here right now," Kate muttered.

"Me too." Jillian untied her apron. "I'm going to check on Zeb. If he's awake, I'll see if he wants something to eat. Be right back."

She returned a couple of minutes later, as Kate was checking the warming table. The chili was staying hot in a covered pan.

"I guess we're ready, but we'll have some bored guests tonight," Jillian whispered to her sister.

"How about board games for the bored?" Kate asked with a smile.

"We can suggest it. There are plenty of table games upstairs, and I'll mention the library shelves in the lounge. Should we announce that supper's ready?"

"I can go knock on everyone's door."

Jillian eyed her in surprise. "Even Luke?"

"I'm just knocking on doors. I'll be off down the hall before he comes out."

"Okay ..."

Zeb wouldn't be joining the others in the dining room, so Kate skipped his room and went up the stairs to the second floor. Luke's room was nearest the landing, and she hesitated. Things could get awkward if they came face to face. Maybe she'd do the third floor first.

She skittered up the stairs and across the lounge, to the door of Scarlett O'Hara, where the Simons were staying. Charles was a history professor from Massachusetts, on sabbatical leave. His wife was an artist, and Kate found conversing with them interesting. She knocked firmly on the door.

A moment later, it opened, and Marie Simon smiled at her. The middle-aged woman wore black pants and a long, white shirt with splashes of red and blue. Her husband was sitting at the desk with his laptop open, and they had all the lights on in the shuttered room.

"Hi," Kate said. "Just wanted you to know that supper is ready. We're serving in the dining room right now."

"Oh, thank you," Marie replied. "We'll be right down. Awful wind, isn't it?"

"Very." Kate turned away and crossed the lounge full of packed bookshelves, to the hallway. Since two rooms up here had plumbing problems, the only other occupied room on the floor, besides the one where she would sleep, was the Anne Shirley Room. Dr. Eliza Rowan was staying there.

When she knocked, Dr. Rowan called, "Yes?"

"It's Kate Gage. Supper is served in the dining room."

"Thank you."

Kate was near the elevator, so she took it to the second floor. Stepping off, she turned left and knocked on the

Galadriel Room's door. The occupant came to the door. "Hello."

"Hi, Mr. Cowper. Supper's ready. Just letting everyone know."

She repeated the performance at the Hercule Poirot Room's door, where a male voice called, "Who is it?"

"It's Kate Gage, Mr. Dryer. Supper is ready in the dining room."

"Okay."

She turned to the door of the David Copperfield Room and knocked. Nobody answered. She paused and knocked again. Max Pelletier, the marine scientist, must be downstairs already—or in the bathroom. If he didn't show up for the meal, they could call his room later.

Luke was the last guest to notify. She hauled in a big breath and walked across the game room's bright, geometric rug and out to his room. She stood for a moment staring at the door. Maybe she should go down to the lobby and call his room instead. He'd hurt her so badly. She was serious about not wanting to engage in a conversation with him.

The door opened, and she stepped back with a little gasp.

"Oh, hi," Luke said with his lovely smile. "Sorry about that. I was just going to get some ice."

"Okay. Well, supper's ready downstairs." She turned away and hurried to the stairway. No elevator this time—he might catch her before the door closed.

"Kate—"

"Gotta run," she flung over her shoulder. She reached the lobby and dashed into the dining room. A few guests were already at the buffet. When she burst into the kitchen, Jillian gave her a critical look.

"Everything okay?"

"Yeah. One guy didn't answer. Uh ... the Copperfield Room."

"Mr. Pelletier."

"Right. I thought maybe he was in the shower."

"Could be. I was just going to add these to the dessert cabinet." Jillian lifted a tray of cookies, plated brownies, and small plastic dishes of whipped cream-topped pudding.

"That's not a bad spread on short notice," Kate said.

Jillian flashed her a smile and headed into the dining room. Kate leaned on the work island and took three deep breaths. Determined not to let Luke's nearness get her down, she went to the sink and started washing pans. Luke had told Jillian he was taking a couple of personal days. But he worked in construction. Could he do that? Maybe the approaching storm had affected the work schedule. Or maybe he'd found a different sort of job. Not that she cared.

A minute or two later, Jillian was back. Kate kept scrubbing at the brownie pan without looking up.

"Did you see Luke?" Jillian asked.

"Uh, yeah, just for a second."

"He asked me if you were all right."

"None of his business," Kate said with a grimace.

"I told him you were fine."

Kate swallowed hard. "Okay. Good."

"He's sitting over near the windows."

"Thanks." She intended to stay in the kitchen, if possible, until he went back upstairs.

The quiet hum of all the electrical appliances and the furnace went silent, and the lights flickered out.

"Oh, man, just what we need." Kate fumbled for the dish towel and dried her hands.

"We'd better get out there and light the lanterns," Jillian said. "Can you help?"

"Yeah." She followed her sister through the dining room door, using her cell's flashlight app to light her way and wishing they'd emptied their freezer down at the carriage house and offered the ice cream to their guests.

"Hey, folks, we've got things under control," Jillian called to their patrons. They'd left one battery-operated lantern burning at the buffet, against the chance the electricity would fail. Kate moved toward the corner where they'd left a stockpile of more lanterns.

"Hold on, and Kate and I will set up the lanterns over here and light the candles on each table," Jillian announced.

Quickly the two of them carried out the tasks, with Jillian making sure she was the one to visit Luke's table. The guests all seemed willing to keep a cheerful attitude, and several praised the sisters for their foresight in setting out the candles as centerpieces "just in case."

"Now, the hot food won't stay hot," Kate pointed out, "so if you want more chili especially, best get it now."

A latecomer, Roger Cowper, the salesman from the Galadriel Room, came in with the aid of his flashlight.

"I almost took the elevator," he said. "Good thing I walked down."

Kate nodded soberly. A guest stuck in the elevator would be a nightmare. "We're grateful you took the stairs," she told him.

"What about our room keys?" asked Dr. Rowan.

"The room locks run on batteries," Jillian said in her teacher voice, so everyone in the room could hear. "They don't need an electric connection to work, so you shouldn't have any problems. But if you do, come and tell me or Kate. One of us will be in the office or the lobby all night."

"Oh, you shouldn't have to sit up for us," Dr. Rowan said from her table with the Simons.

42

"We usually have a night desk clerk," Jillian explained. "But we told him to stay home tonight. It's no problem."

The sisters moved quickly about the room, and when all the candles at occupied tables were burning and the available lanterns shone brightly, they met near the kitchen door.

"Not everyone's down here," Jillian said quietly.

"Who's missing?" Kate peered around. Luke was where she expected him, and she didn't let her gaze linger.

"Pelletier and ... Dryer."

"Who?"

"The latecomer," Jillian said.

"Well, I told him we were serving, so he knows about it."

"I'd better go fix Zeb's tray." Jillian sounded quite concerned, and Kate wondered just how sick Zeb was and if it had been a good idea to bring him into the inn. She knew Jillian would wash her hands diligently, but still.

"I'll keep an eye on things out here."

Kate went to the office while Jillian retreated to the kitchen to fix Zeb's tray. It wouldn't hurt to remind the guests that the elevator wasn't working now. She took a sheet of copy paper and a marker to prepare a sign for the elevator door reading "Please use the stairs."

When she returned to the dining room, Mrs. Simon flagged her down. "Kate, will it get cold tonight?" That was a fair question in springtime Maine.

Kate followed her sister's example and spoke up so everyone could hear. "Every room has extra blankets in the closet, and if we can, we'll get the generator going to run the furnace."

"Oh, good, you have a generator," Mr. Simon said jovially.

"Well, it's small," Kate told him. "We usually use it for our cottage, but if we can, we'll hook it up here tonight. My brother told us it would probably run the furnace and maybe the lights, but not everything. That means there might not be any hot water tonight or hot food until the power comes back."

"But there will be cold water?" Mrs. Simon asked.

"Uh ..." Jillian was passing through with Zeb's tray, and Kate shot her a desperate look.

"We're not sure yet," Jillian said. "This is actually the first time we've had to use the generator for the inn since we opened about a year ago. We're on a learning curve, but we'll do our best to make you comfortable."

"I'm just glad to have a dry place to sleep tonight," Roger Cowper said.

"I'll call Rick," Kate whispered.

Jillian nodded and hurried into the hall, toward Zeb's room.

They might need their camp stove, Kate thought. They could make coffee in their campfire coffeepot in the morning if necessary and cook some bacon on the propane stove. She ducked into the kitchen to make her call.

"I'll try to get over there," Rick said. "Right now we're helping the marina staff secure some boats. Maybe Luke knows how to run a generator. You'll have to keep it outside— the porch is fine, and there's an outlet on the side porch."

Kate hesitated. "We'll ask him."

"Let me know if you get it going."

Kate returned to the dining room to try to forestall any fears the guests had. Maybe she'd wait for Jillian to ask Luke about hooking up the generator.

"Folks, we brought in extra wood for the fireplace in the living room." She pointed to the large room behind the dining room. "We've also got some lanterns in there. If anyone wants to play board games, we have a large assortment one floor up, in the game room, or you might just want to sit by the fire and chat."

"So, you and Jillian don't actually live here?" Marie Simon asked.

"We live in the old carriage house, behind the inn." Kate pointed in the direction of the bay and their snug home. "We're both staying on hand here tonight, though. It will save us from going back and forth in the storm."

The diners finished eating and began to filter out. Luke kept his distance, and Jillian returned, assuring Kate that Zeb was doing fine.

As the sisters began clearing dishes and wiping down the tables in the dining room, Kate noted that the Simons and Eliza Rowan wandered into the next room, where Charles Simon began laying a fire. He soon had a blaze on the hearth.

"Did you get ahold of Rick?" Jillian asked as she and Kate carried trays of dirty dishes to the kitchen.

"He says not to try to set up the generator ourselves, since we've never done it. He'll try to get over later, but he suggested we ask Luke if he knows how. Right now, the officers are all out helping people with real emergencies."

"We can do it." Jillian seemed almost offended that her brother might think running generators fell exclusively into men's domain. "Of course, if there are vehicle accidents or people who need to evacuate their homes, we want him to be with them, doing his job. We can cope here."

"Do you want to ask Luke? If he's not up to speed, maybe one of the other guests can help." Kate turned up the lantern on the counter beside the dishwasher.

"I'm afraid Luke is our most likely candidate since he was in construction." Jillian shook her head. "I wish Rick had done it earlier."

Kate shrugged. "We didn't need it earlier. It wouldn't have made sense to start it up before the outage."

Together they loaded the dishes, even though they couldn't

run the dishwasher yet. They had plenty of clean crockery for breakfast, but if they had to provide lunch for everyone, they'd have to use that generator or start heating water on the propane stove and washing plates and coffee mugs by hand.

"We do have a small stock of disposables," Jillian said, as if reading her mind.

"I thought we might set up the camp stove on the porch in a pinch," Kate said.

Jillian nodded. "Is it still in the storage room?"

"I think so, but let's wait a bit and see if Luke can help with the generator or if Rick can come back."

"Okay, but people might want coffee or hot chocolate later."

Kate sighed. "It's a hurricane. They need to take Mr. Cowper's attitude and be glad they're nice and dry tonight. Hey, should we put away the food?"

"Check if everyone's done."

Kate went to the swinging door and pushed it open. Max Pelletier was turning away from the buffet table carrying a plateful of food.

"Oh, there you are. I was just going to call your room and see if you wanted to eat. I hope the chili's still warm."

"It's warm enough, thanks."

Kate nodded and retreated to the kitchen. It was going to be a long night.

5

The next time Jillian ventured into the dining room, Dr. Rowan had left the living room, and Luke had joined the Simons. She paused in the wide doorway arch, watching the firelight flicker on their faces as they chatted amiably.

"Can I get you folks anything?" she asked.

Marie Simon laughed. "Marshmallows?"

"Afraid not, but that's a good idea. We should stock some in the future. My brother hopes to get here a bit later and help us get our generator set up. If we can't do that, we'll at least get out our Coleman stove and heat some water for hot drinks."

"Don't worry about us," Charles said. "We're fine."

Jillian left them, glad they were so amenable. She thought about asking Luke to start working on it, but she decided to hold off. Kate was uncomfortable enough already, without having Luke in and out of the storage room off the kitchen.

Maybe she'd call Lee Wilding again. She headed for the office. When she lifted the desk phone's receiver, silence met her—no comforting dial tone. Her heart lurched. She took out her cell and opened a new contact, copying his number from her address book. Immense relief flooded her when it rang. They weren't totally cut off.

"Jillian? Everything all right?"

"Yes, Lee. I just wanted you to know that I brought Zeb over here to the inn. I didn't like him being over there alone, and it's gotten pretty nasty out."

"Thanks so much for doing that. It's bad here too. Is he awfully sick?"

"I think it's a bad cold, but it could be the flu. He's had the shot, though. I know—I drove him to the appointment for that last fall."

"Good to know. And thank you again."

"Well, he ate a little supper, but he's mostly sleepy. I'm making sure he gets plenty of fluids. He took some ibuprofen a couple of hours ago. He had a fever when I first brought him here, but that seems to be under control."

Silence.

"Lee?"

She pulled the phone from her ear and stared at the screen. Call dropped. Jillian wasn't really surprised, given the weather. She glanced ruefully at the dark monitor of her desktop computer.

With a sigh, she pocketed her cell and went back to the kitchen. "I called Lee, but we got cut off," she told Kate. "The landline's down. And the Internet, of course."

"I figured on that," Kate replied. "I hoped we'd keep the phone, though. Do you think we'll be able to call out on our cells if we need help?"

"I don't know. I just hope Rick gets here."

"Yeah, it's getting cooler. I haven't opened the refrigerator since the power went out."

"Good," Jillian said.

"What should we do with the chili?"

"There's not a lot left. Maybe a covered dish on the side porch?"

"The wind might carry it off."

"True. Well, you said it's cool in here. Maybe just stick it in the storage room for tonight. If we get the generator going, we can put it in the fridge."

"I think we're okay for breakfast."

"Me too—for one day. If we can't shop or bake tomorrow, it might get tricky."

"We should have stockpiled more."

"There's plenty of food," Jillian said. "No one will starve, but we just might not be able to serve all the usual dishes." She looked around the kitchen. "If we can use the generator, it won't run everything for this big place. What's most important?"

"The pump. Running water."

"Yeah. Toilets. And the stovetop, I'd think."

"What about the computer?" Kate asked.

"If we can, but we should consider the guests' comfort over our convenience."

"Hmm. Lights, for sure. Hot water if possible. And by morning, we may be begging for the furnace."

"It's not going to freeze tonight. Still ..." Jillian picked up one of the lanterns. "Are we all set? I can take first turn on the desk."

"Okay. Come get me at midnight if I'm not down here."

"Right—oh! Luke was by the fireplace with the Simons."

"Thanks for the heads-up. Do you think we should ask him now about the generator?"

"Maybe so."

"Well, you ask him. I'm going upstairs." Kate picked up a lantern and an extra battery, and they walked out through the dining room together. Jillian paused at the living room doorway.

"Hey, everyone. I'll be at the desk this evening. Just let me know if you need anything. And Luke, how well are you acquainted with generators?"

"Not real well, but I'm willing to take a look."

"Mmm, I'm still hoping my brother will get here soon. Let's give it another half hour."

Luke nodded. "I'll either be here or up in my room."

While Jillian spoke to them, Kate slipped out into the lobby.

"Hey," she stage-whispered as Jillian came out there. "Look at this."

"What?"

Kate pointed to one of the lobby desk's drawers. In the dim light of the small lantern she'd positioned on the far end of the desk, Jillian thought the drawer was open a crack. She reached out with one finger and tugged the handle. The drawer slid open.

"It wasn't locked?" she whispered.

"No, it was like that." Kate's face was drawn, and her brown eyes were troubled. "I tested it, and it opened, but I put it back the way it was so you could see it. Who was the last one to check in?"

"Mr. Dryer. I checked him in, remember?" Jillian frowned. Had Dryer shown up in the dining room for supper at all? Maybe he was exhausted and went right to bed. "But I locked the card drawer after."

"Are you sure?"

"Yes. Well ... ninety percent." They gazed at each other.

"Why would someone want to get in the card drawer?" Kate whispered.

"I don't know. I mean, none of the key cards in the drawer

can be used without being coded. We're always careful about that."

"Right," Kate said. "Do you always deactivate the cards people turn in? I don't ..."

"They're automatically deactivated at check-out time."

"What if they check out early?"

Jillian hesitated. "Well, we can go into the system and deactivate any keys we want to." How many guests left early because of the oncoming storm? She hadn't bothered to deactivate their cards. "But still—who would steal cards on the off chance one will still open a door?"

They stood in silence for a moment.

"Okay, let's not panic," Kate said.

"I'm *not* panicking. But I'm also sure I locked that drawer."

"How about we count the cards?"

"That won't help. We have a bunch of extras in there." Jillian felt a little sick. If only she didn't have that five-to-ten-percent doubt about locking the drawer. "The power's out. I can't go into the system now and deactivate anyone's card." Her stomach clenched as she realized she wouldn't be able to activate any new ones either, if another storm refugee showed up.

Kate frowned. "If we had Internet, we could check and see if Mr. Dryer's card was the last one activated. So, how many people were planning to stay tonight but left early?"

"Two? Yes, two."

Kate shrugged. "I don't think there's much we can do. I mean, if the power was on, we could, but ... Maybe we should just keep an eye on them. Which rooms were they in—the people who left?"

Jillian's brow wrinkled. "Yours and ... hmm, maybe Jeeves?"

"That's the room you're in now," Kate said. "Liz Bennet's

still empty. The couple in my Hornblower was going to leave anyway."

"Right. I'm pretty sure I didn't deactivate the Hornblower card, but it would have done it automatically at noon anyway —checkout time."

They gazed at each other, and Kate said, "So, your room and Liz Bennet. I think those are the only ones that might not have had their keys deactivated."

"Wait, when I made the new key for myself to use, it deactivated the old one for Jeeves."

Kate smiled. "So, the problem's half solved. Liz Bennet's the only one that would be vulnerable."

Jillian wasn't so sure. "Did you ever see Mr. Dryer come down to eat?"

Kate's expression was troubled. "No. he's the only one who didn't show. But he answered when I knocked on his door. I told him we were serving supper, and he said, 'Okay.'"

"And he said he'd look forward to supper. Do you think we should check on him?"

"I guess we should have before we cleared all the food away."

"Maybe he brought something with him. He'd been planning to drive through to Portland." Jillian eyed her closely, trying to gauge Kate's anxiety.

"Well, the desserts and snacks are still out. It's his own fault he missed the window for hot chili."

In Jillian's ears, that didn't sound very convincing.

"I'll run up to Poirot," Kate said. Before Jillian could respond, she was halfway up the curving stairs.

Jillian sat down at the front desk. The rain still beat on the shutters and the porch roof. Faintly, she heard her sister calling to the guest upstairs. After a couple of minutes, Kate came slowly down the steps.

"He's not answering the door."

Many thoughts zipped through Jillian's mind, and she rejected most of them. Could he have fallen asleep so early, with the storm raging? He couldn't be in the shower with the power off. Maybe he was stoned. She shuddered at the thought.

"Do we have a cell phone number?" Kate asked.

"I don't think so—but if we do, it's in the computer, and I can't access it."

Kate went to the front door and unlocked it. When she released the latch, the door flew in toward her. Kate braced herself and gazed out into the parking area.

"Help me shut this."

Jillian got up and went to her side. Together they closed the door, and Kate locked it.

"His car's still out there."

"Okay," Jillian said. "I'll go up." She took out the master key that would open every guest room door.

"I'm going with you," Kate said.

Jillian hesitated, then nodded. Kate grabbed the lantern off the desk, and they plodded up the stairs. When they reached Hercule Poirot, she knocked firmly. "Mr. Dryer?" She listened carefully, but there was no answer. Jillian knocked again, so loudly that everyone in the inn probably heard it.

Still no response. Kate's face was white in the glare from the lantern.

Gulping in a big breath, Jillian reached for the master key. As she pulled it out of her pocket, her cell rang. She stuck the key card in Kate's hand and looked at her phone.

"It's Craig." She swiped the screen and put it to her ear. "Hi, Craig."

"Hi. Just checking up on you. Everything okay there?"

"Well, no." Jillian shot a glance at Kate. "We don't have the generator up yet, and we were just about to open a guest's door because he didn't come down to eat supper. We've knocked twice, and he's not answering us. Our landline phones and power are out, so we can't call his room."

While she spoke, Kate was tapping the battery-operated lock with the master key. Jillian put out a hand to stop her, but the door was already opening.

"The power's out all over town," Craig said in her ear. Just hearing his voice comforted her.

Kate stepped into the guest room, holding the lantern high. "Jillian! Get in here!"

Jillian caught her breath. "Hold on, Craig. Something's not right."

She took three steps into the room and paused beside Kate. Alan Dryer lay on the queen-sized bed, unquestionably dead.

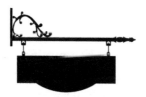

"Uh, Craig?" Jillian felt as if all the blood was draining from her head, leaving her dizzy and disoriented.

"What is it?"

She pulled in a breath. Craig was like a rock in the quicksand that threatened to swallow her.

"I ... I think the first course of action in our protocol for unattended deaths is to call the police."

"What? You've had a death there?"

"Yes."

Kate grabbed the phone from Jillian's hand. "Craig? It's Kate. You need to get over here. One of our guests is dead."

Jillian glared at her, but when Kate said, "Okay, just a sec," and moved closer to the bed, she was just as glad that she wasn't the one following Craig's instructions.

"There's blood." Staring down at the rug, Kate shifted her feet a couple of inches. "Quite a lot of blood." She looked back at Jillian. "Don't come any closer."

Jillian nodded.

Into the phone, Kate said, "Are you sure I need to do that? He's just staring at the ceiling. Well, all right." She reached for Dryer's hand. "Ugh. No, he's ... he's cold and ... and ... just take my word for it. Okay, we'll do that. Right. One of us will be down in the lobby when you get here. 'Bye." She tapped the screen and handed Jillian the cell. "Sorry. I took it because you looked kind of shocky."

Jillian inhaled slowly and met Kate's gaze. "What did he say?"

"He'll be right over, and he's putting out a radio call for any officers nearer the inn to get on over here. He's not sure how long it will take them—some of the streets are blocked. There's water over the road down by the marina, and there are trees down ... well, anyway, he said to get out of the room and lock it and not let anyone else go in."

"Right. Let's go."

They went out into the alcove off the game room, where the doors to Hercule Poirot and David Copperfield faced each other. Jillian checked to make sure the door locked behind them.

"Maybe we should have looked around to see if ..."

Jillian stared at her. "What?"

"Well, if there was anyone in the bathroom, or ... I don't know." Kate's eyes were huge.

"Do you think he killed himself?" Jillian whispered, casting a sidelong glance into the dim game room. Nobody was in there, at least as far as she could tell.

"How should I know? But the blood was on his—his body." She waved her hand over her torso. "You know, his chest area. I sure don't think he cut his wrists or anything like that."

This was too much like the day Jillian had discovered the body of another man downtown. She put a hand on the wall—

something she often told Kate not to do, for fear of discoloring the paint—to steady herself.

"You told Craig one of us would be downstairs."

"Right. To let the officers in."

Jillian nodded. "And answer any questions the other guests have. One of us should stay up here, though."

"Why?"

Putting a hand to her forehead, Jillian thought for a moment. She raised her gaze to Kate's and whispered, "Because somebody else in this house knows he's dead in there. We need to see if anyone comes poking around."

Kate stood there for a long moment. "Okay. I'll ... sit in the game room. You go down."

"Are you sure?"

"Yeah."

Jillian touched her shoulder. Kate had told her in the past that she was the strong one, but she had no doubt that Kate was braver than she could ever be. Maybe a little reckless at times, but brave.

"Okay, Katie. But keep your cell out. Call me if anything odd happens." She never called her younger sister Katie anymore, but this situation had shaken her, it was true.

"I will, but you know you can hear me down there if I yell." Anyone standing near the balcony railing could see down to the front desk and the main door.

Jillian nodded. "Okay, but ..."

With a tight smile, Kate said, "A password."

"What?"

"If I yell, 'Lightning,' that means get up here fast. Or if I text you ... uh ... SOS."

"SOS?"

"Sure. Nobody would hear me, but you'd get the message."

"As long as the cell towers stay up." Jillian gazed at her,

unwilling to leave her younger sister. "Maybe we should both go down."

"No, you go. I'll be fine. In fact, I'll set the lantern right here ..." Kate strode to a coffee table by one of the seating arrangements in the large room. "I'll take a pack of cards and play some solitaire." If anyone comes in, I'll just tell them I'm killing time."

Jillian winced at her choice of words.

"You'll be able to hear our voices if anyone does come into the room," Kate said. "I'll talk extra loud."

For a moment, Jillian pulled her close. "Don't do anything reckless," she whispered. She turned and headed for the stairs. At the landing, she turned on her phone's flashlight and hurried down. She'd better quit using that app, or it would drain her battery.

As soon as she reached the desk, she took a flashlight from a drawer and, by its light, brought in a lantern from the dining room. At least they'd had the foresight to stash light sources all over the office, kitchen, and common areas.

Huddling over the front desk, she waited. A faint glow shone above her, through the railing spindles. Kate's lantern. Normally, Rick could get here from the police station in about five minutes. She couldn't count on that tonight. Jillian tried to breathe slowly and regularly, but each inhalation seemed to catch in her throat. The wind howled on the other side of the front door, and the rain still pattered down, but she thought it had abated somewhat.

The murmur of voices came from above, and she jerked her head up.

"Oh, hi, Marie," came Kate's bright greeting to Mrs. Simon. "Yeah, we've got Scrabble. It's right over there on the shelf. Here, I'll show you."

Jillian could hear their footsteps. She frowned. She'd left

the Simons in the living room, near the fireplace. How did Marie get up one level to the game room without her noticing? Maybe she'd gone to her third-floor room first, while the sisters were exploring Alan Dryer's room, and then stopped off at the game room on her journey back down. Had she overheard anything?

She stood and went to the dining room door. Yes, the fire was still flickering on the hearth in the living room, and she could hear quiet male voices. Charles Simon and Luke Brantley were still in there. She slipped back onto her stool behind the front desk as Marie came down the stairway carrying a familiar brown box.

"Playing games?" Jillian managed a smile.

"Yeah, we thought it would pass the time."

"Good idea."

"Do you have to sit there all night?" Marie asked.

"Kate and I will swap off."

"Can I get you anything?"

"No, I'm fine."

As Marie walked through the deserted dining room toward the cozy fireside, Jillian had a sudden urge to check on Zeb. Alan Dryer had been killed in his room. Was Zeb all right? She forced herself to sit still. She would check on him as soon as Craig or another officer arrived.

Ten long minutes later, Rick blew in with Craig, bringing a slosh of water with them that puddled on the lobby's tile floor. They stood catching their breath, with drops plinking off their raingear.

"What happened?" Rick asked.

Jillian put a finger to her lips and leaned in close to them. "We don't want the guests to hear, and the sound travels from here up to the second floor."

Craig glanced up at the railing on the landing above them. "You said one of the guests is deceased."

She nodded. "Kate's up in the game room, outside his door, playing solitaire and trying to look innocent."

Craig smiled, but Rick rolled his eyes heavenward.

"Should we just go up the stairs?" Rick eyed her as though she was a child, not his elder sister.

"You'll have to. The elevator won't work. And Kate has the master key."

"Are you all right to stay here?" Craig touched her sleeve solicitously.

"I—I'd like to check on Zeb again. You know I brought him over here, right?"

"You told me," Rick said. "Go ahead, but I'd kind of like to have someone near the front door."

"I'll wait, then. You need to get up there. Send Kate down when you don't need her anymore."

Rick hung his dripping raincoat on the coat tree under the stairs, and Craig followed his lead. The two men jogged up the stairway, and despite the raging wind and rain, she could hear the murmur of their voices as they conversed with Kate.

Everything went quiet, and she assumed they'd entered Dryer's room. A few minutes later, Roger Cowper came down the stairs.

"Hey," he said to Jillian. "I don't guess there's any coffee, but maybe something else to drink?"

"Yeah, there's bottled water and some bottled soft drinks near the juice dispenser. I'm afraid they won't be cold."

"That's okay." He meandered into the dining room and came back with an open bottle of Coke. "So, what's the word on the power outage?"

"Nothing so far. I don't expect they'll start repairs until the storm clears." She didn't tell him that her brother was upstairs that very moment, or he'd want to know when they'd have the generator up and running.

Instead of going upstairs, Roger went into the living room. Jillian leaned forward to look, and the Simons and Luke were still in there, playing Scrabble. They all looked up and greeted Roger as he entered.

Kate came scurrying down the stairs, and Jillian gave her the quiet sign. "Luke's still in yonder with Mr. and Mrs. Simons. Mr. Cowper just went in there too."

Kate glanced through the dim dining room toward the living room and came quickly around the desk, to a point where she wouldn't be in anyone's line of sight from beyond the doorway.

"Craig says he'll call the medical examiner, but he likely won't be able to get here right away. He and Rick had to detour because of the flooding near the marina, and apparently there's a big tree down on Main Street."

"So ... what? We just leave the dead body there indefinitely?"

Kate shrugged. "I guess it's more important to help people who are alive and in danger than to risk lives to take a body to the morgue."

Jillian sighed. "So, we can't do anything about it right now."

"Right. Rick and Craig are going over the room."

"Did they say anything about how he died?"

"Not really, but I think we'd have heard a gunshot if that were the case."

"Yeah. Unless the killer had a silencer."

Kate shivered. "I don't like to think about someone coming in here with a gun in their suitcase. Until we hear otherwise, I'm going with suicide or accident."

"You know that doesn't make sense."

"Prove it."

Jillian met her sister's stubborn gaze. "Let's not fight over it. I need to go check on Zeb. Can you stay here a few minutes? I'll try not to be long."

Kate nodded soberly. "What do I say if someone sees the cop car or the guys?"

"I don't know. We'll have to tell them at some point."

Kate made a face but sat down behind the check-in counter that was their front desk.

"Go."

Jillian fished out her key for Zeb's room and hurried down the hall. She tapped softly on the door and then opened it a few inches. "Zeb? It's me."

"Jillian." His voice was gravelly, and she hurried in.

"How are you doing? Can I get you a drink of water?"

She handed him a bottle of water and then helped him get to the bathroom and back to his bed.

"Are you comfortable?" she asked.

"So comfy I might forget what my hammock back home feels like. What time is it?"

"It's quarter to eight. Think you'll be able to sleep some more?"

"Maybe."

"I'm sorry there's no TV tonight."

Zeb smiled. "I'm okay without TV. It might be nice to have something to read if I can't sleep, though."

"Sure. What would you like?"

They settled on that morning's paper and an Agatha Christie novel Zeb had never read. Jillian hurriedly explained to Kate as she went through the lobby to the stairs. The door to Alan Dryer's room was still shut when she reached the second floor, and she assumed Rick and Craig were inside. She went on up to the third level, where they had an extensive library in the lounge.

She found the Agatha Christie and pulled out an old sailing manual that had been a favorite of her dad's as well. Zeb never got tired of talking about boats, and she guessed he'd thumb through that. She snagged the morning paper from the front desk and nearly ran down the hall to make the delivery to Zeb.

"Oh, thank you, dear. These look interesting." Zeb was sitting up in bed now, and his face wasn't flushed. "And just so's you know, I took a couple more of those pills."

"That's fine," she said. "Head still aching?"

"Some, and the throat's a little sore. I hope I don't give it to you."

"I'll wash my hands first thing."

Zeb gave her his angelic smile. "If I ever had a daughter, I'd want her to be like you."

He was one of the sweetest men Jillian had ever met. She wondered how the men who served under him had seen him. He was actually quite mild-mannered, and she couldn't imagine him cursing and fuming. Yet, she'd seen him frustrated and discouraged. He could probably bark out orders with the best of them.

"If you weren't so germy, I'd kiss you," she said.

He wagged a finger at her. "I'll remember that later."

———

Kate was tempted to go up and knock on the door of the Poirot Room, but she made herself stay put. She considered reading an e-book on her phone, but that would run the battery down. She supposed she and Jillian could recharge their phones with the mobile chargers they carried in their vehicles. But her Jeep and Jillian's car were down in the garage, near the carriage house, and she wasn't about to get soaking wet unless it was an emergency.

"Kate! What's going on?"

She jerked her head up, and her pulse rocketed. Luke strode into the lobby.

"Nothing. Just taking a break while Jillian tends to Mr. Wilding."

"Marie said she saw two cops come in a while ago."

"Oh. Well, that was Rick and his friend."

"Are they here to start the generator? I could help."

She hesitated. Talking to Luke was the last thing she wanted to do, but she didn't want him to start a big fuss either. "Look, we're trying to keep this quiet, at least for now, but I'll tell you. Please don't spread it around."

"What?" His dark eyebrows quirked.

Feelings from the past ambushed Kate as she gazed up into his glittering brown eyes, and that in itself sparked anger in her. She bit her lip and decided to take the plunge. Maybe telling Luke would distract them both from the idyllic past and excruciating breakup that lay behind them.

"One of the guests died."

"What?" He whispered harshly. He glanced over his shoulder. "Who? Wasn't everyone there at dinner? Except your old neighbor, I mean. Was it him?"

"No. It's Mr. Dryer, the guy who came in late without a reservation."

"I guess I didn't meet him. What happened?"

"We don't know yet." Kate swallowed hard. Rick would be furious if she gave out any details. "Rick and Sergeant Watkins are handling it, and a medical examiner will come as soon as he's able. The storm, you know?"

Luke nodded.

"So, we're hoping we don't have to tell everyone before they can ... can remove the ... you know."

"Okay."

"Don't tell the others. Promise?"

"I guess so, for now. What should I tell Marie and Charles?"

"Nothing."

"I can't do that. I expressly came out here to find out why the police were in the house."

Kate let out a puff of air. "I guess you can explain that our brother is a cop, and say he brought another guy here to check on us. You could say they're helping with something."

"They'll think it's the generator."

"That generator's on the side porch. They're up on the second floor. Anyway, I don't know if we can get the generator running tonight."

Luke frowned and was silent for a moment. "I could help. In fact, I could probably do it on my own. I just haven't done it before, without someone who knew the ropes."

"Not yet," Kate said. "They have to ... do things upstairs. Maybe later. I'll ask Rick when he comes down."

Luke nodded soberly. "Okay, I'll try not to let it slip. But when this is over, I want the whole story." He smiled, as if there was still some understanding between them.

"Maybe Jillian can give it to you."

"Oh, come on, Kate. We have to talk sometime."

"No, we don't."

His brow furrowed. "I don't know if your sister told you or not, but Tara and I are history."

"I don't want to hear it."

Scowling, he flounced away toward the living room.

Kate consciously relaxed her clenched fists. Would he tell the others to spite her? She didn't have time to worry about

Luke and the stress he was causing her before Jillian returned. She rapidly told her sister about the conversation.

"Okay, so Luke knows." Jillian's flat tone told Kate she wasn't happy.

"I didn't give him any details. Did you tell Zeb?"

"No. I didn't want him to fret."

"I'm sorry. I had to tell Luke something. He says he'll keep it quiet until we announce it."

Jillian gave her a skeptical nod. "Here's hoping."

7

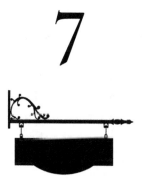

F ootsteps on the stairs drew their attention. Kate was relieved when Craig appeared, using his flashlight. He snapped it off when he reached the relative brightness of the lobby.

"Hi. Glad I caught both of you." He glanced across the hall and asked quietly, "Can we go into the office for a minute?"

"Sure," Jillian said.

Kate quickly opened the door behind the front desk, and the three of them went inside.

"Oops, forgot the lantern." She ducked out past Craig and brought the light in and set it on Jillian's desk. She and Jillian sat down, but Craig remained standing.

"Rick's still up there," he said. "As we feared, the M.E. can't get here right now. I'm afraid we'll have to leave the body where it is, probably until morning."

"That's creepy," Kate said.

"Who's in the room next to him—the David Copperfield Room?"

"Max Pelletier," Jillian said. "He's a marine biologist."

"That's a little offbeat. Why's he here?"

"He came in yesterday. Said he wanted to study the marine life in the bay."

"Interesting. It's a bad time for that," Craig said.

Kate frowned. "At that point, we were all still hoping Cloris would blow out to sea."

"No such luck. It's hitting full force tonight."

"He said something about mollusks," Jillian offered.

Craig looked at her and back at Kate. "Rick thinks one of us should stay here tonight, given the circumstances."

"And I think we'd appreciate that," Jillian said. "But Diana and the kids will need Rick."

"My feelings exactly. I told him I'd stay."

"We've got exactly one empty room," Kate said. "I mean, besides the two with plumbing problems." Her lips skewed.

"I may just sit up in the lounge up there."

"It's the game room," Kate said. "The lounge is above it, on the third floor."

"Okay, the game room."

"Well, we can give you the Liz Bennet Room, so you can have a private bathroom on the same floor and a place to stretch out if you want," Jillian said. "With power out, we can't activate new key cards, but that master key we gave you guys will open any door. Liz Bennet is down the hall from the game room, beyond the elevator, and to the left."

"Thanks. Now, you said two rooms are out of order— where are they?"

"Up on three," Kate said. "Scout Finch and Rip Van Winkle. They have a jack-and-jill bathroom."

"What's that?" Craig asked.

"They each have their own toilet area and sink, but they share the tub and shower in the middle."

"So, whoever's in one room has access to the other?"

"Well, they could, if one of the occupants didn't lock the doors in between," Jillian said. "We try to give those rooms to families or people who know each other. But as Kate mentioned, right now, no one's in them because the tub drain is plugged up."

"Okay. And the master key will open those as well?"

Jillian nodded. "You want to see them?"

"I just thought it might be a good idea for us to take a look at any empty rooms, as well as your storage room and so on."

"Are you looking for the killer?" Kate whispered. This was getting unreal.

"More like a weapon."

Both women stared at him in silence.

"We're troubled by the wounds," Craig said. "There's blood on the rug, and there's a lot on the bed, where the victim is lying. Someone ..." He hesitated then plunged ahead. "Someone padded the bed with towels and an extra blanket. Not a lot of blood soaked through to the mattress, which is good news for you."

"But it's odd," Jillian said.

"Exactly."

Kate's mind whirled. "So ... you're suggesting that he died on the floor and was moved to the bed?"

"No, we're not jumping to conclusions, but there's quite a bit of blood on the floor."

"We saw it on the rug near the bed," Jillian said.

"And we also found a small smear on the doorjamb inside the room," he said.

Kate blinked. "Didn't notice that."

Craig gave them a sad smile. "The woodwork in that room is stained dark—walnut, I'm guessing—and you two were focused on the victim. Rick and I have had time to look around carefully."

"We tried not to step on the patches on the rug," Jillian said. "I didn't go that close, but Kate did."

"I was checking to make sure he was dead, like you told me," Kate reminded him, trying not to sound accusatory. "I was mostly gawking at Mr. Dryer. He was very obviously not breathing and ..." She shuddered.

"What kind of weapon are you looking for?" Jillian asked.

"Probably a knife of some kind, but the autopsy will tell us a lot more."

Kate pulled in a big breath. "Should we check our knives in the kitchen?"

"That's a good idea. And it would help us to have a list of all your remaining guests."

"I'll get that for you," Jillian said. She started to rise and checked herself. "Oh. One of them's a doctor."

"Really?"

Jillian nodded. "Eliza Rowan."

"Hmm. I'll see what Rick thinks. Since the M.E. will be delayed, it might be good for someone else with medical experience to take a look. I want to let Rick go as soon as I can."

"Is he needed on rescue duty?" Jillian asked.

"We've only had a couple of real emergencies. Dave and Geordie are out at a fender bender near the highway right now. The chief is at the station tonight, and our other officers are handling things so far. We haven't had to evacuate anyone, but some families down in the low spots have moved to higher ground. I'm surprised none of them came here for refuge."

"I'm glad they didn't," Jillian said. "We've got enough to handle tonight."

He reached for her hand and gave it a squeeze. "Hey, it's okay. We'll get through this." With a smile, he turned and left the office.

Kate's stomach churned. "A guest was murdered in our inn, Jillian."

Her sister came over and put her arm around Kate's shoulders. "We'll be okay. Craig and Rick will sort it out. Right now, we have to check the knives and make a list of guests."

As usual, Jillian looked calm and self-assured. "I'm glad Craig's staying. Will you do the knives? Luke's still in the living room, and I don't want him to see me go past."

"Sure. Make the list of the guests' names and the rooms they're in, and then take it up to Craig. And don't forget Zeb."

"Right."

The list took only a couple of minutes, and she double-checked it with Jillian when she came out from the kitchen.

"Looks good to me," Jillian said. "All our knives are where they should be too."

"I wish we could lock the door between the kitchen and the dining room."

"I know. It seems odd that we can't. I mean, there are locks on almost every door—the storage room, the linen closet, the office."

Kate nodded. "Anyone can get into the lobby, the dining room, the living room, the game room, and the lounge. But it doesn't seem right for the guests to be able to go into the kitchen. We can't watch that door all the time."

"Absolutely right. I never really thought about it before. But in theory, we've always got someone in the lobby who can tell if anyone's in the dining room or living room." Jillian's brow wrinkled, and Kate figured she was calculating the cost of adding a lock to the swinging kitchen door.

A peremptory knock came on the hall door to the office, and Kate jumped up and opened it. Rick stood outside.

"Hey," Kate said.

He strode into the room. "Craig's telling me to go home,

but I don't want to leave until I know you two are okay with that."

"You should go." Jillian stood. "We'll be fine, and you ought to get some sleep. I'm sure there'll be lots for the whole department to do tomorrow."

"I'm sure, but ..." He shook his head. "Diana did call me. She wants me to come home. The kids are nervous, and she says there's no school tomorrow. I think she's more emotional because she's pregnant."

"She's probably a little jittery," Kate said. "But what about the generator?"

"Go," Jillian said. "We're okay."

Kate frowned at her. She couldn't see missing this chance when Rick was right here. "We'd be a lot better with some lights. Not to mention water."

Rick wavered. "I'll bet Luke and I can get it running in under five minutes. Where is he?"

"In by the fireplace with some other guests," Jillian said promptly.

"Okay, I'll tap him for some help. I left a can of gas in the storeroom earlier."

"It's still there," Kate assured him.

"Great." Rick strode out into the hall.

Kate wanted to follow him, but that would mean more contact with Luke.

"I'll go," Jillian said. "You sit tight."

"I can sit in the lobby."

They both left the office, and Kate took up her post. She was startled a few minutes later when the overhead light came on and the computer terminal began humming. A muffled cheer reached her from the game players in the living room.

Jillian hurried out of the dining room. "We're all set. Can you believe it? Rick checked the wattage on the generator, and he thinks we can do lights and hot water if the guests are okay without running the furnace."

From the doorway, her brother said, "Yeah, Jill thought hot showers and flushing toilets were more important to the guests than a couple extra degrees tonight. I flipped a few breakers off, but you should be all set."

"Thanks so much," Kate said. Behind Rick, she saw Luke slip through the dining room to rejoin the Simons.

"All right, but I told Craig to call me immediately if he needs me to come back." Rick's face slackened. "Oh, I almost forgot. Your Dr. Rowan?"

"What about her?" Jillian asked.

"She's a podiatrist."

"Oh."

Kate grimaced. "I knew she was a medical doc, but I didn't ask what her specialty was."

"Craig said we ought to have her come in anyway." Rick shrugged. "He figures it's wise to have somebody medical go in and see the body before it gets any colder. She's still a full-fledged M.D., just hasn't seen sickness or death since medical school—only feet. And she may have some insights."

"She might tell some of the other guests," Jillian said. "She's been spending time with the Simons, for instance."

"Well, it may be time to clue them all in." Rick glanced at his watch. "Anyway, she's up there with Craig now. Here's Dryer's room key. It was on his dresser." He laid the key card on the desk. "Craig said to give it to you, so there's no chance someone else gets hold of it."

"Thanks." Jillian picked it up.

"Now, I'd better go if I'm going." Rick put on his raincoat and let himself out.

"Thanks," Kate called after him.

"Give our love to Diana," Jillian added.

He managed to shut the door alone, which told Kate the wind had slackened, at least for the moment.

"It will be nice to be able to make coffee and eggs for breakfast," she said.

The sisters gazed at each other.

Jillian said soberly, "Time to have a meeting and let the cat out of the bag."

———

Twenty minutes later, all of the Novel Inn's guests except Zeb were gathered in the living room. Charles Simon had built up the fire, and several people pulled chairs closer. Dr. Rowan had come down and told Jillian that Sgt. Watkins would appear shortly, so she made sure all the guests were accounted for and went ahead with her spiel.

"We've asked you all to come down here to explain two things. First, as you know, the generator is up and running. We've got enough gas to keep it running all night. But it's not powerful enough to run the heating system. We've got lights and running water, but no furnace. So do get out your extra blankets tonight. Our weather radio says it shouldn't get down below forty degrees outside, and I'm sure it will stay warmer than that in here."

"What about food?" Marie asked.

"We'll be able to cook breakfast as usual, and there's enough power to keep the refrigerator running. As long as you're stuck here, we'll try to feed you, but I'm not sure if we'll be able to do any shopping, so meals may get interesting. It will be whatever we can manage."

"That's fine," Charles said.

"And we appreciate all you're doing," Luke added.

Craig came to the doorway and nodded gravely at Jillian.

She took a deep breath. "And now I'm going to introduce Sgt. Craig Watkins, of the Skirmish Cove Police Department, to tell you about our second topic."

Craig stepped forward, and she sank gratefully into a chair in a corner where most of the guests wouldn't see her unless they turned their heads. She was tired of being in charge.

"Thanks for coming in, folks," Craig said. "There's been an incident here at the inn, and I know some of you are wondering what's going on. I'll just say it: One of the guests has died in his room."

Nobody gasped or cried out, which didn't surprise Jillian. Most of them knew, or had at least a suspicion.

"The deceased is Alan Dryer," Craig went on. "Some of you may have met him earlier, although I understand he arrived only this afternoon. He was staying in the Hercule Poirot Room, on the second floor. We've locked his room for now. We had hoped the medical examiner could get here, but he can't in this storm. I'm sorry, but we have no choice. We have to wait until the proper officials can get in here with their equipment to remove the body."

"Wait, I have to sleep next door to a body?" Max Pelletier said.

Craig frowned at him. "That's correct, if you're in the David Copperfield Room."

Jillian cleared her throat. "We do have one more room on the same floor. If you would feel better, Mr. Pelletier, you can move your things into the unoccupied room around the corner."

Max's brow furrowed. "I guess I'm okay. I mean, you'll have police here and everything, right?"

"That's correct," Craig said. "I will be staying here on watch all night, and we'll keep Mr. Dryer's room locked. In the morning, we'll see if we can get a hearse here to take him away."

Max didn't look happy, but he sat back in his chair.

Marie Simon raised her hand, as if they were in a classroom. "Can I ask how he died? I mean, it's not some virus we're all going catch, or something like that, is it?"

"No," Craig said quickly but calmly. He nodded toward Eliza Rowan. "You are fortunate that one of your fellow guests is an M.D. Dr. Rowan has examined the body for us. Since she's not licensed in the state of Maine, the coroner will have to issue the official death certificate. But she has pronounced Mr. Dryer dead. At this time, it is an open investigation, so I can't discuss the cause of death. I will note, it was *not* from disease. The autopsy will tell us more."

Roger Cowper jerked his head up. "What are we talking about here—suicide?"

"I can't discuss it," Craig said.

"So, do you need to put him in the cooler or something?" Max asked.

From the other side of the room, Kate met Jillian's gaze, her face pale. Jillian tried to convey support. *It's okay. Stay calm. Some people don't think before they speak.* Kate wriggled in her chair and pulled in a deep breath.

"No need for that." Craig sounded affable but firm, and again Jillian was glad for his presence and his air of authority. "As Mrs. Tunney said, it will be cool here tonight. That's good in this case. And I assure you, we'll remove Mr. Dryer as soon as we possibly can."

Luke opened his mouth as though he would speak out, but then he closed it.

Craig took a few more questions, then said, "Folks, I suggest you all go to your rooms. I'll be upstairs in the game room outside Mr. Dryer's door. If anything comes up, find me there. If I have to leave that room for a few minutes, Jillian or Kate will be at the front desk in the lobby. Good night." With a smile, he turned away.

Jillian stood, trying to look self-composed. She doubted she could have dismissed them all so definitely. Kate hurried out, and Jillian figured she would duck into the kitchen. Luke stared after Kate for a moment, then turned around and met Jillian's eyes.

Craig walked over and said, "I'll head upstairs. I hope everyone goes to bed, but some might be restless."

"Okay. We'll be alert. And thanks, Craig. I don't know what we would have done without you."

"Glad to help." He touched her arm for a second, then followed the guests through the dining room toward the stairs.

Luke and Max were the last two to leave. As they entered the hall, Luke said to Max, "Did you say you're in the room next to where the body is?"

The two men went into the lobby and toward the stairs. Jillian wished Luke wouldn't show such an avid interest in the murder. But mostly, she was glad Max hadn't insisted on changing rooms.

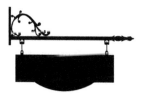

J illian sat up with her e-book reader in her office. Kate went upstairs not long after the guests had retired, and all was quiet. The historical romance she'd started didn't hold Jillian's attention. Her mind wandered to the murder, and to Craig. Was he sitting up there in the game room keeping watch? Or was he busy collecting more evidence?

She wished she could sit and talk to him easily, the way they sometimes did in the evening. They'd go out for coffee, or Craig would sit down with her here, in the office or out near the fireplace. They were still getting to know each other, but so far she liked everything she'd learned. She'd opened up to him more than she ever had with anyone outside her family, and she was comfortable with him. They were growing close, close enough to trust each other fully.

At ten thirty, she heard soft footsteps. They halted at the top of the stairs. She got up and went into the lobby. Looking up, she saw Craig peering down over the railing. He smiled, and a wave of warmth swept over her.

"Everything good?" she whispered.

He nodded. "I hoped to get to talk to you, but I don't think I should leave my post.

"I could come up for a while," Jillian said. She would either see anyone heading for the stairs or hear them walking around in the lobby.

He nodded, and she went back to close and lock the office door, then tiptoed up to join him. He smiled and took her hand.

"Over here." He led her to a couple of armchairs near the shelf unit holding games. It was farther away from the entrance to Dryer's room than the sofa, but also farther from the guest room next to it.

From here, they could plainly see the victim's locked door, and also the top of the stairway and the near end of the hall, along which Luke Brantley and Roger Cowper's rooms were located. The Elizbeth Bennet Room, which she'd designated for Craig, was also down there, around the corner.

Craig leaned in and whispered, "I did a little more searching in Dryer's room and studied his belongings more closely."

"Find anything?"

"Not a lot. Rick gave you the room key Dryer had left on the dresser?"

"Yes."

"If you'd rather, I could use it and give you back the master key."

"We have another master. Besides, you might need to unlock other doors. I put Dryer's card in a plastic bag in my desk in the office, in case you needed it for fingerprints or something."

Craig shrugged. "We know he handled it, but I suppose it wouldn't hurt to check it."

"The killer might have touched it," she whispered.

"Possible. And another thing—his wallet was also on the dresser. There wasn't any cash in it."

She thought about that. "Some people don't carry cash these days."

"No, but travelers usually have a little at least. Tips, and so on."

"What about credit cards? I recall him giving me a Mastercard when he checked in."

He eyed her sharply. "Not a Visa?"

Jillian shook her head.

"Because I found a debit card that's a Visa, but no Mastercard."

"Are you sure?"

"Yes. Are you?"

She nodded. "It was definitely a Mastercard, and he charged it as a credit, not a debit. Maybe he put that card somewhere else."

Craig's lips thinned. "I didn't find it in his room."

"Why would someone steal a Mastercard but not the debit?"

"There may have been other credit cards in the wallet too. We don't know what's missing. Only what's still there."

"His driver's license?"

"That was there, and an insurance card, and a store discount card."

"Odd. Most people have several credit cards. I know I do."

"Did you notice if he was wearing any jewelry?" Craig asked.

Jillian closed her eyes and tried to focus on Alan Dryer's hands as he passed her the credit card. "A ring, I think." She moved her hands slightly, reenacting his motions. "On his right hand. A big, chunky ring. Maybe a class ring."

"Not one you recognized?"

"No. It wasn't a school from around here. It could have been some other thing—an association or a sports ring, I suppose."

"And no wedding ring?"

She hesitated. "I'm not sure."

"How about a watch?"

"Not that I noticed, but that would probably have been on his left hand. He carried a cell phone, I remember that, so maybe he didn't wear a watch."

"We found his phone," Craig said. "And he wasn't wearing a wedding ring. I was just testing you. His ring finger doesn't have an impression from one. But his right hand does. He'd definitely been wearing a ring recently, no doubt the one you saw."

"So, they stole his ring, along with his credit cards and possible cash."

"That's what I'm thinking. I checked his pockets. Nothing there but car keys and a Kleenex. Nothing significant in the bathroom or in his suitcase. Just normal, everyday clothes, an electric razor, and toiletries."

"Would someone kill him for a ring?" she asked.

"I don't know."

Something niggled at the back of her mind. "Wasn't there a big jewelry robbery recently? We heard something on the radio."

"Yes. There was a smash-and-grab heist yesterday in Bangor."

"That's it. Kate was griping that the announcer said the clerk 'did not survive,' instead of saying flat out that he died. But ..."

"What?" Craig asked.

"Two things. First, would someone who knocked over a jewelry store and committed murder in the process take a huge chance to get one man's ring? And second, Dryer said he came up from Castine, not down from Bangor. He mentioned driving on to Portland, but he stopped here because of the weather."

Craig nodded pensively. "According to his driver's license, he lives in Auburn."

"So why was he going to Portland, not straight to Auburn, which is closer?"

"Did he say what he does for a living?" Craig asked.

"Afraid not."

"As soon as we're done with this hurricane craziness, we'll get his background. They're ready at the station to start doing that—and getting information on all your other guests—as soon as they can. Right now, it's emergency calls only."

"Have there been many car accidents?"

"A few. There's also been one electrocution and a few injuries from flying debris and broken glass. Our officers have also had to help some people down near the marina evacuate."

"I thought Rick said no evacuations."

"A few had to. Some got out on their own, but I believe a couple of patrol officers are down there."

"So, it's worse than it was earlier. I'm kind of surprised they haven't sent anyone here for shelter. But we're pretty much full now."

"Yeah."

They sat for a moment in silence.

"Do you have safes in the guest rooms?" he asked. "I don't recall seeing one in Dryer's closet."

"No. We have the big one in the office. My dad said those little ones are ridiculously easy to open. He never wanted to invest in them."

"Do you know if any of the other guests have valuable jewelry? Mrs. Simon, maybe?"

"I commented on her necklace yesterday. It was very

attractive, but I don't think it was very valuable. She's an artist, you know. She said a friend of hers made it."

"Did it have stones?"

Jillian shook her head. "Enameled metal, I think. And nobody's asked to have anything put into the office safe."

"That was my next question."

———

Rick paced his bedroom in his bare feet, trying not to disturb Diana's fretful slumber. He could go downstairs, but then he wouldn't be handy if she or the kids woke. He should lie down and try to sleep, but he had too much on his mind. The storm, the murder at Novel Inn, Diana's pregnancy.

This was a horrible time for morning sickness. He wouldn't wish it on any woman. Still, he wanted to be out with his fellow officers, helping people in the community. No, that wasn't the strict truth. He paused by the window and stared out into the unrelenting rain. He wanted to go back to the inn, where the murder investigation was lagging.

But Craig was there. He'd take care of things. Rick sighed and turned back toward the bed.

The door burst open, and his thirteen-year-old son stood in the doorway in his pajamas.

"Dad." The boy's voice cracked in the darkness.

"Yes, Joel?"

"I just ..." Joel's chin ducked. "Can I sleep in here?"

"Well, apparently you can't sleep in your own room."

"It's the wind," Joel said.

"Yeah, I thought it would die down by now, but it's still pretty fierce."

"I slept for a while, but then I woke up, and I can't get back to sleep."

Rick sighed. "I know the feeling." He waved toward the bed. "Climb in on my side."

Another form appeared in the doorway, ghostly in her pale pink pj's.

"Hello, Ashley," Rick said.

"Hi." Her voice was small, as though she was ashamed of acting like a toddler. "I heard voices."

Diana stirred as Joel slid onto Rick's spot on the other side of the king bed.

"What's going on? Rick?"

"It's just the kids," Rick said.

Diana gave a little moan and shifted toward the middle of the mattress. "Climb in. It's just one of those nights."

Rick made the decision. No way could he rest with two teenagers poking them. "Look, I'm going down—"

A huge crack outside was followed by a crash above him, and the bedroom window shattered. Rick leaped back as screams pierced the night.

9

Kate woke at quarter to twelve and groped for her phone. She turned off the alarm and took several slow breaths, waiting for her pulse to slow. Jillian must be exhausted, and it was time to relieve her. Kate climbed out of the big bed and stumbled to the bathroom.

As she brushed her teeth, she wished the shutters were off the windows so she could use the telescope tonight. Oh, well, rain still seemed to be peppering them. The clouds would hide the stars tonight. She'd have to plan a special time on a clear evening when the Hornblower Room was empty. Maybe she and Jillian could invite a few friends for a stargazing party.

She pulled on her jeans with a sigh. At least they had running water now. The guests would leave, remembering their little adventure at the Novel Inn. Kate shivered and listened to the wind howl. She tugged a hoodie on over her shirt, then headed for the stairway.

At the second-floor landing, she peered into the game room. Craig sat on the sofa. He lifted a languid hand, and she waved back and went on down to the lobby.

Jillian blinked at her from behind the front desk, where she sat huddled with an afghan from the living room sofa around her shoulders.

"Oh, good. I think I read the same page five times." She pressed the off button on her reader.

"Everything's quiet, I guess?" Kate asked.

"Yeah. I'll check on Zeb when I go past his room."

"Okay. I saw Craig on the sofa upstairs, so I guess all is calm up there too. Good night."

As her sister walked quietly down the hall, Kate settled in, then gave herself a mental kick. She hadn't brought anything to read. After a moment, she got up and opened the office door. Jillian had some reading material in there, she was sure.

Kate's search turned up a guide for small hotel owners and several back issues of *Country Living*. Jillian said the magazine gave her ideas for decorating. Kate hoped she wouldn't overhaul another guest room anytime soon. She opened a cupboard where they kept a "lost and found" box with a few things guests had left behind. They kept the items in there for several months, in case a former patron called and asked for something.

Under a single glove and a Red Sox cap, she found a stuffed kitten and a paperback book. *Silence Can Be Deadly*. She'd never heard of the author, but it sounded suspenseful and would probably keep her awake for a while. She took it with her to the lobby. Instead of the stool directly behind the computer terminal, she settled into the more comfortable chair Don used in the wee hours, when the whole house was quiet.

Yep, the rain still pattered steadily on the porch roof, but it didn't sound nearly as violent as it had earlier, and the wind had slacked off some. Amazing that she'd been able to sleep up on the third floor, where the noise was louder. She turned on the weather radio just long enough to learn the rain would continue most of the day. With a sigh, she flicked it off and opened the mystery novel.

She was only ten pages into the book when she heard stirrings above her. She looked up. Craig was leaning over the railing.

He gave her a smile. "I don't suppose there's coffee down there?"

Kate jumped up. "I'll make a fresh pot and bring you some. I could use some myself."

"Thanks. Black is fine."

He moved away from the railing. He must have stayed awake so far without the benefit of caffeine. Kate felt guilty. She'd make up for it on her shift. She scurried to the kitchen and set a small coffeepot brewing.

"Thank you, Lord," she breathed. "Thank you for running water. Thank you for the generator. Thank you for Craig." She poured a mug for each of them and took the pot to the dining room, where it could remain warm for refills.

Craig thanked her profusely when she took him his mug.

"There's more," Kate said. "Just let me know if you want a refill. And here—I brought you a couple of cookies."

He grinned. "Perfect."

Below, she settled into her chair again with her coffee and the mystery. It soon pulled her into the story.

———

"Okay, that should do it." Rick stepped back from the window that he'd covered with a plastic shower curtain and a heavy blanket. "I'll see about fixing it as soon as the storm clears."

Joel, who was holding Rick's heavy-duty flashlight, played

the beam over the severed tree branch that had shattered the window.

"Do we have to sleep in here with that?"

Rick sighed. After the scare, he and the kids had tried unsuccessfully to shove the big limb out the window. He finally had to run down to the garage for a handsaw to cut off the part of the maple branch that had crashed inside.

The rest of the limb had fallen away outside, thudding on the lawn below. He hoped it didn't do any more damage, but he'd have to investigate that later. Now the master bedroom had a good-sized branch lying on the carpet between the bed and the damaged window frame. Bare, wet twigs draped over the foot of the bed.

"No," he said, reaching for the flashlight. "I think you should go back to your own rooms. It'll be safer there, since the wind is blowing toward us from the bay, and your rooms are on the back of the house."

"Mom, will you come with me?" Ashley's voice still sounded a little shaky.

"Sure." Diana swung her legs off the edge of the bed and grabbed her pillow.

"Dad?" Joel asked.

"What?"

"Will you come in my room?"

Rick sighed. "I thought I'd take the couch downstairs."

"I have twin beds." Joel was wheedling now.

Rick hesitated. He didn't think they all needed to retreat to the basement, but how safe were they? Any more damage to the house was likely to focus on the upper level.

"Tell you what, you kids can settle on the living room floor with sleeping bags if you want. Your mom could take the couch."

"I think Ashley's room will be more comfortable," Diana said. She plodded over to him and leaned in for a kiss. "Try to sleep, wherever you end up, honey." She and Ashley headed down the hallway.

"Okay. But I'm getting up in a couple of hours and going back on duty," Rick called after them.

"Do you have to?" Joel asked.

"Yeah, buddy. There are a lot of people out there with worse damage than us."

Diana and Ashley were already halfway down the hall to Ashley's room.

"I'm coming with you, Dad." Joel's rock-solid tone told Rick the boy was covering his fear.

He ruffled Joel's hair. "Okay. You get your pillow, and I'll go get you a sleeping bag out of the laundry room closet."

Joel insisted on sleeping on the carpet. Rick started to protest but decided to let him. That would leave the couch free for him if he thought he could sleep. Once he'd settled Joel on the floor, he paced the room quietly. Occasionally he went to the dining room window facing the water, peering out toward the bay, but he couldn't see much beyond the rain sheeting down the glass.

He couldn't leave his family right now, but he itched to know what was going on outside his home—specifically at the inn. Were his sisters safe?

After an hour, he tiptoed into the kitchen and used his radio to call the police station.

"Yeah, Rick," came David Hall's voice. Dave was the newest member of the department, but he'd been with them for nearly a year now.

"How's it going, Dave?" Rick said. "Am I needed?"

"The chief hopes you'll report at six. The bridge on the

main road is out just north of town. We may be isolated on the peninsula for a while, and people might need help getting food and water."

"Any evacuations?"

"Uh ... three families from the area near the marina. Two went to stay with family or friends. There's a couple over at the Methodist church, sleeping in their youth room tonight. If it keeps raining, we may need to take a few more out. We've got seven homes on alert."

"I'm pretty sure the Novel Inn is full up," Rick said.

"Yeah, the chief said that's too close to the bay anyhow. If we need hotel rooms, we'll probably go with the one downtown."

"Okay. I'll see you at six o'clock."

"Get some rest while you can," Dave said.

Good advice. Rick went back to the living room, where Joel was snoring softly, snuggled into his sleeping bag on the carpet. Rick stretched out on the couch and pulled the afghan his mother had crocheted down over him. He missed Diana, though she was only up in Ashley's room. He'd get that window fixed tomorrow and the tree branch out. He was sleeping in his own bed with Diana next time.

A baby. Boy or girl? He didn't really care which variety of miracle they received. Its arrival would strain their budget, but he was happy. He was pretty sure Diana was too. Except for the morning sickness.

A couple hours' sleep would be good. The pelting rain had a sort of rhythm on the glass of the unprotected windows, and it soon lulled him into rest.

———

Kate heard the soft closing of a door above. Before she had time to think about it, Luke was jogging down the stairs. She tensed but tried to control her anxiety.

He pulled up short when he saw her peering at him. "Hey. Thought I'd check the generator. It probably needs more fuel."

"Thanks. Are you freezing up there?"

"It's cool, but not life-threatening."

She stretched her arms. "I guess I could build up the fireplace fire. That might help a little."

"Some folks might want to eat their breakfast in there," he suggested.

The clock over the desk said five thirty—time for her and Jillian to start breakfast. They normally began the breakfast service at six. However, she doubted anyone would check out early this morning. If Jillian was sleeping, good for her. Kate would give her a few more minutes. She had no doubt her sister would be out here by six.

Luke stepped toward the front door. He was wearing a light jacket over his casual clothes. Kate hesitated, not wanting to give him any comfort, but if it was her ... She decided to save him a small amount of annoyance.

"You can go out the side door—through the kitchen and storage room. You went that way with Rick, didn't you?"

"Yeah, but I wasn't sure you'd want me to."

"Go ahead. Your room key should unlock the side door when you're ready to come back inside."

"Okay." He left her, headed for the kitchen.

Kate's pulse was tripping again, so she decided not to go to the kitchen until he'd finished his work on the side porch and gone back through. She didn't want to find herself alone with Luke out there. At least here in the lobby, Craig would hear if she yelped.

She looked upward, and sure enough, there was Craig, at the rail again.

"All good?" he asked.

"Yeah, thanks." Had Jillian told him about Luke and the way he'd smashed her heart ten years ago? "You want more coffee?"

"I won't say no."

She fetched it from the coffee station in the dining room this time, keeping two rooms between her and Luke.

"Thanks," Craig said with a weary smile when she reached the game room. He took the mug and cradled it in his hands.

"I was thinking," Kate said. "When we give a person their room key, it will also open the front door and the side door. That's in case they stay out late and the front door's locked when they come home. But the side door ..." She shook her head. "Maybe that's not such a good idea."

"What are you thinking?"

"Well, if somebody wanted to get in without letting the desk clerk see them, they could go to the side porch and sneak in through the storage room and the kitchen. If no one was in there, I mean. Which no one is all night."

"Hmm. I see what you mean. But then they'd still have to pass the lobby desk to get back to their guest room."

"Right." Kate frowned, wondering if it mattered. "I'm going to start the fire in the fireplace."

"I could do it if you want."

"Don't you need to stay up here?"

He looked toward Dryer's room. "How about if you sit up here for five minutes? It shouldn't take me longer than that if there's kindling and everything ready."

"Okay. And there may still be some coals. If not, there's tinder in the metal box to the side."

Craig took a big gulp of coffee and set down his mug.

94

"Oh, and Luke's gassing up the generator."

"I saw him go by and guessed that was his mission." Craig went quietly but swiftly down the stairs.

Kate pulled in a deep breath and sat down on a chair across the room from the two doors opening off the game room. She hoped Craig was as good as his word. Luke could return to his room any minute, and he'd surely see her sitting here.

Certainly not more than ten minutes later, she heard steps on the stairway. She held her breath and puffed it out in relief when Craig appeared on the landing.

"Fire's roaring."

"Thanks. I hope your coffee's not cold."

"I drank most of it. I'll be fine."

She nodded. "Jillian should be up soon, and we'll start breakfast. Do you want me to bring you a plate?"

"Let's see if Rick or another officer shows up. If none of them are here by seven, I'll take you up on that."

Luke paused on the landing.

"Morning," Craig said quietly.

Luke raised a hand in greeting. "The generator's all set for a while."

"Thanks," Kate said. She waited for him to retreat to his room, and Craig gave her a sympathetic smile.

"He took his time doing that," she whispered.

"Duly noted," Craig said.

She went down and met Jillian in the lobby.

"Hi," Jillian said. "Everything under control?"

Kate opened her mouth to reassure her and, to her dismay, her throat tightened and tears filled her eyes.

"Hey, are you okay?" Jillian moved closer and put her arms around her. She rubbed Kate's back for a moment. "What's going on?"

"Nothing," Kate choked out. "It's just …"

"Luke?"

She nodded, dashing away a tear with the back of her hand.

"I'll tell him he has to leave at breakfast time."

Kate waved a hand. "He hasn't overstepped, really. It's just the memories, you know?"

"He treated you terribly," Jillian said.

Kate nodded and couldn't hold back a sob. "I don't know how to pray, Jill. I know I shouldn't keep on hating him, but ... It's hard, you know?"

"Yeah, I know. I'm praying for you too." Jillian glanced upward. "Craig's still up there, right?"

"Yes, and he's had coffee. If no other officers are here by seven, we take him a plate."

"Well, we'd better get moving on breakfast," Jillian said. "It's nearly six, and we don't have anything ready yet."

"They'll understand. I'll get the cold stuff out. You start the eggs." Kate paused and turned hesitantly at her sister. "Can we use the stove?"

"Rick said we can use a burner, but not to try using the big oven. The microwave's okay, though. Maybe we should start the bacon in there, though it will splatter."

"And we'll clean it." Kate squared her shoulders and led the way through the dining room.

"Oh, the fire's going," Jillian said.

"Craig did it. We may need to add wood."

"Let me check."

Kate went on to the kitchen while Jillian tended to that task. Soon both were hard at work preparing the meal. Kate replenished the pastry and muffin cabinets and restocked the individual cereal boxes in the rack. She put out milk and juice and made sure there was plenty of coffee and hot water. Assorted tea bags, check. Hot chocolate mix, check. She got out butter and cream cheese, and the refrigerator seemed fine. No need to open the freezer compartment.

As Jillian carried a pan of scrambled eggs to the buffet, Dr. Eliza Rowan came in from the hall.

"Good morning," Jillian sang out.

"Good—oh, dear." Dr. Rowan stepped closer to them and lowered her voice. "I—I think someone's been in my room."

10

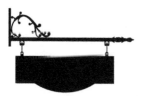

Jillian stared at the doctor. "In your room?"

"When?" Kate asked. "Just now?"

"No, I think it was yesterday—last night, when I was playing Scrabble with the Simons. I just noticed this morning that my things were out of place. Someone rummaged through them, I'm sure. And the book I was reading was on the nightstand. I'm sure I'd left it on the desk."

"Is anything missing?" Jillian asked.

"A turquoise bracelet that I'm rather fond of. I didn't bring any valuables other than that, and I had my handbag with me every time I left the room."

"Is the bracelet valuable?" Kate asked.

"I paid over three hundred dollars for it when I was in Arizona last year."

Jillian's heart sank. "Sergeant Watkins is still here. He's up in the game room on the second level, keeping an eye on ... on Mr. Dryer's room. You should tell him."

"I will." Dr. Rowan pivoted and left the room.

Kate gritted her teeth. "Are we responsible?"

"We may have to contact our insurance company," Jillian said.

Luke stepped forward from beside the coffeemaker. "Hey, I couldn't help overhearing. Someone ransacked her room?"

"That's a little dramatic," Jillian said. "She thinks someone else has been in her room, and her bracelet is missing. But it's possible she only misplaced it." *We can hope*, she told herself, but Kate wouldn't be convinced.

"It's odd," Luke said. "Someone else being able to get into her room, I mean."

"Well, yes," Jillian conceded. It *was* odd, especially when the maid hadn't been in that day.

Someone rang the doorbell. Normally no one used it, except after the door was secured at night. "Excuse me," she said, but she had no doubt Luke would watch her open the door with interest. Kate, she realized, had fled to the kitchen as soon as Luke made his presence known.

Rick stood on the front porch in his rain gear.

"Hi," Jillian said. "I should have given you a master key last night."

"It's okay. Is Craig still on watch?"

"Yes, he's up in the game room. But the doctor, Eliza Rowan, just went up to tell him she thinks someone was snooping around in her room yesterday while she was down here playing Scrabble by the fireplace. And a special bracelet of hers is missing."

Rick checked his movement to gaze at her keenly, but then he continued stripping off his rain gear. "I'll go up. Craig's probably ready for a break."

"We gave him access to the Elizabeth Bennet Room, if he wants to get a shower or a nap there."

"Okay. We'll see."

Jillian eyed the dripping raincoat he hung under the stairs. "I guess it's still raining."

"Obviously. There's a lot of flooding near the marina, and a few other places in town. The main bridge is out, and the one on Seaside Drive is underwater, so we had to post that."

"Wait. We can't get off the peninsula?"

Rick's mouth tightened. "There's still the small bridge on Spruce Road, but it's a roundabout way to get here. Don't look for the medical examiner anytime soon."

Jillian blew out a breath. "Have you been up all night?"

"No, no," Rick said. "I got a little shuteye. I just touched base with Dave at the station before I came over here. The chief went home to get some rest, and Dave's covering the desk. So ... like I said, probably no word from the medical examiner for a bit."

"Rick, what do you think happened to that man?" Jillian lowered her voice and swept a glance toward the hall and the stairway. Luke was nowhere in sight, and she assumed he was helping himself to breakfast.

Rick sighed. "We told you last night—Craig and your Dr. Rowan both believe he was stabbed."

"Yes. We checked our knives. But why? Why kill him? Craig said he's missing a ring."

"People kill for lots of reasons. Greed is one. To cover up other crimes is another."

"So ... maybe Alan Dryer caught the thief in his room?"

"Could be."

She studied Rick's face carefully. "How are you doing? How are Diana and the kids?"

"Still sleeping when I left, but we had a bit of excitement in the night. The kids were scared and came into our room, and then a big branch blew off that maple tree out front and broke the bedroom window."

"Oh, wow. No one was hurt, I hope."

"No, we're okay, but I've got repairs to tend to when the storm's gone out to sea. And there's no school, of course. The kids will drive Diana nuts today."

"How's she doing?"

He tipped his head to one side. "She seems to be having more morning sickness with this one than she did with the others."

"That's too bad. I'd say bring them here, but ..."

"Yeah, I don't think so. Not with a dead man in the house."

As Rick started up the stairs, Jillian called, "I'll bring you some coffee."

She took up a tray with two steaming mugs and two muffins. Craig and her brother were talking in low tones in one corner.

"You go ahead," Rick said to Craig, reaching for the tray. "I'll stay here as long as I'm needed."

"I'll check in with the station. If they don't need me downtown, I may take a nap here. It's easier than fighting my way home right now." Craig took his coffee cup and went down the steps with Jillian.

"You implied last night that Mr. Dryer was stabbed," Jillian said when they reached the bottom. Several more people were moving about and chatting in the dining room, so she lowered her voice as they stood in the lobby. "Rick says Dr. Rowan thinks so too."

"Yes, that's our best guess. We won't know for sure until there's an autopsy. But it looks like, after the initial attack, he was moved to the bed—hence the blood on the carpet. Which you'll probably have to replace, by the way."

Jillian made a face. "Yeah, I assumed as much. And I think you're right about what happened. But it's bizarre. I mean, who would put an extra blanket and towels on the bed before putting a bloody body on it? A woman?"

"Possibly. But she would have to be stout to lift a body alone. Dryer's not huge, but he must weigh one-sixty or one-seventy. We haven't seen any sign of another guest with blood on their clothes, but they couldn't have moved him without getting messy."

"True. So, does moving him show that the killer was remorseful and didn't want to cause us more trouble? It doesn't really make sense."

Craig sighed. "I don't know."

"Are you going to search all the rooms?"

"It may come to that." He lifted his mug to his lips.

"And no chance at all that it's suicide?" Jillian whispered.

He shook his head. "No. Not with the position of those wounds. And besides, there's no weapon in the room. I made a pretty thorough search. I didn't find anything the killer could have used, and nothing suspicious in Dryer's suitcase."

"He only had one small roller bag when he came in," Jillian said.

Craig nodded. "Well, as I said, we don't know what was there when he arrived, only what's there now."

"What about Dr. Rowan's claim that someone was in her room?"

"Yeah, I went with her to take a look. It's inconclusive. Sometimes people forget little details."

"She seemed sure." Jillian remembered her own initial certainty about the key card drawer, and then the way she'd second-guessed herself. "She did report a turquoise bracelet missing, right?"

"She did." Craig's eyes narrowed. "I don't want to cast aspersions on a victim, but there have been times when people reported items taken when they weren't really stolen. We can fingerprint her room, but it will take time. And she claims she didn't notice until this morning, and yet she's been handling her belongings for hours since the alleged crime. I can't say she's telling the truth, but I can't say she's not either."

"I didn't see the bracelet she's talking about," Jillian mused.

"She told me she had it in her luggage and hadn't worn it since her arrival."

"Why didn't she carry it around with her in her handbag?" Jillian rubbed her forehead and sighed. "Okay, I don't suppose I would carry my extra trinkets around. It's probably true—she might not have opened whatever case it was in since yesterday. But, Craig, this could be an insurance nightmare for us."

"Worse than the murder?"

"Well, no." She gave a tight smile before continuing. "But it might be better for us to just reimburse her for the bracelet."

"Don't do that yet. I told her we'd try to get some prints, but that it would take second place to the murder investigation. She said she understood. But now that Rick's here, maybe we can do that."

"You need to sleep, though."

Craig shrugged.

"Listen," she said, "I don't think Kate and I mentioned this before, with all the distractions, but the drawer where we keep the extra key cards was open a little bit last night. And we keep it locked."

Craig eyed her thoughtfully. "What are you saying?"

"I'm not sure. If somebody managed to take a card, it wouldn't have done them any good. All the cards deactivate automatically at noon—that's checkout time—on the day the guest is scheduled to leave. Kate and I talked it out. The only room that possibly hadn't been deactivated yet when it happened would be the Elizabeth Bennet Room."

"The one you gave me."

"That's right. The guest who was staying there left yesterday morning but wasn't scheduled to leave until today. Which means the card may have stayed active, since I didn't manually decode at the time, and I couldn't after we lost power."

Craig exhaled slowly. "I don't think anyone's been in there who shouldn't be—but then, there was nothing in that room before I went in to use the bathroom. I don't have any luggage or anything."

She spread her hands in helplessness. "I think the room is probably okay, and if that card is still floating around, it will deactivate in a few hours. The thing that really bothers me is, who got into the drawer? And now Dr. Rowan ... How? We don't leave an active master key in that drawer."

"Let me think about it."

Gazing into his grave brown eyes, Jillian knew he'd figure it out—if she and Kate didn't find a solution first.

Max Pelletier came down the stairs and nodded at them. "Morning." He went into the dining room.

"I've got to go help Kate," Jillian said.

"Of course."

The next two hours flew by. Breakfast was a bit haphazard, but no one complained. Finally all the guests but the Simons had finished and left the room, and the sisters began their cleanup routine.

"The worst of the wind is over," Kate said. "We should open the shutters, at least upstairs in the occupied rooms."

"We'd better ask Rick. I don't want to do it too soon. And I need to take Zeb a tray." Jillian glanced at the clock. "Goodness, it's after eight."

"Here, I've got a few sausages left," Kate said.

"He likes the muffins a lot. Good thing you cooked more

yesterday before we lost the oven." Jillian put together a tray and fixed Zeb a cup of hot tea the way he liked it. She hung up her apron. "Back in a few."

"I'll go out front," Kate said.

When she reached the door of the Anna Karenina Room, Jillian balanced the tray carefully and tapped on the panel. She didn't hear a response, but she tried the handle. The door was locked. Her heart pounding, she fumbled in her pocket for the master key. They could *not* have another death here. Not now, and not Zeb!

She held the card to the lock. The door swung open, and she nearly dropped the tray as she hurried inside. He was in bed, and she could hear his breathing clear across the room. That was a mixed blessing. His breath whooshed in and out nosily. Each inhale sounded almost like a gasp.

Jillian set the tray carefully on the desk and walked over to the bed. Zeb's face was flushed, and he'd flung off the duvet, even though the room was cool. She gazed down at the elderly man, so dear to her. He wore a white T-shirt and plaid pajama pants, and white stubble obscured his chin. Would he end up with a Santa Claus beard? She counted his respirations. Fast, and definitely labored.

As she wavered between waking him and trying to call a doctor, Zeb blinked and opened his eyes.

"J-Jillian."

"Yes, I brought you breakfast. Do you feel up to it?"

He grimaced and swallowed hard. "Water."

She hadn't brought any plain water. "I've got orange juice and hot tea, but I can get some water. It will only take a minute."

He shook his head. "Tea." He struggled to sit up, and she grabbed the extra pillow and wedged it behind him. She brought the mug of tea over and placed it in his hands, not quite letting go as he raised it and took a sip.

"Ah." He looked up at her, the lines of his face more relaxed. "I was so dry." His face contorted, and he coughed. Jillian set the mug down and grabbed a box of tissues from the nightstand. Zeb took one and coughed into it.

"Zeb, there's a doctor staying here, and I think maybe she should take a look at you."

"No. I want my doctor. Dr. Coolidge."

"I can try, but I'm not sure he can get here. A lot of the roads are closed, and the landline phones are still out."

Zeb frowned. "I think I'll be okay once I eat." He swung his feet over the side of the bed, and Jillian reached to steady him.

"Do you need to use the restroom?"

"Aye."

He got shakily to his feet, and Jillian took his arm, walking him slowly to the bathroom door.

"I'll be okay," he said gruffly.

"Of course."

She backed away, and Zeb shut the door between them. She clenched her teeth, hoping he would truly be all right in there alone. It would be so easy for the old man to lose his balance.

Taking advantage of the opportunity, she took out her cell and called Kate.

"What's up?" Kate said.

"Zeb's breathing hard this morning, and he's kind of wobbly. He wants Dr. Coolidge."

"The phone's still out," Kate said.

"Do you have his cell number?" Jillian asked. Kate had formerly worked for Dr. Coolidge and his partners as the office manager.

"Uh ... I might still have it. Let me see."

Jillian held her breath. Kate hadn't been very happy with her former bosses last summer. It was entirely possible she'd deleted all her contact information for them out of resentment.

A few seconds later, Kate's voice came through. "I've got it. I'll see if I can talk to him and call you back."

As Jillian put her phone away, the bathroom door opened, and she walked beside Zeb on the short trip back to bed.

"Do you want to sit up in the chair?" She nodded toward the rolling chair near the desk.

"I don't think so." Zeb hacked out a cough.

"Kate's trying to reach Dr. Coolidge."

He nodded and grabbed for the tissue box.

After Jillian settled him in bed once more, with an extra pillow from the closet behind him, she brought the breakfast tray over and settled it on his knees.

"Is it cold in here?" Zeb asked.

"A little. The power's out, and we're using the generator. It's not big enough to run the furnace."

"Oh, that's right. You told me last night. My feet get cold easy." He went to work on the food, ignoring the sausage. He finished the scrambled eggs and ate half a muffin. When he'd swallowed the last of his tea, he waved a hand, and Jillian took the tray away.

"Is there anything else I can do for you?" she asked.

He coughed and rooted about on the covers for his last tissue. She grabbed the box and held it out.

Zeb blew his nose and gazed up at her. "Yes, there's something."

"Anything, Zeb. You name it."

"Can you help me make a will?"

11

A will? Jillian caught her breath. "I ... I guess so. But, Zeb, you're not dying."

"We all go sometime, and I want to make sure. Besides, I don't feel ..." He started hacking again and reached for the tissues.

When he calmed down again, she reached for the pillows propping him up. "Why don't you rest for a while? If you still want to do that later—"

"No, I want it settled."

Jillian frowned. "Surely you've made a will already. I mean, you were in the Navy. When you enlist, don't they make you ...?"

He shook his head rapidly. "Way back, fifty years or more ago, I made one. And I put my parents as my heirs. They're long gone now. I need to make a new one."

That made sense, but it still chilled her. Perhaps she could distract him for a while, and he'd put it out of his mind.

"Zeb, Sergeant Watkins asked me to ask you a question."

"That Watkins boy? He's a police officer?"

She smiled. "Yes. He's here at the inn. In fact, he stayed here last night."

"Whatever for?"

"Well, I didn't want to upset you, but one of our guests died."

The wrinkles on Zeb's forehead sank even deeper into his skin. "Who? Someone I know?"

"That's what Sgt. Watkins wants to know. The man's name was Alan Dryer. He came in during the storm yesterday afternoon and asked for a room. None of us knew him. Apparently he lived in Auburn."

"Never heard of him." Zeb coughed again.

Jillian's cell rang, and she answered it.

"I finally got Dr. Coolidge," Kate said. "He can't come. He's at the hospital in Bucksport, and he can't leave right now. Besides that, he said the roads are awful. He's planning to stay there all day."

"Just great." Jillian reached out to feel Zeb's brow.

"Should I call one of the partners?" Kate asked. "I have Dr. Englebrite's number."

"Let's wait," Jillian said. "Zeb seems a little better, now that he's eaten breakfast. He's coughing a lot, but I think his fever's gone down. Maybe he was just overheated under the covers. Although ... he said his feet were cold. We have a heating pad, right?"

"Uh ... yeah, I think there's one down at the house. It was Mom's."

"Yeah. I might run down and get that."

"I can go for it if you want," Kate said.

"Are you sure?"

"Yeah, it won't take ten minutes. I'll tell Rick I'm going, and I'll make sure the office is locked."

"Thanks so much," Jillian said. She ended the call and

turned to Zeb. "Dr. Coolidge is out of town. We can try to get someone else—"

"I'll be fine," Zeb said. "So ..."

Jillian arched her eyebrows at him. "Yes?"

"About my last will and testament."

"Oh. Right." She couldn't think of another reason to delay. "If that's what you want, I'll go get some paper."

"Isn't there some in here?"

"Just little notepads. We need something bigger, I think."

"All right, you go. But don't be long. I want this written down."

"Aye, aye, sir." She gave him a wan smile and headed for the doorway.

She took his tray to the kitchen and had just unloaded it when Kate scrambled in the back door carrying a plastic grocery sack.

"Here's the heating pad." She tossed the sack on the counter.

"You're soaked," Jillian said.

"Yeah, it's pouring again. I grabbed an umbrella down there. It's in the storage room now, if you need to go out." Kate peeled off her dripping jacket. "Hey, are you sure you don't want another doctor?"

Jillian sighed. "Zeb says he'll be fine. But he wants me to take down his will."

"What?" Kate's face scrunched up. "His will, as in, if he dies?"

"Yeah."

"Wow, that's off-putting."

"It makes me ... I don't know—sad, scared, uneasy—all of the above." Jillian took the heating pad out of the bag. Together they walked out to the lobby. "He doesn't want a doctor, but he wants to make a will. He must be thinking about ... well, you know. That this could be the end for him."

Kate pursed her lips and blew out a breath. "It's something everyone needs to do. I keep telling myself I should. Have you got one?"

"Well, yeah. After Jack died, I wanted to make sure that, if anything happened to me, Megan would get what little I owned."

"There are places online where you can find templates for a simple will. I tell you what ..." Kate sat down on the stool and began clicking on the computer keyboard. "Go give him the heating pad, and I'll look one up for you."

"Thanks. That would be helpful, but I thought you couldn't get Internet right now. I was able to turn on the computer earlier, but I couldn't get online."

"Oh, yeah." Kate's discouraged features brightened. "Hey, I know. You could use yours as a pattern. It's fairly simple, right?"

"Well, yeah, but it's down at the house." Jillian frowned.

"Where is it?"

"I don't want you to go down there again. I'll go myself."

"Hey, no sense in both of us getting wet. Besides, I think I'll drive my Jeep up here this time. Then we'll have it handy if we want to run back and forth."

Jillian thought about it for a moment. "Okay. I put mine in the file cabinet by Dad's old desk. And, hey! We've got Mom and Dad's wills in there too. If you can find all three, I'll look them over. That should give me a pretty good idea of what to do for Zeb."

"Good thinking. I'll be back soon."

Kate headed out through the dining room, and Jillian walked down the hall to tell Zeb there would be a short delay. "I'll help you as soon as I refresh my memory on what a will looks like," she told him with a smile as she plugged in the heating pad.

"All right, young lady, but we're doing this today."

"Yes, sir." She gave him a saucy salute and went back to the lobby and into the dining room.

———

Roger Cowper was near the coffee station, helping himself to a Danish pastry and coffee.

"Hi, Mr. Cowper. How are you doing?" Jillian kept moving, not really expecting an answer.

"I'm good. Do you know when the rain's supposed to end?"

"Uh ..." Jillian reached the swinging door and turned back toward him. "Not exactly. I heard it will probably continue all day."

He frowned. "I was planning to leave this morning. Maybe I'll just head out and take my chances."

"A lot of roads are closed, and some of the bridges are out. Maybe you should go up to the game room and talk to my brother. He came in a little while ago, and he could get an update for you by radio from the police department."

"Okay." Roger sipped his coffee but made no move toward the stairs.

Jillian pushed on into the kitchen. She loaded dirty dishes into the dishwasher while she waited for Kate. Was Roger avoiding a conversation with a police officer, or did he just want to finish his coffee first? She grabbed a cold bottle of water for Zeb from the refrigerator and went out to the lobby. Roger was gone, and she hoped he was upstairs, talking to Rick.

A few minutes later, Kate blew in the front door, having parked the Jeep out front. "Here you go!"

She handed Jillian another plastic bag. Jillian peeked in and recognized the three thick envelopes.

"We can use the computer to type it up," Kate said as she hung up her dripping coat. "We just can't go online."

"Okay. After I write up what Zeb wants, I'll type it and print it out." Jillian sat down for a minute to scan the documents.

"I glanced at Mom and Dad's," Kate said. "They're pretty simple, especially Mom's. 'I, being of sound mind ... yada, yada, yada ... leave all my worldly goods to my husband, or if he predeceases me, to my children, and so on.' And if he wants to make any special bequests, you just write them at the bottom. Dad did that for a gift to their church. I'm pretty sure you need two people who aren't heirs to witness Zeb's signature."

"That pretty well sums it up, I think." Jillian took a clipboard and some paper and pulled a pen from the holder on the desk. "You okay for another half hour or so?"

"I'll call you if I need you."

Jillian paused. "Have you seen Craig?"

"He was down here right before you came out of Zeb's room. He said he thought he'd get a shower."

Relief washed over Jillian. Maybe he and Rick would both stay for a while. "So, he's up in Liz Bennet, then."

"I'd say so."

"Good." Feeling just a tad guilty for monopolizing two of Skirmish Cove's tiny police contingent, Jillian took her writing materials, with the wills in the sack to guide her, and headed back down the hallway.

"There you are," Zeb said as she entered his room.

"Sorry about the delay. Kate found some family wills that we can use as our framework. Here's my mom's, for instance." She took out the envelope that held her mother's will.

"How does it read, if you don't mind me asking?"

She pulled a chair over and read him the standard opening

paragraph. "And then you tell who you want to inherit your estate. If you want to make more than one bequest, we just make a list. It seems pretty simple."

"Okay. Most everything will go to Lee."

She smiled. "I figured. I know Lee's special to you."

"Not only that, he's the only kin I have left."

"Really? I know he's your brother's son, and your brother passed away, but ..."

"He's an only child," Zeb said.

"But don't you have any other siblings, or nieces and nephews, or cousins, even?"

Zeb shrugged. "Not that I'm close to. There might be a cousin here or there, but I haven't been in contact with them for years. Now, I want Lee to have my house. I don't care if he sells it, but I want him to have the land. There's some value to shorefront property."

"Well, yes." Balancing the clipboard on her knee, Jillian began to write on the paper. "What's his full legal name?"

"Ormond Lee Wilding."

Jillian smiled, understanding why Lee went by his middle name. She checked the spelling with Zeb and went on to write out a clear statement saying all of Zeb's worldly goods except any listed below would go to Lee.

"Okay. Any other bequests?" She sat with the pen poised over the clipboard.

"Yes. I'm leaving my set of signal flags to ..."

Jillian wrote it on the paper and waited for him to finish the sentence. She looked up and met his gaze.

Zeb smiled. "To you."

"Oh, Zeb! That is so special. And fun! Thank you." If he hadn't been sick, she'd have kissed him. The flags could be used as decorations in the Hornblower room, or the lounge, or even the carriage house. Or maybe they could erect a flagstaff in front of the inn and run up messages important only to the Gage siblings. However she used them, the colorful flags would bring her dear friend to mind for many years to come.

The old man's eyes were a bit duller than usual, but she glimpsed the twinkle she loved. "You're the one person I know well who would appreciate them."

"I will, for sure. And I'll treasure them." She wrote her name on the paper and waited expectantly. "Anything else?"

"Yes. Five thousand dollars."

"To whom?"

"Jillian Gage Tunney."

She paused, dismay ambushing her. "Oh, no, Zeb. Don't do that."

"Why not? You're my best friend."

Acknowledging that with a smile, she shook her head. "Leave it to Lee."

The crow's feet at the corners of his eyes deepened. "By the time I depart this world, young lady, I might not have anything left in my bank account. Right now, there's a bit of a stash, but I realize that could be used up on my care in a hurry. I've made my decision. If there's anything left, Lee will get the property and whatever else there is. I want to give you a little something besides the flags."

"I really—"

"Write it down. If you won't, I'll get someone else. That Watkins boy, maybe."

Jillian sighed. The first sheet of paper was full, so she pulled out the second one. She hoped there would be space for signatures at the bottom of this one. She wrote down the bequest with misgivings.

"Okay, I did it. Anything else?"

His face scrunched up until his eyes were slits. "Don't think so. Leave it here for me to go over, and you can go find some witnesses. They don't have to read it, do they?"

"No. You can cover the top part, so all they see is the place to sign and the date." She eased the extra sheet of paper from the clip and laid it over the ones revealing the bequests. "Like that." She handed Zeb the clipboard.

"Okay, go on."

"Anyone in particular you'd like to witness it? I don't think my siblings qualify, since I'm named in the will."

"Whoever."

"All right, I'll be back as soon as I can."

When she reached the lobby, Craig was coming down the stairs, his hair looking shiny and soft. He smiled when he saw her.

"I thought you'd take a nap," Jillian said.

"Maybe later. Thought I'd sneak another muffin if there are any left."

"Sure. After you eat it, would you want to witness the will Zeb just made?"

His eyebrows flew up, and she hastily explained the circumstances.

"He specifically mentioned you as 'that Watkins boy,' and I thought of you as a possible witness."

Craig grinned. "That's me. Sure, I'll do it."

"We need one other person not related to me."

"Not related ..."

"He's leaving me his signal flags." She didn't feel comfortable mentioning the money.

"Oh." Understanding flooded Craig's handsome face. "How about Dr. Rowan? She wouldn't be afraid of germs, and she'd understand about ill people wanting to make sure their affairs are in order."

"Hmm, okay. I'll see if she's in her room. Help yourself to whatever's in the pastry case."

"Thanks. I'm laying off the coffee for now, and maybe I'll be able to sleep after we fix Zeb up."

Ten minutes later, Jillian, Craig, and Eliza trooped into the Anna Karenina Room. Zeb sat up, leaning on his pillows and surveying them with bright eyes.

"I think you know Craig Watkins, Zeb," Jillian said. She waved toward Eliza. "And this is Dr. Rowan. They've both agreed to act as witnesses for you."

"Dandy. Do I sign it first?"

"You sure do." Jillian noted that he'd covered most of the paper with the blank sheet. She stood aside and watched as he wrote his name with a flourish.

"Who's next?"

"Me, I guess." Eliza reached for the clipboard.

As she took it, the paper shifted a little. Jillian was certain the handwritten portion extended farther down the page than the last bit she'd written. Had Zeb added a clause? She frowned but said nothing.

Eliza signed her name and handed the clipboard to Craig. He wasn't a scribbler but took his time writing his name carefully and putting the date beneath it.

"There you go, Mr. Wilding." He handed the whole thing back to Zeb.

"I thank you all." Zeb nodded his head at all of them.

"You're welcome. How are you feeling?" Eliza asked. "I understand you've been ill."

"I'm doing better, thank you."

"Glad to hear it. I'd be happy to come see you if you feel you need a look from a physician."

"I'll keep it in mind," Zeb said.

Eliza hesitated then turned toward the door. "If there's anything else I can do, let me know."

She went out, and Zeb pressed down on the clip and tugged the papers out.

"Would you like me to help you?" Jillian asked.

"No, thanks."

"All right then." Her face felt like plastic as she smiled. What was the old fox up to?

"You can take the clipboard and the pen." By that time, he'd folded up the bottom third of the papers. No way was he going to let her see what he'd added to the document.

She leaned over and took the clipboard and the pen. A moment later, he held out the papers he'd folded in thirds. "Would you please put that someplace safe? And no peeking."

Jillian took it. "All right. Can I bring you anything else, Zeb? Some tea or juice, maybe? Or a muffin?"

"I think I'm good until eight bells."

Craig laughed. "We'll tell the sailors in the galley you'll be ready for your rations then."

"Thank you, young fella." Zeb reached to remove a pillow from the stack behind him. Craig stepped up to help him and set the extra pillow on the unused side of the bed.

"I'll put this document in the inn's safe," Jillian said. "When you're ready to go home, either Kate or I can get it out for you."

"Thanks." Zeb was already snuggling down under the comforter, and his eyes were closed.

Jillian looked at Craig, who nodded and turned to the door.

In the hallway, he gave her a tired smile. "That went smoothly."

"Yes. Do you think I should tell his nephew he made a will?"

"I don't see why. Isn't he coming up to visit after the storm's over?"

"He said he would."

"There you go. Either Zeb will tell him then, or you can. And if, heaven forbid, it's needed sooner, we'll both know where it is."

"Right." Jillian drew in a deep breath. "Now you should sleep."

"I'll give it a try, but I have a feeling they'll need me soon. The chief said earlier that he's sending Geordie home at ten o'clock. He'll probably want me out on the street for a few hours."

"Craig …"

He eyed her sharply.

"Rick says a couple of bridges are out. We're nearly cut off. Can't reach any bigger towns except by a roundabout route, and who knows if that's safe?"

"He's right. But the rain should stop tonight, or at least by tomorrow, and then the water will go down. It may take a while to repair the main bridge, but if so, we'll just have to live with the detour for a while."

In her mind, Jillian pictured a ferry service starting on the shore.

With a reassuring smile, Craig left her, striding toward the stairway. Jillian entered the office and took a business-size envelope from a drawer. As she stood looking down at the papers, the urge to open them was almost overpowering. Maybe she should have asked Craig to stay with her until she'd secured Zeb's will, for accountability.

Lord, give me strength.

She stuffed the papers quickly into the envelope and licked the flap. Laying it on the desk, she pressed the flap down firmly, then picked up a pen and wrote "Zeb Wilding" on the front. A few seconds later, she had the safe open and laid the envelope inside, on top of the deed to the inn, their extra checks, password list, and the key to their safe deposit box at the bank.

For a moment, she crouched, staring at it. She closed the door and twirled the dial. With a sigh, she straightened. Zeb's will was finished and secured. Now she had other things to think about.

12

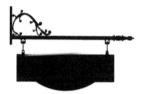

Rick paced the game room slowly, deliberately. He hated this type of duty—waiting, making sure nothing happened. Craig had gone to one of the guest rooms to try to catch some Zs. His sisters were no doubt in the kitchen, scaring up lunch for their guests, who couldn't leave if they wanted to.

That was good, in a way. Nobody could leave the building where the crime took place. The police hadn't been forced to tell them they couldn't leave—yet. Someone would get restless and want to go, especially with the temperature hovering near sixty degrees inside. He'd kept his jacket on.

Luke Brantley came up the stairs. He started to pass the opening and go toward his room, but he caught sight of Rick and stepped into the game room.

"Hey."

"Hello, Luke."

"I just put more gas in the generator."

Rick nodded. "Thanks. Have the girls got enough fuel to keep it going for a while?"

"Yeah, I think they'll be okay for tonight anyway. Maybe another night. But if the power outage continues, I don't know."

"Well, they might have to shut off the hot water." Rick grimaced. "I'm not sure they'll have enough food for everyone for many more meals either. They don't usually serve three meals a day."

"How far away is the nearest grocery store?" Luke asked.

"Not too far, but I doubt they're open. Most of the gas stations are closed too. And supply trucks can't get here while the main bridge is closed."

"Hmm." Luke scowled and stared at the carpet as if trying to think of a solution. He looked up suddenly. "Hey, I was wondering about something."

"What's that?"

"There's a guy here, Max Pelletier. I saw him coming down from the third floor last night."

Rick glanced toward the closed door of the David Copperfield Room, where Pelletier was staying. "There's a common room up there—the lounge. Anyone can go up there and watch TV or get a book or just sit and talk."

"Oh, okay. That makes sense."

Rick thought of the secret rooms on both the upper levels, but no way was he going to mention those. "I'd be surprised if you could get TV right now, though."

"Yeah, even if the broadcast stations are operating, I wouldn't want to put a strain on the generator just so's everyone could watch TV," Luke said.

"The girls have a battery-powered weather radio in the kitchen."

Luke nodded. "They brought it out in the dining room during breakfast. Sounds like the storm won't end for a while. It may be another day or two before the roads are passable."

"I know the power company's ready to send teams out to work on getting the lines back up, but I don't think it's safe for them yet. Last I heard, they were handling emergency-only situations." Since Luke didn't turn away, Rick waited. Something else was on his mind. He hoped it wasn't a man-to-man talk about his younger sister. He had no desire to hash over Kate and Luke's relationship.

Finally, Luke took another step toward him. With a glance toward Copperfield, he said quietly, "I guess you guys are checking into all of us? I mean, that guy wasn't killed by some outsider. We all know that."

That was it. He was afraid of what they'd find in his background. A criminal record, maybe?

"It does seem unlikely that some psycho came in here during a hurricane and committed murder, then left." Rick cocked his head to one side. "Is there anything we should know up front, Luke?"

"I've had a couple of traffic stops over the years. Nothing major. But—well—a couple of months ago, Tara and I had—a loud fight. The cops came."

"Any charges from that?"

"No. I moved out that night."

"Hmm. You told us you'd never met Alan Dryer before."

"True."

"Then, as long as you're honest with us, you shouldn't have anything to worry about."

"Oh, I'm not worried. I just ..." Luke stepped back. "Okay, then. Guess I'll head for my room."

Rick watched him go, the wheels turning in his head.

———

Jillian checked the coffee urn and headed for the kitchen to talk to Kate about the lunch preparations.

"Jillian? I wondered if I could have a word with you."

She turned to the living room archway, where Luke stood watching her. She didn't want to talk to Luke. What could he possibly need to say to her? Was it about the generator? If so, the news was probably not good. Or was it about Kate? She wanted to stay well out of that.

"I'll be right there." She plodded into the kitchen.

Kate had cold cuts, bread, and condiments spread all over the work island and was constructing a mountain of sandwiches. She glanced up. "Hi. I hope this will work, with soup and chips."

"I'm sure it will be fine. Do you need me to do anything?"

"Not right now." Kate glanced at the clock. "Maybe in half an hour?"

"Sure." Jillian went back out and wound through the tables, approaching the living room. Luke was sprawled on the sofa, flipping through last month's issue of *Down East* magazine. He set it aside when she entered. The room was pleasantly warm, and it appeared that he'd tended the blaze in the fireplace.

"What's up, Luke?" Jillian sat down opposite him in an armchair, but she didn't settle back, not wanting to appear too comfortable. She'd make sure this was a short conversation.

"When we spoke yesterday, we agreed that I would check out today. But your brother tells me it might be best to hold off another day—or at least a few hours. It's still raining. Some roads have been cleared, but others have gotten worse. Apparently there's quite a lot of flooding in some areas, and the big bridge is out."

"Yeah." Jillian crossed her arms, thinking about it. So far,

Luke had kept his word for the most part. He hadn't bothered Kate. He'd helped them out with the shutters. If the generator needed attention, he was a good man to have around—although she was sure Rick or Craig could handle it as well.

"I'll pay your usual room rate, plus whatever you think is fair for the extra meals," Luke said.

She met his gaze. "Understood. And you'll keep out of Kate's way when you can?"

"I will. I'll admit, I'm still hoping she'll change her mind and sit down with me sometime, but I'm not going to push her."

"You'd better not." Jillian sat forward. "If you upset her, you're out of here. Period."

He lifted a hand. "I get you. I just ... I don't particularly want to go out into this weather, and I don't have any place to go."

"Don't you have a job?"

He hesitated. "We can't work in this weather. And anyway, I'm on leave."

"You got fired," she said with certainty.

"No, no. Really." He sighed and shook his head. "There was some trouble at work, and the boss told me to use my vacation days. I'm hoping everything will be sorted out by next week."

Jillian eyed him keenly. "What did you do, Luke?"

"Nothing. I swear."

"Then what does he think you did?"

"*She*. My boss is a woman. And I'd ... rather not discuss it."

"Great. Just great." Jillian heaved herself to her feet. "One more night, Luke. Tomorrow, you're out of here, even if we get a tornado, an earthquake, and a blizzard at the same time."

Without waiting for his reaction, she strode from the room. She didn't want to face Kate until she'd calmed down, so she went out to the front desk. Was she being too hard on Luke? Would the guests even be allowed to scatter yet? It had been less than twenty-four hours since Alan Dryer was murdered, and the police hadn't taken detailed statements from everyone yet because they were shorthanded.

She sat down and closed her eyes for a moment. *Lord, give me grace. Help me to treat Luke the way you want me to. And please help us with the food problem.*

Soft footsteps sounded on the stairs, and she opened her eyes. The Simons came down into the lobby. Both were bundled in layers of sweaters and turtlenecks.

"Hi," Marie said, halting in front of the desk. "We were supposed to check out today, but we're thinking it might be best to stay one more night, if you can handle us."

"That's fine," Jillian said. "We're pulling together meals for everyone—nothing fancy—and we hope we can get some fresh supplies in today."

"Well, we were headed for Route 1, but that didn't sound promising on the weather radio at breakfast," Charles said. "Apparently a major bridge is out."

"Yes, but the roads to Bangor seem to be open if you take a detour to get off the peninsula," Marie added. "We could take the longer way around, I guess, but we're comfortable enough here for another night. That seems a better option with so much flooding going on."

"We'll do everything we can to make your stay pleasant." Jillian turned to her computer monitor, praying she could use her booking program. It came up, and she added another day to the Simons' stay. Their extended stay would make up for one of the cancellations she'd received, but the inn would still probably lose a lot of money this month.

The couple thanked her and went into the dining room.

By the time she'd finished changing the booking, Kate stood in front of the desk. "Hey. I covered the sandwiches and put them in the fridge. I'm going to run up to my room for a minute. Is that okay?"

"Sure," Jillian said. "The Simons are staying over, and Luke. He promised to keep out of your way."

Kate frowned. "I'm not crazy about it, but I guess we can't really ask anyone to leave right now. Especially with a crime investigation underway."

"That's right. I'm sure Rick and Craig would like to keep all the suspects under our roof a while longer."

"Rick told me earlier that when Craig wakes up, they'll interview people individually. They want detailed statements on everybody's movements up until we discovered the body. The state police can't get here yet, so they told our guys to go ahead."

Jillian sighed. "That's good, I guess, but I can barely remember what I did ten minutes ago, let alone last night. It's all a big blur."

"Write down everything you remember." Kate headed for the stairs.

Jillian turned back to the booking program and added a night to Luke's stay. The landline was still not working, and she thought about how she could find out if any local stores were open. In the future, they needed a better plan for feeding guests in an emergency.

Footsteps sounded on the stairs above, and then Kate's excited voice reached her from the game room. Rick answered her in his lower tones, but Jillian couldn't make out their words. Shoving back her chair, she stood and stared up at the second-floor railing.

A moment later, Rick appeared above her.

"Can you come up here for a minute?" he asked.

Without answering, she dashed for the stairs. When she reached the landing, a wide-eyed Kate pulled her into the game room, away from the stairs and the railing where people below might hear them.

"My room's been searched," Kate whispered.

13

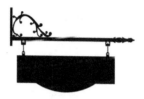

"**N**o!" Jillian looked to Rick for reassurance.

"Let's just stay calm," he said. "I'm going to wake Craig up, and then we'll go take a look at Kate's room. First, how do you know it was searched?" His gaze drilled into his younger sister.

"My stuff isn't the way I left it, and my toothpaste was on the floor in the bathroom."

Rick's eyes crinkled. "That's not much."

"Oh, and the bed. It's messy. I always make it up the right way—Jillian and I worked hard to learn how to do it right."

"Okay. Messy, how?"

Kate's eyebrows drew together. "The pillows. One's under the spread. I left them both on top. And I only had a few things in there last night—Jillian brought me an overnight bag. I didn't bother to put things in the dresser. I figured we'd sleep at the carriage house tonight. But I could tell someone had been through my bag."

"One of you stay here. I'll go get Craig." Rick started for the hallway, then turned back. "Oh, and a little bit of good news. The medical examiner should be here this afternoon. The chief says the road to Bangor is fine up to the bridge, but from there, he can take the detour. It's only ten or fifteen minutes longer, and the M.E.'s office is putting a priority on this case. So he's coming."

"Good," Jillian said. "We can't keep a body here much longer."

He went to the stairway, and Kate flopped down in one of the armchairs. "This whole thing rots."

With a sigh, Jillian sat on the sofa. "Yes, it does, but with God's help, we can handle it."

"They could have taken a boat across the bay and picked up the medical examiner over there." Kate sounded pouty. Glancing around, she leaned in toward Jillian. "One of our guests is doing this. Plundering the rooms. And probably the same person killed Alan Dryer."

"We don't know that it was the same person."

"Really? What are the chances of us getting two guests who are criminals the same week?"

Jillian clenched her teeth. Her sister had a point. "I suppose someone might see it as an opportunity. Someone's dead, so the police aren't paying any attention to what else is going on, so they start pilfering."

Kate's lips twisted. "That's not very likely."

"Craig and Rick aren't blind. If anything, they're more alert right now than usual, and they're pretty sharp on a normal day."

Kate gave a reluctant nod. "You're right. So, who do you think's doing it?"

"I couldn't say."

"Sure you could, to me." Kate's sober brown eyes demanded an answer.

"Well, we know it's not Zeb."

Without hesitation, Kate said, "Agreed. What about the rest?"

"I don't know. The police are doing background checks on all of them, but it's slow going between the power problems and all the people they've had to go help. They may not be able to complete the investigation until the hurricane craziness is over."

"So, everyone has to stay until they complete the investigation? Even Luke?"

"I don't know. They'll at least have to stay reachable. Right now, every officer in Skirmish Cove except Rick and Craig is out helping people—accidents, stranded people, some who need evacuating."

"There must be someone on the desk at the police station," Kate said.

"I think the chief's there. And maybe a dispatcher or someone like that."

"They use the regional dispatch center."

"Well, yes." Jillian frowned. She really should learn more about the department and how things worked there if she was going to spend a lot of time with Craig. And she hoped she was. Every day it became more apparent how much Craig meant to her.

"Do you think they're looking up these people while they sit around the inn?"

"Honestly, I have no idea. I hope so."

"We can use our computers, now that we have the generator going."

Jillian shook her head. "I was able to use the booking program, but we still can't get online. I think the towers are down or something."

Kate scowled.

"Okay, who do you think is behind it?" Jillian asked, though she wasn't sure she wanted to hear the answer.

"I think we should keep an eagle eye on the Simons," Kate whispered. "With one of them providing a diversion, the other could be up to something."

"I ... I thought they were nice."

Kate sighed. "They probably are. I like Mrs. Simon. Haven't talked to Mr. S. very much, but they are polite, and they don't seem to be complainers. Well, I suppose one of us should go check on the dining room. And we've got lunch covered for today, but what about supper?"

"I'm not sure. I guess we can open the chest freezer, but how much meat is in there?"

"We had quite a bit of hamburger in the one down at the carriage house, and a steak or two. Maybe some pork chops?"

Jillian put a hand to her forehead. Whatever they'd stashed for the two of them wouldn't go around to feed all the guests. And meanwhile, they apparently had a sneak thief, or at least a sneak. So far, nothing except Eliza Rowan's bracelet seemed to have been stolen. But Kate was worried. Did she think Luke had killed Dryer? Jillian could almost picture him snooping in Kate's room, trying to find out about her life since the breakup —but murder?

When Craig and Rick came in from the hallway, Craig smiled at the women. Jillian jumped up.

"Rick told you?"

"Yes. Kate, you come with me and show me everything that's out of whack in your room. Rick will stay here." Unspoken was the need to keep an eye on Dryer's room and make sure no one tried to enter it.

Kate and Craig started for the stairway, and Jillian turned to Rick. "I'd better go down and clear off the breakfast buffet. We'll be putting out lunch soon. Can I bring you something?"

"I'll come down and eat as soon as Craig's done."

"Okay."

"Oh, and I checked in with Diana," he said.

"Your cell phone's working?"

"Nah, at least it wasn't a few minutes ago." Rick touched the radio on his belt. "I had Geordie put me through. We've got a receiver at home."

"How are she and the kids doing?"

"Okay. We had that scare last night when the branch smashed our bedroom window. I was hoping I could work on that this afternoon, but it sounds like I need to stay here a while."

"Don't stay for our sake."

"Got to. There's too much going on here for one officer to handle alone, and it sounds like it will be a while before we get some help."

She couldn't disagree. "We're really glad you're here. I don't know what Kate and I would do without you and Craig."

"I hope Diana and I don't have to sleep in with the kids tonight." Rick gave her a wry smile. "Anyway, I told her about the meal problem here. She says if I can drop by for it, she can send over several loaves of bread from our freezer. And we've got plenty of venison and chicken breasts."

"It might not be a good idea to open your freezer right now."

"Our generator's running it."

"Oh. Lucky you. Maybe we should get another one."

"Two the size you've got would run this whole place, I'm sure—that or one big one, but they're expensive. Anyhow, she's also got a lot of canned stuff she put up last summer. Canned green beans, corn, tomato sauce, applesauce."

"We've got frozen blueberries and hamburger in our chest

135

freezer at the carriage house," Jillian mused. "Maybe we should open that and leave the big one here shut."

Rick shrugged. "I think I left the breaker on that runs that, but I can check. We don't know how long this outage will last. Just let me know if you want the stuff from Diana. I'll swing by the house this afternoon."

"Well, the bread would help us a lot. And maybe the chicken. We'll have to feed twelve tonight—thirteen if you and Craig both stay here."

"I think we can handle that. She said there's plenty."

"Well, Kate and I can eat peanut butter and jelly if we need to, but the guests ..."

"Right."

"We'll pay you back."

Rick grinned. "You feed me half my meals anyway."

———

"And I'm positive I didn't leave it that way." Kate stared at the bed she'd slept in.

"Maybe someone was checking under your pillow," Craig suggested.

"Then he got a fistful of nothing."

Smiling, he knelt beside the bed. He lifted the pillows and spread back the covers, then ran his hand between the mattress and box spring.

"I'm not finding anything."

"I told you, I didn't put anything there."

Craig got to his feet. "So, based on what you've told me, they rifled your bag, snooped in your bed, and at least entered your bathroom."

"Yeah. But why?"

"That's a good question. I wonder if whoever came in knew you were the one staying here."

"Or maybe they thought the room was empty. We only had six guests until Zeb came. Well, seven with Dryer, but he was dead before this happened. Maybe someone was checking out the empty rooms for some reason." Kate glanced at the binnacle and the large, mounted telescope. "Some of the things in here are fairly valuable. We got an appraisal of eight hundred dollars for that antique compass. Do you think they were planning a heist?"

"Maybe. Could be that when they saw someone was staying in here, they backed off. You'd have noticed immediately if one of the decorations was missing."

"Maybe." Kate looked around again. She checked off those items every time a guest left the room. "Probably. Certainly the telescope. And that compass wouldn't be as easy to steal and hide, now that it's in the wooden case Zeb made for it. You couldn't tuck it into a suitcase easily. And with cops in the house and the roads impassable ... You could be right."

"Has anyone left this morning, or tried to check out?"

"I don't think so, but you should ask Jillian. She said the Simons and Luke are staying an extra night because traveling's so awful. I'm not sure, but I think one or two others may have expected to leave today."

"Okay. I'll make sure all the other guests are staying over tonight. That would be Cowper, Pelletier, and Rowan, right? Anyone else?"

"Just Zeb and you guys."

Craig nodded.

"So, will the state police come in here and take over the case after you've done all the work?"

Craig gave her a tight smile. "It could happen. Wouldn't be the first time. But they're spread pretty thin right now, as I understand it. For now, it's all ours. We may wish it was otherwise if we can't figure out who's the culprit."

"One more thing," Kate said.

"What?"

She gazed earnestly at him. "The door was locked. The windows are still shuttered, and we're on the third floor. I had a room key. Jillian had a master key, and you have one. No one else's room key would work on this door. So how did he—or she—get in here?"

Craig surveyed the large room. The air vents were way too small for anyone to crawl inside. This room had no door to an adjoining room.

"That's a very good question."

———

All of the guests were eating lunch when Rick and Kate came down the stairs. Jillian, who had split her time between the kitchen and dining room, was ready for a break.

"I wish I could stay," Rick said. "Something fishy is going on here, and it will take more than one of us to keep an eye on everyone. Unfortunately, the chief needs me to go rescue some idiot who tried to drive through a foot and a half of water."

"Can you grab a quick lunch?" Jillian asked.

"No, I'll stop by my house when I've sorted out the motorist. I need to touch base with Diana anyway. There's no school, and she and the kids are stuck there."

"I wish we could help, but ..." Jillian gave a little shrug.

"Craig's upstairs," Kate said. "We should take him a tray."

Max Pelletier came out into the lobby. "Hey, Officer, I wondered how the roads are. I'd like to head out this afternoon if I can."

Rick eyed him soberly. "It's not good out there, Mr.

Pelletier. I'm heading out now to help stranded people. And it would help the police department a lot if you and the other guests stayed here until we can do some in-depth interviews."

"You mean, about the dead guy?"

"That and other things."

Max frowned. "Sure. I volunteer to go first."

"Well, it may be a little while, but stick around."

"Okay. Whatever you say."

Kate had zipped into the dining room, and as Max drifted out, she passed him with a covered cardboard cup of coffee for Rick. "Here you go. Keep safe."

"Thanks." Rick took it and raised it slightly in a silent toast. "You two be careful. I'll come by later with the bread and chicken. I don't know when."

"Take your time," Jillian said. "With Diana's contribution, we'll make it through supper. If it looks like everyone will be here through tomorrow, we'll have to get more creative."

"We're low on desserts. I think I'll make some no-bake cookies for tonight," Kate put in. "But we'll survive."

When Rick opened the front door, they could see that a drizzle continued, and water still flowed from the downspouts. Rick left, and Kate fixed herself a plate and brought it to the front desk. She settled on the stool and picked up her spoon.

"Go on. I know you're dying to talk to Craig."

Jillian attempted a scowl but couldn't manage it.

"Okay, but give a yell if you need me. I'll be right up there." She waved toward the landing rail above.

She fixed a plate of sandwiches, a bowl of soup, and a cup of coffee the way Craig liked it. When she plodded up the steps, he stood from his comfortable perch on the sofa.

He met her near the landing and reached out for the tray. "Thanks."

"What did you find out in Kate's room?" She sat down next to him so she could speak quietly.

"She didn't tell you?"

"Rick was leaving. She didn't say much."

Craig sipped his coffee. "A few things were out of place, but she didn't think anything was stolen."

"That's good." Jillian focused on his face. A day's stubble only added to his rugged good looks. He regarded her soberly with soft brown eyes. "Craig, do you think Luke maybe sneaked in there to see if he could ... I don't know, maybe to find out what's making her tick these days? He's definitely trying to get back on her good side."

"And that would be a bad thing, I take it."

"She doesn't want to pick up with him again. He's separated from his wife, and soon to be divorced. Kate already didn't trust him because of the way he hurt her before. Now she's even less eager to stay in touch with him."

Craig took another drink from his cup. "We'll do a complete background check on him, the same as the other guests, but we already know a few things. Maybe I'll interview him first."

"Oh, that reminds me. Max Pelletier was asking when he can leave. Rick told him to stick around to be interviewed in depth."

"Okay, I'll put him second in line. Because once the M.E. has been here, I'm not sure we can make them stay. I'd better get those interviews done as quickly as possible."

"Don't rush it," Jillian said uneasily.

Craig smiled, melting her heart. "Don't worry. We'll be careful. I hope Rick can come back and sit in, but if not, we're agreed that I should go ahead." He took another gulp of coffee. "I suppose I should have gone out on rescue work and left him here. He has more experience as a detective."

"Your department doesn't have detectives."

"I wish we did. Rick would be first choice. But our budget won't stretch that far. I keep wondering how long he'll stay in Skirmish Cove."

"What do you mean?"

"At least one bigger town has approached him."

"Wouldn't he have to take a test or something?"

"He already has, and he qualifies."

Jillian stared at him. "He didn't tell us."

"Sorry, I probably shouldn't have spilled the beans."

"But this is his home."

"I know." Craig gave her a tight smile. "The town fathers say we don't have enough felonies to justify funding a detective squad—or even one detective."

"I disagree. Look at what's happened this past year."

"Our crime rate is up, for sure. But Rick could earn a much better salary in another place—say, Bangor or Portland. Even Augusta and Waterville pay more than we can."

She sighed, saddened by the thought that Rick might move away. "Well, anyway, you're the sergeant."

"That doesn't mean I shouldn't be out there in the field." He watched her for a moment.

Jillian didn't trust herself to speak. She cared deeply about Craig, but also for her brother.

"How are *you* doing, Jill?" he asked softly.

"Me? I'm fine."

"You're looking out for everybody. Kate. Zeb. All your guests."

Her stomach tightened. "Yeah, speaking of Zeb ..."

"What about him?"

"That will he made?"

"Yes? You helped again by writing it up for him."

She nodded. "I basically copied off my folks' wills and filled in what he wanted. Then I went to scare up some witnesses."

"Right. Me and Dr. Rowan."

"Correct, but when I came back into his room ..."

"What?"

"He'd changed something."

"Are you sure?"

She hauled in a deep breath and held it for a moment, thinking. "Yeah, I'm sure. He'd asked me about shielding the paper, and I told him the witnesses didn't have to see the actual text—the bequests in particular."

"I noticed he'd covered that part with another sheet of paper. That's all right, though, isn't it?"

"Sure. But I had a glimpse of the last line, or part of it. He'd added something. I'm sure of it. It was in his own shaky handwriting, not mine."

"Well ... that's okay too, right?"

"Yes, but ..."

"It bothers you that he added a bequest that you don't know about."

Her cheeks burned. Was she angry? Feeling silly for caring so much? "I just ... he had made a bequest to me, Craig. Before that, I mean. I wrote it down for him."

"And you told me he's leaving you his set of signal flags."

Miserably, she met his gaze. "There's something else. He also made me put down that he's giving me five thousand dollars."

Craig's warm smile washed over her, calming her. Yes, she felt a little foolish, but that was okay with Craig. She wouldn't want anyone else to know, however.

"That's generous of him—a very nice gesture."

"Yes. I protested heartily. Not about the flags, but the money. I told him to leave it to Lee. But he was adamant."

"From what I know of Zeb Wilding, he's a stubborn man."

"Very." She managed a smile. "He admitted that all of his money might be used up on his care before he goes. I told him not to worry about that. But the house and land will go to Lee, and that will be worth quite a lot."

"I should think so. It's a fantastic location, there on the bluff."

"It is. And if he wanted to leave something else to another person, I shouldn't worry about it."

Craig studied her face for a moment. "You're worried he left something else to you."

She inhaled slowly. "I guess I am. I don't want Lee to feel slighted."

He reached for her hand. "Don't fret about it, sweetheart."

That melted her completely. She dove into his arms.

"Thank you. I needed an objective perspective."

Craig held her close, with his cheek leaning on the top of her head. "Here's my opinion: Zeb is wise in choosing his friends. He might want to give his telescope or his chess board to one of his buddies. Or not. Trust him to know his own mind, and let him do what he wants."

His arms tightened about her, and Jillian rested there for perhaps half a minute. Then she sat up, smiling, and ran a hand through her hair.

"Thanks. I'm sure there are dirty dishes awaiting me downstairs, and Kate and I will need to plan supper."

"Come back here." Craig drew her to him and kissed her. When he sat back, their eyes met. "Okay, go do your innkeeper thing."

14

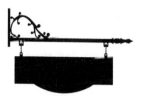

Kate flipped through one of her mother's cookbooks. No one had complained about the scanty lunch—sandwiches, soup, and chips. But something was going to have to change before suppertime. Counting on Diana's offer of chicken breasts, she browsed some poultry recipes.

The doorbell rang. Jillian was also in the kitchen unloading the dishwasher, and Kate said, "I'll get it." She hurried out to the lobby and unlocked the door. A middle-aged man stood there with a black case in his hand.

"Hi, I'm Dr. Smithson. I'm here to examine the deceased."

"Right. I'm Kate Gage. Come right in." She walked with him to the bottom of the stairway. "Sergeant Craig Watkins is right up these stairs. If you go up to the first landing, you should see him in the game room. He's keeping an eye on the victim's door."

"Thank you." He plodded up the stairs.

Kate waited until she heard Craig greet the doctor, then dashed to the kitchen. Jillian now sat at the work island, poring over their recipe boxes.

"The medical examiner's here," Kate said.

"Hooray." Jillian sounded distracted rather than elated at the news.

"Craig can start his interviews." Kate watched her to see if this lifted her sister's spirits.

"That's good. I guess you'll be happy when he tells Luke he can leave."

"Well, yeah."

Jillian straightened on the stool and met her gaze. "Zeb told me we can borrow from his stored food, and I think we might need to take him up on it."

"I hope he's got something good."

"Well, if Rick comes through with the bread and chicken he promised, we can get by tonight," Jillian said. "Who knows? We may be down to just us tomorrow."

"If not, what do we need for tomorrow? It's possible we might have to feed twelve for lunch again."

"Veggies. Milk. Butter. Juice. Sugar." Jillian gazed up at the ceiling. "And something to serve tomorrow morning. We're low on eggs and bacon."

"Apparently the two grocery stores in town won't open until at least tomorrow, maybe Friday. Do you want to go over to Zeb's, or should I?"

"I'll go. I want to check on Zeb first and tell him what we're doing. He'll be glad we're making use of his food."

"Hey, we opened our freezer. Didn't we have veggies in there?"

Jillian shook her head. "Not in this one. We've got a few small packages for you and me, down in the carriage house freezer, but not enough for twelve people. I don't figure it's worth opening that one, when our house isn't on the generator. If we don't get the electricity back for a week, all of that food would spoil."

"We should have bought another generator." Kate held up both hands. "All I can say is, as soon as this mess is cleaned up, we need to work on a better emergency plan. We should have enough food on hand all the time for a full house, for at least a week."

"You're probably right, but if we stock up like that, we'll probably never need it again."

"So? We'll date everything and rotate the stock."

"Yes, Mother." Jillian gave her a flippant smile. Usually she was the one giving the orders.

"Sorry," Kate said.

"No, you're absolutely right. We were caught off guard. Next time, if there is a next time, we'll be better prepared. And the freezer should be okay tonight. If we don't get the power back tomorrow, we should probably open it and bring that food up here."

The dining room door swung open, and Craig walked in.

"What's the word?" Jillian asked.

"Dr. Smithson is completing his exam, after which he'll issue the death certificate. He's already called for a hearse, and they'll come for the body as soon as they can—probably within the hour."

"Really?" Kate perked up at that. "The roads are clear?"

"They're coming the long way around, but he convinced them it was necessary to get the body to the morgue."

"Where's the morgue?"

"They're taking him to Augusta."

Kate stared. She'd expected him to say Bucksport, or maybe Bangor.

"Why is that?" Jillian asked. "I thought maybe a local mortuary would take him until the bridge is fixed."

"Because it's a murder, and the state police are taking over the case. An S.P. detective will be here soon."

Jillian nodded. "I wondered about that. Aren't you required to hand this case over to the state police?"

"Yes and no. Things are so chaotic right now, with the storm and with the bridges out ..."

"But you were going to start the interviews," Kate said.

"I still am," Craig assured her. "We can't let anyone leave until Detective Seaver gets here, but I can take statements. In fact, Seaver wants me to. And if he's okay with them when he gets here, the guests can go."

"I know at least two of them who'll be glad." Jillian stacked a few recipe cards and laid them aside. "I should go talk to Zeb."

As she rose, Craig's radio crackled.

"Hold on a sec." He turned away and spoke to the dispatcher. He came back to the sisters grinning. "They've got electricity at the police station. It's not far away. Yours might be on too. I'll go disconnect the generator and flip on the main breaker ."

He strode into the storage room, and the sisters waited in silence. Kate sent up a prayer, hardly daring to hope.

A humming started. Kate felt a rush of warmth on her ankles, from the vent below the counter by the sink. At the same time, the clocks on the oven, microwave, and coffeemaker started blinking.

"Hey! It's back on! For real."

Jillian whirled and grinned at her. "Now, *that* is terrific news."

Craig came through the storeroom doorway. "Tada!"

Jillian beckoned to him. "Great! Come with me, Craig. I'll help you find Max Pelletier for his interview. Maybe we'll have a few less people here for supper."

———

An hour later, Detective Seaver still hadn't arrived. Craig had spent half an hour with Max, who was outraged that he still couldn't leave and stormed off to his room when the interview was over. Now Craig was deep in conversation with Charles Simon. Jillian had offered him the use of the office, but Craig didn't want to leave the second-floor landing and the entrance to Hercule Poirot unattended, so he was taking statements in the game room.

Jillian and Kate settled in the office to write down everything they could remember about the previous afternoon and evening.

"My brain hurts," Kate said at last. "I've written down anything that might be important, and a few things that almost certainly aren't. I'm tired."

"I know. Sorry."

Kate sighed. "I wonder if Max can hear what Craig and Charles are saying from in his room."

"I doubt it would matter." Jillian sat back and reviewed her own account. "I'm finished. Do you mind if I go sit with Zeb a while? I know there's stuff to do, but I've been putting it off."

"Go." Kate tossed her pen on the desk. "I'll come get you if I need you. We need to start supper soon, but I'm still hoping Rick will deliver that chicken."

"Hmm." Jillian tapped the keys on her computer. "The market promises to reopen at eight tomorrow morning."

"Good, but that won't help us tonight."

Jillian's cell rang, and she answered it with a smile. "Hi, Craig. Do you need your next victim?"

"I just got word that the hearse is on the way, but that detour will take them a while. They won't be here for at least another half hour."

"Okay. Kate and I have been jotting down statements about the murder and the rooms that have been entered. I'd say 'broken into,' but we don't have any evidence that anything was broken. Or stolen."

"I'm glad you've written things down. We need to know about anything odd that's happened in the last two days. I'm asking the guests if they've noticed anything. Some may not have realized their rooms were entered. I guess there's no sign of the state police yet?"

"Nobody's come in."

"Okay, I guess I'll talk to Dr. Rowan next. Is she in her room?"

"Yes, the Anne Shirley. It's on the top floor. I can call her room for you."

Craig thanked her, and Jillian placed the call. Eliza sounded relieved that something was happening at last.

When she hung up, Jillian put her statement in Kate's hands. "I'm going to see Zeb."

"Okay."

Scarcely fifteen minutes later, Kate tapped on Zeb's door and opened it. Inside, she found Jillian playing a card game with him.

Zeb smiled as Kate came through the doorway. "We've had a bit of excitement here. I don't usually see such activity."

"I'm glad it's nearly over. Jillian, now that the power's back on, we should do some baking and catch up on the paperwork." Of course, Kate meant computerized records, but Jillian would understand that. The truth was, Kate was getting antsy about the meal they had to serve in less than two hours. If the chicken didn't arrive soon, they'd have no time to cook it.

Jillian stood. "Yes, there's a lot of catching up to do. Anyone checking out yet?"

"No, Craig says he can't let anyone leave until Detective Seaver gets here. I expect a few will want to leave as soon as he arrives."

"I thought he'd be here long ago." Jillian scooped up the deck of cards and slid it into its box. "I'll see you later, Zeb."

The sisters walked back toward the office.

"I heard Dr. Rowan say she might start packing earlier," Kate confided.

"I hope she can leave soon. Although I have mixed feelings about seeing people go," Jillian said. "It's good in a way, but I feel as though we've grown attached to them."

Kate nodded. "We've shared a traumatic experience."

The front door opened, and Rick came in with a cardboard carton in his arms.

"Here's the food. Where do you want it?"

"I'll take it." Kate held out her arms.

"It's heavy. I might as well take it to the kitchen for you."

Jillian led the way, opening the swinging door and directing him to place the box on the counter. Kate went right to work, shifting the packages of chicken into the refrigerator.

"Ooh, Diana sent canned peaches too. Lots of them."

"Great." Jillian stacked the loaves of bread on their work island.

"Listen, the rain's tapering off and should be done before morning," Rick said. "Do you want me to take down the shutters?"

Jillian looked at Kate. "What do you think?"

"It might raise morale. It would be nice to be able to see out again."

"Shutters down it is, then." Jillian started out through the dining room, and the others followed her. "Are you still on duty, Rick?"

"Yeah, I'm—"

He broke off as they crossed the dining area toward the lobby. The front door was open, and a man in rain gear was entering.

Jillian hurried forward. "May I help you?"

"I'm here for the state coroner's office."

"Oh, yes. I'm Jillian Tunney, and these are my siblings. We're the owners of the inn."

"Ah." He held out a clipboard. "We'll take the remains, but I'll need one of you to sign here."

"I'll do it," Rick said. "You gals might want to try to distract your guests for a few minutes."

Somehow the word got around that a hearse was in the parking lot. Guests began filtering onto the second-floor landing or down to the lobby.

"Hey, everyone, there's plenty of coffee and hot chocolate," Kate called in as cheerful a voice as she could muster.

A couple of people fixed beverages for themselves, but most stayed put to watch as Dryer's remains were trundled out of the Hercule Poirot Room on a stretcher and into the elevator.

"Thank God the power came on before they moved him," Jillian said.

Kate couldn't imagine the mortuary workers transporting the body down the winding stairway with everyone staring—or maybe she could. The scene had been awful enough with the elevator back in use.

"Guess we should get that chicken in the oven," she said.

"Mmm. But we need to watch the front desk too."

Rick had moved down the hallway to take a phone call, and he walked toward them pocketing his cell. "I've got to go up and brief Craig. We have a complication."

"What is it?" Kate asked.

"Back in a minute."

Her infuriating brother bounded up the stairs without giving her an answer.

Rick pushed open the swinging door. "Something smells good."

"It's the chicken. We had to start supper," Jillian said.

"That's okay."

"Since we've got the oven back, I'm making brownies and cherry cobbler," Kate said as she measured flour into a large mixing bowl. "What's going on?"

"It seems the state police can't send a detective here tonight after all. They've got too many other cases going on. There was a huge pile-up on I-95, and there've been a couple of hurricane deaths south of here, plus a murder in Naples."

"Wow." Jillian gazed at him in sympathy. "So, what do you do now?"

"The chief talked to the S.P. supervisor and told him we could handle it. But nobody can leave tonight."

Kate let out a little moan.

"That's not going to go over well with a couple of our guests," Jillian explained.

"Maybe not, but it's good in a way. Nobody can disappear on us."

"Max isn't going to want to pay for another night," Kate said.

"Well, don't say this too loudly, but the chief said if it caused a big problem, the town would have to pick up the tab."

"That's got to be a first," Jillian said.

Rick grimaced. "The budget's tight, but under the circumstances, it may be necessary."

"When can we clean the room?" was Kate's question.

"*That's* your priority?" Rick scowled at her.

"I can't help the way my mind works," Kate protested. "We need to know if the Hercule Poirot Room will need a new carpet. A new mattress seems imperative, but I'm just not sure how we can squeeze out enough money to spring for a new carpet. And since you're a partner in this business, you should care."

"We need to keep it sealed for another day or two, until we're sure we're done," Rick said soberly.

Jillian laid a hand on his sleeve. "Then that's what we'll do. Just tell us what you and Craig need."

"We've got a couple more statements to take. Now that the body's gone, I figure Craig and I can sit down together someplace private and hash it all over. We'll probably both be here all night."

"Do you need a room?" Jillian supposed she and Kate could give up their rooms and go back to the carriage house—or bunk together. And there was Elizabeth Bennet, the room they'd let Craig use. But they needed to know which rooms needed cleaning right away.

"There are two beds in Liz Bennet, right?" Rick asked. "We can swap off for naps in there."

Jillian tried not to let her relief show. No rushed cleaning. Without an officer sitting in the game room all the time, she hoped the guests wouldn't feel they were under constant surveillance. Still, Rick and Craig would stay close enough for her and Kate to call them in quickly if something else happened.

Which it wouldn't.

She hoped.

"All right," Kate said. "We're fixing an evening meal for all of the guests. You're welcome to eat here as well."

"No charge for you and Craig," Jillian said quickly.

"I should hope not, since I brought you the main course."

Jillian nodded her concession to that. "We'd like to help you wind this up any way we can. And if you want to use the office, that's fine. Maybe you should hang a Do Not Disturb sign if you don't want us barging in."

"Thanks." Rick glanced at his watch. "It's getting late, so we'll probably take you up on the offer of supper. Then we'll decide if we need to spend more time in Dryer's room, or if we should search any other rooms."

Jillian supposed that might be the logical thing to do. Kate had kept busy as they talked, preparing her dough for the cobbler. Jillian opened the oven to check on the brownies she was baking on the rack below the chicken.

"I'll tell Craig we can use the office, and then I'm going to track down Roger Cowper for an interview," Rick said.

"Galadriel Room," Jillian called after him as he strode toward the door. Rick waved and disappeared.

While the brownies cooked, she fixed a coffee tray and added extra cups for the interviewees. When she reached the office, both doors were closed, but no sign hung on the handle. She tapped on the hall door, and Rick called, "Come in."

He was interviewing Luke. That surprised her, as she was sure Craig had talked to Luke in depth earlier. She'd understood that Roger would be next. Rick didn't explain, but both men stopped talking as she entered. She set down the tray.

"Anything else I can bring you?"

"No, this is great," Rick said.

She returned a tight smile and turned away, avoiding Luke's gaze. As she closed the door, Rick said, "Tell me about this domestic charge the Bangor police ..."

Her mouth went dry, but she didn't linger. Shutting the door carefully, she hurried to the kitchen. Kate was baking up a storm, and Craig sat on a stool at the island, with his own coffee before him.

"Craig, did you know Luke Brantley had a domestic charge against him?"

"Yes, I found out earlier. When Rick arrived this afternoon, he gave me an update on the background checks." Craig took a sip of coffee.

Kate stopped stirring the batter in her mixing bowl. "Domestic? As in domestic abuse?"

"More like a fight between married people. At least, that's the way Luke tells it." Craig gritted his teeth for a moment, as if undecided on how much to reveal. "In January, Luke pounded on his wife, but she fought back—enough to give him a black eye. The neighbors called it in. Both refused medical treatment, and neither pressed charges. The responding officers decided to give them a stiff warning and let it slide."

"Shouldn't someone have been arrested?" Kate asked.

"It's a judgment call, depending on how badly the people are injured. Luke apparently said his wife—Tara, is it?"

Kate nodded.

"He said Tara started it, and she didn't deny it. That was all at the time, but Geordie found out she filed for divorce two months later, after another argument."

"Okay. Well, that doesn't make him a murderer."

"No, it doesn't."

Jillian was surprised that Kate would go even that far in defending Luke.

"Oh, and he has a recent OUI on his record," Craig added.

"Operating under the influence?" Jillian said.

Kate's face fell. "I can't say that really surprises me. Drinking was something we never agreed on. You could say it contributed to our breakup."

Craig's radio beeped, and a garbled voice said something. He seemed to understand it and stood. "Excuse me." He walked to the other end of the kitchen and talked for a couple of minutes. When he came back, he said, "That was Geordie. I don't suppose your landline is working yet?"

"I don't think so." Jillian went to the kitchen extension and lifted the receiver. "Nope, no dial tone."

"Okay." Craig sighed and sank onto the stool he'd occupied earlier. "I'm not sure what to do."

"Anything we can help with?" Jillian asked.

His lips skewed. "I probably need to talk to Rick, but I'll wait until he's done with Luke. I had a little trouble understanding everything, but I'm pretty sure Geordie said ... " Craig looked up apologetically. "I'm not sure I should discuss this with you. In fact, I probably shouldn't. But she *is* staying here, on your property."

"She?" Kate asked. "What's going on?"

Craig pulled in a deep breath. "Geordie said—I'm pretty sure he said—Dr. Rowan lost her license to practice medicine in Massachusetts because of a medical blunder."

Kate's face froze. "You mean she's not allowed to be a doctor anymore?"

"Not without some new training and supervision, I think. I'm not exactly sure what the law is in Massachusetts."

"What about other states?" Jillian asked.

"I don't know. She was probably only licensed there in Massachusetts. She told us she's not in Maine, but it's possible she's okay in some other states. I'm just not sure."

They were all silent for a long moment. Finally, Jillian spoke.

"I wouldn't think it would have a bearing on the crimes here, would you?"

Craig shrugged. "If I understood correctly, her mistake caused a patient to lose his foot."

Kate stirred her bowl of batter slowly. "Do you think it's possible Alan Dryer knew about it—or something worse she did—and threatened her?"

"Maybe he was blackmailing her not to tell about her

medical gaffes," Jillian said.

"Yeah, that." Kate waved her wooden spoon at her sister with approval.

Craig smiled. "I don't know. It's a matter of record."

"Well, maybe she did other things that aren't on the record," Kate said a little belligerently. "Maybe she's accidentally killed other patients. If she wants to get relicensed or get approved in another state—like Maine, for instance—maybe she was desperate to keep him from telling the medical board, or whoever would do something about it."

"That's a little far-fetched," Jillian said.

Craig gave a wan smile. "A little. I wanted to do some cyber checking on her, but I think I'll wait until we have better communication."

"You can get online now," Kate said.

"Really? I thought the Internet was still down. Here at the inn, I mean."

"I brought in our email a little while ago," Jillian said.

"In that case, would you mind if I had a session with your computer?"

"Sure. Do you want to use the one in the office? There's also a terminal on the front desk."

"Front desk, I guess. Rick's busy in your office."

Jillian straightened and pulled out her master key. "We keep the keyboard and the hard drive locked up when we're not using them. Let me open the cupboard for you and start it up."

As they stepped out of the dining room, they saw Zeb coming down the hallway.

"Hi," Jillian called in surprise. "Can I get something for you, Zeb?"

"That depends. Do you have a chess game?"

"We sure do. It's upstairs, but one of us can bring it down

here for you."

"I was wondering if one of the other guests might like a match."

"That sounds like a great idea," Craig said. He swiveled and looked behind him. "A couple of folks are in by the fireplace."

Zeb nodded and moved on into the dining room. Jillian set Craig up with the computer. As she finished, Charles came into the lobby.

"Mr. Wilding says you have a chess set upstairs? We thought we'd have a match."

"Certainly," Jillian said. "Would you like me to get it for you?"

"Just tell me where it is."

She gave him instructions, and he hurried up the stairs.

Meanwhile, Craig radioed Geordie and was soon logged in to the police department's network. The office door opened, and Luke came out, followed by Rick. Luke passed them with a tight nod and hurried up the stairs. Rick came to stand beside Craig's chair.

"How's it going?" Craig asked.

"Let's get this done. And it might be a good idea for you to sit in."

"Okay." Craig shot Jillian a glance. "Geordie gave me some intel about Dr. Rowan. And also Roger Cowper."

"Cowper told me he has a police record," Rick said. "Auto theft, but it was fifteen years ago, when he was a teenager. He swears he's been clean since then. But he seems wary, and I wondered if he was holding something back."

"He is. He was expelled from college on a hazing incident."

"Oh, man." Rick rolled his eyes. "Everybody's hiding something, it seems."

"Maybe more than we know yet. Who do we want on the hot seat next?"

15

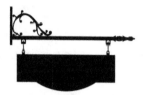

J illian took the first shift that evening. Don Reece emailed her, saying he thought he could be there Thursday evening for his usual shift on the front desk. She assured him they'd be all right one more night but would be glad to see him when he returned. She was bone tired, but in a way, she was glad they wouldn't have one more person to keep track of and explain things to tonight.

With the furnace running once more, she didn't feel the chill that evening, but she noted on their indoor-outdoor thermometer that the temp had fallen to thirty-eight degrees outside. Frost wasn't unusual this time of year—in fact, many years they got a full-fledged snowstorm in April. She wondered how cold it would get before dawn.

Luke had rounded up a crew to remove the shutters with Rick's approval. With Max, Charles, and Roger, the downstairs storm shutters had come off and been stored in less than half an hour. Not trusting any of the men with a master key, Jillian had told the guests to open the shutters on their own bedrooms but to leave the rest upstairs for the staff. She and

Kate did their own, and Charles had helped Eliza Rowan with hers.

She went to the front door and peered through the glass, listening. Dripping sounds were unmistakable, but perhaps the rain had stopped.

She'd barely sat down at the front desk, hoping Kate was sound asleep, when Craig slipped down the stairs.

"Everything okay up there?" Jillian asked.

"Yeah. We're taking turns checking the common areas. Marie Simon was in the lounge a few minutes ago, looking for a book to read."

Jillian nodded. The third-floor lounge was just outside the Simons' Scarlett O'Hara Room. "Roger was down here about half an hour ago, getting a snack and some coffee. I guess everyone's a little restless tonight."

"Yeah."

"Would you mind if I checked on Zeb?"

"No, go ahead. I thought I'd get coffee."

"I might join you. Although, I don't think I want coffee now. I plan to wake Kate in an hour or so and hit the hay."

"I'll save you a seat." He smiled and nodded toward the empty dining room.

Jillian walked quietly down the hall. She used her master key to open Zeb's door after a light knock brought no response. The old man was sleeping fretfully, stirring as she peered in but not opening his eyes. She shut the door softly and retraced her steps.

Craig hadn't flipped any wall switches, but the glow from the juice dispenser and the light spilling in from the lobby were enough. She filled a small glass with grape juice and sat down opposite him, feeling almost as if they were on a romantic date at some coffee shop.

"What do you think about this?" he asked.

"About the murder, you mean?"

"All of it."

"I'm not sure. I know it wasn't you, me, Kate, Rick, or Zeb. Anyone else in this house is fair game, I suppose. But what about you? I'm sure there are things you know that I don't."

Craig sipped his coffee and sat back in his chair. "Dr. Rowan makes me uneasy. She should have told us she'd lost her license. Especially when I asked her to examine the body."

"That is disconcerting."

"Don't let her in on anything we discover," he said.

"Oh, I wouldn't."

"I know, but ... well, she's the one claiming her room was burglarized. But there's no proof. I've asked her to email us a picture of the bracelet when she gets home."

"She can't access one on her phone?"

"Apparently not, but she says there are a couple on her desktop at home."

"Do you think she only said it was stolen to throw suspicion off herself?"

"Maybe. She seemed truthful when I talked to her, but we know she wasn't telling the whole truth."

"Yes." Jillian sighed. "It's too bad, because I liked her. She was good with Zeb, you know?"

"I thought so, too, and he seemed comfortable with her. So, for now, we're taking her complaint about the bracelet at face value and assuming it was stolen. She's had plenty of time to find it, if it was simply mislaid." He glanced toward the lobby and went on. "Then there are a couple of fellows with records."

"Luke and Roger, right? Anyone else?"

"We haven't turned up much on the Simons, other than confirming that they really are who they say they are. She's an artist, medium-well established, it seems, and his university confirms Charles's position there. Are they just too ... normal?"

Jillian smiled. "I don't think they're what I'd call normal. They're both creative, intelligent people."

"Hmm, yes." Craig took another swallow from his mug.

"What about Max?" She glanced toward the lobby, but no one was in evidence there.

"He's a tough nut to crack. He's holding back too. Not happy to be kept here. And Luke told your brother he'd seen him coming down from the third floor. But you've got a lounge up there, so we can't hold that against him."

"You haven't been able to find out anything about him?"

"Oh, minor stuff. He's held various ho-hum jobs."

"I thought he was a biologist."

Craig's lips tightened. "Now, that's an interesting thing. He claims his degree is from a college that folded four years ago, so we haven't been able to contact them directly. I pressed him on his current employer, and he said he was here freelance. Plans to write a book on mollusks."

"Not sure I believe that."

"Me either, but apparently, it's his passion. He gave me the names of a couple of publications he'd written articles for, and he's able to spout off tons of statistics on how the mollusk population is declining due to global warming and pollution."

"Anyone could bone up a little on stuff like that. Most people wouldn't listen to him long—I suspect it would get boring after a while."

"Yes. He does have a nice camera with him, and he showed me some photos he'd made of clams and mussels on other beaches."

"Hmm. If he'd said whales or harbor seals, that would be more interesting."

"And also easier to check up on, I suspect."

"But really," Jillian said. "Clams and mussels? Who's going to buy a book about those?"

"I have no idea. But squid and octopuses are mollusks too."

"That's a little more interesting. But maybe the marine life isn't his real purpose here. It's awfully convenient that his school went out of business."

"Isn't it?" Craig checked his watch. "I guess we'd better wake up our relief troops."

Jillian pushed her chair back and took his cup. "I, for one, am ready for a few hours of sleep."

———

Kate heard the elevator in the wee hours. She got up from the front desk and tiptoed to the hallway. When the doors opened, Eliza Rowan stepped off and came toward her.

"Hi. I couldn't sleep. All that wind howling and waves crashing."

"I'm sorry."

"Well, I thought some herbal tea or something might help me relax. I don't want any coffee, though. That would just make my insomnia worse."

"Let me help." Kate rummaged in the basket of teabags. "We've got vanilla chamomile and a peppermint."

"I'll take the chamomile. Thanks."

Kate hesitated. She remembered Craig's suspicions of Dr. Rowan. Maybe this would be a good chance to talk to her with no one else around. Of course, she wouldn't mention the fact that they knew she had a problematic past. She poured herself half a cup of coffee and sat down across from Eliza.

"So, where are you from again?"

"Just outside of Boston."

"Oh, you work in a hospital there."

Eliza took a sip from her steaming mug. "I did, but I'm

considering some changes. That's why I took a hiatus." She smiled and took another drink.

Kate nodded. Better not push too hard on that. "How long have you been a doctor?"

"Nine years."

"It must be really interesting." Getting no response, Kate said, "I wasn't very good at science. I took business courses, and before we got the inn, I was an office manager for a medical practice." She laughed. "The medical part didn't rub off on me, though."

"You prefer hospitality?"

"I don't know yet. I didn't mind the office, but I love the chance to work with my sister. So ... you're thinking of moving your practice or what?"

"I haven't decided." Eliza pushed back her chair and stood. "I guess I'll go back up and see if I can sleep now. Is it okay if I take my cup with me?"

"Oh, sure." Kate stood and watched her leave. The doctor was definitely uncomfortable discussing her career. Back at the front desk, she tried to read, but her eyelids kept fluttering down.

Sometime later, Kate jerked awake and realized she'd fallen asleep with her head cradled on her arms atop the front desk. Her cell lay on the desktop, and she nudged it. Five thirty. The elevator door opened down the hall. So that's what woke her up. Since the power outage ended, she thought she'd heard the elevator every time it went up or down.

Jillian appeared a moment later, looking far from rested. "Hi. Everything okay?"

"Yeah, nothing new." Kate stretched her arms.

"Ready to start breakfast?" Jillian asked.

"Not really. I fell asleep right here."

"I believe it. At least tonight, Don will be here, and we can get a good night's rest."

"In my own bed, I hope," Kate said.

"Not enamored of the Hornblower Room anymore?"

"I still love it, but with people sneaking in and out of the rooms here, I'd just as soon be down in the carriage house, thank you." Kate's mind was still fuzzy, but it began to focus on the meal they needed to prepare. "Are we running out of breakfast ingredients?"

"We had plenty of sausage in the freezer. The bacon will probably be enough for today, but that's it."

"Oh, yeah, and we can open both freezers now."

Jillian smiled. "Any time we want. But we might run out of eggs today. And we didn't make any fresh muffins last night."

Kate sighed. "I can whip up a batch, but I'll need a few of those precious eggs. Just let me run upstairs first."

"Go ahead. I'll go scout out what we have. I sure hope we can get to a store later."

Kate ran up the stairs. She was puffing a little by the time she reached the third-story landing. She tiptoed across the shadowy lounge with a glance at the door of Scarlett O'Hara. She hoped she didn't wake up the Simons.

She entered her room and hit the light switch. Blinking in the sudden glare she stared at the chair that was out of place, next to the television stand.

"What—"

Why on earth would anyone put the chair there? She glanced around. Her bed looked the same as when she'd peeled out at 2 a.m., not bothering to make it this time. She took two steps to the bathroom doorway and flipped the light switch. Empty. The shower curtain was pushed back, and she could see there was no one in there.

She checked the closet. Nothing. Her hands trembled as she

closed the door. It didn't make sense. Craig and Rick probably wouldn't believe her if she told them the chair had been moved, but she knew it had. If it was there when she got up, she'd have stumbled over it.

Her gaze flickered from item to item, her brain ticking off the catalog of the room's props. Telescope. Framed Navigational chart of the western Mediterranean. Decorative shelf holding eight vintage volumes of C.S. Forester's Hornblower books. Mounted poster of Gregory Peck as a dashing Captain Hornblower. Binnacle and compass. She caught her breath.

Slowly, she advanced and put out a finger to touch the frame of the binnacle. The top walnut rim had been pried off and lay on the rug behind the stand. The compass was gone.

She turned and dashed to the door, making sure to close it firmly behind her so that the lock engaged. Running across the lounge, she almost slammed into a man.

"Whoa, whoa, whoa." Rick grasped her upper arms and steadied her. "What's the hurry?"

"I—you—" Kate was shaking all over. She gulped in a breath. "Someone stole the compass."

16

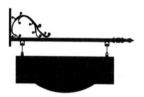

K ate was taking her time. Jillian quickly inventoried their supplies. She set out all the premade pastries on hand, started fresh coffee, and filled the juice dispenser. She decided not to make omelets, as it might take too many eggs, cutting Kate short for her baking. She'd make one conservative batch of scrambled eggs. First come, first served. Latecomers would have to rely on cereal and waffle batter.

At last, Kate barreled into the kitchen, her eyes a little wild.

"You won't believe this."

"What?" Jillian asked placidly. Her mind was on biscuits. They didn't usually do sausage gravy, but maybe today was a good time for that.

"The compass," Kate said. "It's gone."

Jillian stared at her.

"Someone stole it out of my room," Kate went on. "It was there when you woke me up at two, but it's gone now."

"The whole thing?"

"Not the binnacle case. Just the compass, out of the top."

"But ... how could they open it?"

"Ripped it off with some kind of tool. Rick's up there now."

Jillian sank onto a stool at the island. "Zeb will be devastated."

"We'd better not tell him," Kate said.

Jillian thought about it for a moment and shook her head slowly. "Your room was locked. Whoever it is must have a master key."

"How? There are only two. We've got one, and Rick showed me the second one. Craig handed it off to him when they changed shifts."

Jillian felt the pocket of her jeans. Her master key was secure.

"I don't get it. I just don't get it."

"Me neither," Kate said. "You didn't make a third one before the power went out."

"I've *never* made a third one. Sometimes I've thought about it—just in case we lose one. This is a good argument against that." Jillian heard footsteps in the dining room and glanced at the clock. "It's time to start serving."

"Not a word to anyone," Kate hissed. "Rick says they'll check everyone's luggage before they leave."

"Right." Jillian deep-sixed the sausage gravy idea and shoveled the eggs into a warming pan. "We're a little low on some things. This is it for eggs. I left you half a dozen for baking. If we can get to the market, we'll buy more, but ..."

"Yeah, that's fine. Is this the waffle batter?" Kate picked up a container of thick, cream-colored liquid.

"Yes. Can you bring it out?"

They found Roger in the dining room, fixing his coffee and eyeing the few Danish pastries and muffins critically.

"I'm sorry," Jillian said. "We've got eggs, bacon, sausage, and waffle batter, but we're a little low on pastries today."

"Understandable."

"Yes, well ... Uh, Kate's going to make some blueberry muffins, but it will be half an hour or so before they're ready."

Kate nodded to her as she set down the covered bowl of batter, then she scurried back to the kitchen.

"Oh, and there's yogurt over there." Jillian pointed, feeling a little helpless. She was used to having plenty of food to offer their guests.

Neither of the sisters left the food preparation until all of the dishes were on display. Because there was no fresh fruit, Jillian added canned fruit salad to the buffet. At last, she caught Kate's sleeve and whispered, "I'm going to see if Zeb's awake. If he is, he'll be hungry. The eggs and yogurt are going fast, and I want him to have some protein. Can you start thinking about what we'll serve for lunch?"

When she tapped softly on the old man's door, he called, "If you're Jillian, come on in."

She smiled and opened the door. "Well, good morning!"

Zeb was sitting on the edge of the bed wearing trousers and socks and buttoning up a clean shirt.

"You must be feeling better," Jillian said. "I was going to see if you wanted some breakfast."

"I *am* better. So much better that I thought I'd amble down to your dining room and save you fixing a tray."

"That's terrific, if you're sure you're up to it."

"I am. Just bring my shoes from the closet, would you, please?"

A minute later, they walked together down the hallway.

"You look great, Zeb," Kate called when they walked into the dining room.

"Why, thank you, my dear."

"Let me carry your plate," Jillian said. "You just tell me what to put on it. We have a limited selection today, but we're hoping to get to the store later."

Kate frowned. "Rick just told me the Shop 'n Save isn't open yet. They had some window damage. They hope to reopen tomorrow."

"Okay," Jillian said. "Is the corner market open?"

"I'm not sure. I told Rick we'll be getting desperate by suppertime, and he said he'd check around or have Dave Hall do it. I think they're making a list at the station of places people can get food and bottled water."

"At least we've got water. And we won't starve." Jillian smiled apologetically at Zeb. "We may be reduced to canned corn and instant mashed potatoes, though."

"Well, I've got quite a stash," Zeb said. "We could go over and forage in my pantry."

"Oh, no, Zeb. I don't want you to do that," Jillian said quickly.

"Why not? You're putting me up and feeding me. How many people have you got here?"

"Six guests besides you," Kate said. "With Jillian and me and a police officer, that's ten."

"Well, I have plenty of canned stew and spaghetti, and there's a lot of stuff in my freezer." Zeb frowned. "You think it's all right, don't you? I didn't open it after the power went out."

"It should be fine," Jillian said. "The corner market promised to open this morning. It's not quite eight, but I'm going over there as soon as I can. We've got hamburger in our freezer at the carriage house. If the corner store has eggs and milk and a few other essentials, we'll get by."

"Well, if there's any question, you can have the meat and stuff from my freezer, and canned goods from the pantry." Zeb gave her a firm nod, letting her know he would brook no arguments.

"Let's wait a bit and see what we can get from stores, but I appreciate that." Jillian took his arm. "Come on, let's get some breakfast. I don't know about you, but I'm hungry."

As they moved to the buffet counter, she noticed that Luke was watching them closely. Jillian ignored him and slowly walked along the counter with Zeb, adding scrambled eggs and the last strip of bacon to his plate and pouring waffle batter into the compact waffle iron to cook while she settled him at a table. She went back to fetch tea and maple syrup for him, and when she returned to Zeb's spot, Luke was standing by the table.

"Excuse me, Jillian. I don't mean to bother you, but I need to have a private word with you."

Jillian met his gaze. Was he going to pump her for information about Kate? Somehow, she didn't think so. Luke had stayed within the boundaries Kate had set for him during his stay.

"Okay, just a minute. Let me make sure Zeb's got everything he needs."

"Oh, I'm fine," Zeb said cheerfully.

"Your waffle ..."

"There is that." Zeb frowned toward the waffle maker.

"It'll be ready in a sec," Jillian said. "Maybe we could talk in the living room, Luke." She nodded toward the open arch between the dining room and the cozy room with the fireplace.

"I'll wait in there. Come find me when you're done here." Luke snagged his coffee mug from his table and ambled into the next room. He took a seat in one of the armchairs before the windows. Jillian noted that no rain was blurring them this morning.

She waited for Zeb's waffle, greeting Max Pelletier and Eliza Rowan as they sauntered in. Finally, the light went off on the cooker, and Jillian delivered the hot waffle to Zeb.

"Here you go. I brought some butter, too, and you've got your syrup."

"Perfect," Zeb said with his twinkly smile. "Now go tend to business."

Sprawled in his chair before the empty fireplace, Luke straightened when Jillian entered the living room.

"Hey. I thought you'd want to know. Something's missing from my room."

Jillian's heart skipped a beat. She sat down carefully in a nearby chair. "What sort of something?"

"There was a book, an old book. I don't know if it was valuable ..."

"*Around the World in Eighty Days.*"

"Yeah. Since it was in a locked case, I thought ... Well, I was browsing through the paperbacks last night, but the old hardcover looked really cool. I figured it must be worth protecting from careless handling, or you wouldn't have put it in the case."

With a sigh, Jillian met his gaze. "You're right. It's not a first edition, but it's very old. I spent a couple hundred dollars on it. Could be worse. But I'll tell the officers right away. Can you let them take a look around your room, in case anything else isn't as it should be?"

"Sure." He blinked at her. "I'll go up there now. Tell them to come whenever they're ready."

He seemed so sincere. So ... innocent. Jillian found it hard to believe he wasn't being truthful. But if someone was stealing items from several rooms, wouldn't that be the way to take suspicion off himself—to present himself as another victim?

"Do you have any idea when it disappeared?" she asked.

"Not really. I just noticed it a few minutes ago. It was there before supper last night, but I didn't think about it when I went to bed. I'm afraid I didn't notice if it was there or not."

"Okay. Thank you, Luke." She stood on shaky legs. Better take the elevator.

She got off on the second floor, but no one was in the game room. Back at the elevator, she went on up to the third story. As she crossed the lounge, she could see that the door to Kate's room was open. She hurried over and leaned against the jamb. Rick and Craig were examining the binnacle, and Rick was fitting the walnut rim to the main casing.

"I think it can be fixed without much trouble, if we can just find the compass," he said to Craig. "There's one bad gouge, but—"

"Excuse me," Jillian said, and they both turned toward her.

"Hi," Craig said with a smile.

"We've got another theft." She stepped inside and closed the door behind her. "Luke just told me the antique book is missing from the Phileas Fogg Room."

Rick frowned. "I thought you locked it up because Kate made a fuss over how much you spent on it."

"We did. It was in a locked case. I have no explanation, but Luke will be in his room whenever you want to take a look."

"Let's go," Craig said. "We know the compass is the only thing missing in here. But it sounds as if we might have to search all the rooms."

Rick groaned. "Oh, joy."

"Well, you've certainly got to check guests' luggage before you let them check out," Jillian said, more sharply than she'd intended.

"Right. Get us your list of things you check after someone leaves, to make sure they didn't swipe anything good." Rick swept an arm toward the door, inviting Craig to lead the way.

The three of them went to the elevator together.

"Who else knows?" Craig asked on the way down.

"Just me, I think," Jillian said. "Unless someone heard Luke talking to me. There were folks in the dining room, and we were in by the fireplace. It's possible somebody heard when he told me."

The elevator stopped on the second-floor hallway. The men hesitated, waiting for her to go first.

"Do you need me?" she asked.

"You could do a quick sweep of the other decorations," Rick said.

She walked behind them to the door of Phileas Fogg, where Rick knocked. Luke opened the door wide.

"Hi. Make yourselves at home."

While the men beelined to the display case, Jillian looked around, spotting the cushions, movie poster, framed elephant and tiger prints, and the shelf of Jules Verne books. None of them was worth much. The Indian-inspired fabrics did a lot toward setting the tone for the room.

"Everything from the checklist is here, except the book Luke mentioned," she said. The glass-topped case at one end of the desk was conspicuously empty. She walked over to join the three men. "Is it locked?"

"I tried it, and it's not," Luke said. "My fingerprints are probably on the edge of the lid. Sorry about that. But I know it was locked yesterday."

"Seems our burglar is a talented lock picker." Craig bent close to examine the lock and the wood around it. "Ah. He was in a bit of a hurry here. There are a couple of scratches in the wood."

Jillian leaned in to look. "You're right. I'm pretty sure those weren't there before."

"Well, Luke," Rick said, "we know you have an OUI and a

domestic dispute on your record. Anything else you'd like to tell us about?"

"What? No!" He seemed a bit confused and angry, and Jillian didn't blame him.

"Okay then. Have you checked all your personal belongings to be sure everything's there?"

"Yeah. I didn't bring much." Luke looked helplessly toward the duffel bag on the luggage stand.

"All right, let's have you not touch that display case anymore until we can get a fingerprint kit up here and check it," Craig said. He turned to Rick. "You said you have yours in your vehicle?"

"Yeah, I'll go get it."

Jillian followed her brother into the hallway. "Rick, doesn't this seem bizarre to you?"

"In what way?"

She walked with him to the stairway. "Why would someone keep pilfering stuff when there are two policemen in the house? It seems crazy to me."

Rick made a disgusted face. "Maybe the thief heard the state police aren't coming, and he figures we're country bumpkin cops who will never figure it out."

"He's wrong," she said with conviction. "You and Craig are the best there are."

"Thanks for your vote of confidence, but I'm not so sure. I think we should search the other rooms right away."

"You can search mine anytime."

"Great. I was thinking more of the two with plumbing problems. Luke thought he might have heard something up overhead last night. Isn't the room above his one of the ones that's out of commission?"

"Yes. Scout Finch."

Rick started down the stairs. Jillian walked with him as he

talked. "The thief has to make sure the guest is out of his room for a while before he can slip in there and steal something."

"So, mealtimes?"

"That's probably safest in this situation. But in the two rooms that are out of commission, he can sneak in there anytime without fear of being discovered." Rick walked across the lobby and paused with his hand on the front door handle. "I'm going to get my kit. You pull up that list of valuables. You can go with Craig to check those two rooms while I try to lift some prints in Luke's room."

After alerting Kate, Jillian went back to the third floor. She opened the door to the Scout Finch Room, then stepped back and let Craig enter first. He did a quick check to make sure no one was in the room or the bathroom. The connecting door to the shower area was unlocked, and he checked that. The door to the adjoining bathroom beyond, which served the Rip Van Winkle Room, was locked.

"Want me to open that?" Jillian asked.

"Not yet. First, let's confirm that the items on your list for the Scout Finch Room are all there."

"Okay." She consulted her clipboard, naming off the items they verified each time a guest checked out of the room. She ticked them off as they spotted them.

"All here," she said when she'd finished.

"Good."

"So, on to Rip Van Winkle?"

Craig shook his head. "I've been thinking about this. The guests know we're going to check their luggage. We need to think about where they would hide their loot so we wouldn't find it if we searched their rooms."

"Their cars?" Jillian asked.

"Have you kept track of who goes in and out?"

"Tuesday, pretty much nobody went outside except you

and Rick. After Luke helped with the shutters, I mean. Yesterday ... well, they came and took Dryer's body away. And sometimes Kate and I are both in the kitchen. A guest could sneak out to his car then, and I suppose we'd never know." She looked anxiously at Craig. "Will you have to search their cars too?"

"I hope it won't come to that."

"But you can search their luggage, right?"

"Technically, we'd need a warrant. You can give us permission to search the hotel rooms, but their personal belongings are theirs, not yours. I've talked to the chief, and we're applying for a warrant now."

"My dad called the police once or twice over the years to check a guest's luggage. We've never had to do it in the year since we reopened the inn."

"I'm glad you haven't."

She nodded. This was a murder they were talking about, not just the theft of a trinket or two.

Craig studied the ceiling and moved slowly across the two sections of the bathroom, then into the Scout Finch guest room.

"What are you looking for?" she asked.

"If you had drop ceilings, I'd be poking around to see if there was anything above the tiles. But these look solid."

"Yes, I think they're the original ceilings. Of course, they've been painted several times. And there may have been some repairs before we got the place."

He nodded and walked slowly around the perimeter of the room, moving aside a chair and the luggage stand. Jillian watched silently as he knelt on the carpet and took out his pocketknife.

Using the end of one blade, he carefully removed the screws on a vent cover in the floor. When he pulled the cover up out of its position, he sneezed. Then he pulled a latex glove from his pocket and put it on his right hand. He bent down to look into the ducting, then felt around inside the vent. Shaking his head, he removed his hand.

"Nothing, as far as I can reach. Let's search everywhere in this room carefully. Then we'll do the next room."

Fifteen minutes later, Craig was satisfied that no stolen goods were hidden in the Scout Finch Room. Instead of going out into the hallway, they entered the Rip Van Winkle Room through the far side of the jack-and-jill bathroom. Less chance of being seen by one of the other guests that way, Jillian surmised.

They thoroughly searched the toilet area and moved on into the bedroom, where she consulted her clipboard. "Whoa."

"What is it?" Craig asked.

"We had a really old book of Washington Irving stories there, in the glass case. It was here when my parents bought the inn. I don't know what it's worth, but my dad thought it was special." She threw him a remorseful glance. "I guess we should have had all this stuff revalued."

"Might be a good idea when this is over. Or at least, before the thief goes to court."

"Are you sure you'll catch him?"

"He's got a lot of loot stashed somewhere in this building. He might try to carry it all out in a suitcase, but we're going to get him."

"What if it's already in his car?"

"It's possible. That's why we need the warrant today." Craig checked the heating vent as he had in Scout Finch, but without results. As he replaced the cover, he said, "Know what I'm thinking?"

"What?"

He dusted the knees of his pants and straightened. "You've got a secret room."

Jillian stared at him. "Two, actually."

"*Two*? I had no idea."

"There's one on this level, and one directly below it, behind the elevator shaft. The one up here's actually bigger than the one below it. But ... how would the thief know about them?"

"Let's think about who does know."

"Well, Kate, Rick, and me, of course. And Rick's kids and Diana. And you. And that guy who was here last summer—the man who found the compass."

"Yes. And we don't know for sure that he didn't tell anyone else, or that your parents or the previous owners didn't tell anyone."

Jillian scowled. "Of course. Their kids could know, and they might tell friends." She could imagine Rick's son telling a buddy, though they'd sworn Joel and Ashley to secrecy. She huffed out a breath. "So theoretically, any one of our guests could know about those rooms."

"I think we need to search the secret rooms."

"Okay, but can we do it without anyone finding out?"

"Let's loop Rick and Kate in first."

17

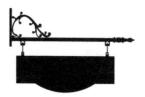

"I don't see that we're going to find anything in either of these rooms." Rick flopped down on a chair in the third-floor secret room. "We've searched them both."

"I know." Craig looked around at the small chamber. "Still, these hidden rooms are there all the time, and nobody finds them unless you tell them where to look."

Rick shrugged. "If they had architectural plans for the house, they'd see there's a gap behind the elevator shaft. I think these were bigger rooms before the elevator was added."

"What year was the house built?"

"I'm not sure exactly, but it was long enough ago for the rich people living in it to have a carriage house."

"Hmm. So probably a hundred years to a hundred and fifty?"

"Yes, and the elevator's a fairly modern one. I suppose there could have been an older model that was replaced later. I just know it was there when my folks bought the place."

"I don't think that elevator's more than thirty years old,"

Craig said. "It should be easy enough to find out, from the information on the control panel."

"I suppose there could be some little secret compartment in one of these rooms, but we've looked under all the shelves and behind every piece of furniture." The levers that opened the doors to the secret rooms were concealed beneath shelves in the game room and lounge. Rick figured that if there were smaller compartments hidden inside them, they'd likely operate on the same principle.

"Did your parents put this stuff in here?" Craig asked, glancing around at the books, desk, and a few other items within the secret chamber.

"No, I think most of it was already here. They didn't use these rooms much. My dad tried using one as a private den, but he didn't like not having a window." Rick stood. "Okay, so what now?"

Craig's eyebrows morphed together. "Your sisters went to the market?"

"Yup. Had to. I think Jillian went, and Kate's watching the front desk, to be sure nobody tries to sneak their luggage out."

"I'll ask for another man, if the chief can possibly spare us one. With only two of us here, there are too many ways to work around us."

"I'll go out and call," Rick said. He didn't think he could get phone service inside the windowless room.

"We need to do a systematic search of every room," Craig said. "We can do that without the warrant, because you three owners have given your permission. But we can't check luggage without the guests' permission."

"Right. So, we need to tell each guest that we have to search their room, and we ask them for permission on the baggage?"

"That sounds right." Craig sighed. "Let's start up here.

There are fewer guests staying on the top floor, so word might not get out as fast if we begin up here. And we've already done the two unoccupied rooms. Jillian and I were pretty thorough on those."

Rick agreed and put through his call. When he was finished, he checked the guest list. "Okay, so we've done Hornblower and the lounge. The Simons are in Scarlett O'Hara, and Dr. Rowan is in Anne Shirley. Those are the only two up here we haven't gone over with a fine-tooth comb." He looked up from the list. "Oh, wait. There's a big, walk-in linen closet on this level too."

"We'll need to look there as well."

They went to the Simons first, since they had the larger room. Charles and Marie went out into the lounge while they did the job. Nothing suspicious turned up, and Rick went out to speak to them.

"How would you folks feel about giving us a look in your luggage?" Rick asked.

Charles looked affably toward his wife. "I don't have a problem with that."

Marie frowned. "Is that customary?"

"No," Rick said, "but the thing is, if we don't search it now, we'll still have to search it before you leave. We've requested a warrant for that. Several valuable items have been stolen, and we need to find them before people start removing bags from the inn."

"Well, I guess it's all right." Marie still didn't seem to like it.

Charles reached over and patted her hand. "They have to, sweetheart. It'll be fine. We don't have anything to hide."

Marie inhaled deeply. "Okay, but this is the weirdest vacation we've ever taken."

"Thank you." Rick tried to keep a straight face and an official demeanor.

He went back into the Scarlett O'Hara Room. Craig was in the bathroom, tapping cautiously on the walls near the shower.

"Permission granted."

"Oh, good." Craig turned toward him. "I don't think there's anything in the walls. And there's nothing behind the mirror or anything like that."

They took the Simons' luggage from the closet and the luggage rack and set the bags on their beds. Carefully, they lifted out all the clothing and odds and ends. Rick examined the roller bag he was checking carefully for hidden pockets or a false panel. It would have to be fairly large to hide a book or a ship's compass.

"Nothing here," he said at last.

"Same."

Craig swapped with him and they went over the bags again, just to be sure. After replacing all the Simons' belongings and returning the luggage to where they'd found it, Rick straightened.

"Dr. Rowan next?"

"Yeah. I'll tell Mr. and Mrs. Simon they're clear and can check out anytime. But the inn owners will have to perform the checklist for their room before they actually leave."

"We just searched their luggage twice," Rick said.

"True, but we won't be with them while they gather their things. Unless you think we should stay."

"No, let's let them take their time and have Kate and Jillian do their usual sniffing around before the check-out is finalized. And I hope the warrant for their cars comes through before anyone actually gets out the door."

———

While Jillian performed a leisurely exit process on the lobby computer, Kate dashed up to the third floor with her checklist. She confirmed that all the Scarlett O'Hara decorations were in place and buzzed Jillian.

"All clear."

"Thank you," Jillian said in a noncommittal tone. She hung up and smiled at the Simons. "You're all set. Here's your receipt." She handed them the paper. "I hope you'll visit us again under more pleasant circumstances."

"You and your sister were wonderful," Marie said. "You couldn't help it that a hurricane happened during our stay."

"Or that a crime was committed," her husband added.

The front door opened, and Geordie Kraus came in, wearing his full uniform and carrying a sheaf of papers.

"Hello, Officer Kraus," Jillian said. "I believe Sergeant Watkins and Officer Gage are up on the third floor. Should I ask them to come down?"

"Maybe the sergeant," Geordie said. "I have some paperwork he's been waiting for."

Jillian was pretty sure he held the warrants for giving guests' luggage and cars a once-over. She waved toward the Simons. "This is Mr. and Mrs. Simon. They were just about to leave us."

"Oh." Geordie hesitated, and his face flushed. "I'm sorry, sir. Ma'am. I need to ask you to wait just a couple more minutes."

While he explained the situation to them, Jillian put in a quick call to Craig. Turning away from the others, she said softly, "Can you come down quick? Geordie's here with your paperwork, and the Simons are just about to leave."

A few seconds later, Craig walked swiftly down the staircase.

"Officer Kraus," he said cheerfully.

"Hi," Geordie replied. "I—uh—brought over your paperwork. From the courthouse." He raised his eyebrows.

Craig nodded. "Thank you so much. Mr. and Mrs. Simon, there's just one more thing, before you go. I promise it won't take long. I believe your car is right out front in the parking area."

"Well, yes." Charles seemed a little flustered, but he let Craig steer them out the door with their bags.

Geordie threw Jillian an apologetic glance. "I'd better go help him. Is Kate okay?"

"She's fine." Jillian smiled. Geordie had a serious crush on Kate. She hoped their date for the next evening could go as planned, and that they'd both have a good time.

Geordie ducked his head and hurried out onto the porch. Jillian deactivated the key cards they'd returned and watched from the window as the two officers performed a search of the car. The Simons were soon on their way.

"All clear?" she said as Craig and Geordie entered.

"Couldn't find anything suspicious, and I'm confident we didn't miss any place big enough to hide the things that are missing," Craig said.

Jillian was about to speak when she heard the elevator open. Dr. Rowan came down the hall, trundling a suitcase. Rick followed her into the lobby and stopped beside Jillian.

"Dr. Rowan is cleared. I told Kate."

Jillian nodded. That meant Kate was going down the checklist in Anne Shirley as they spoke.

Again, she took her time checking out the guest. The desk phone rang.

"Officer Gage, could you take that?"

Her brother looked a little surprised but lifted the receiver.

"Okay. I see. Yup. Thank you." He hung up and nodded at

Craig, motioning toward the dining room. Craig stepped across the hall with Rick.

"Did one of the officers explain to you that they'll have to take a quick look at your car before you go?" Jillian asked.

Dr. Rowan frowned. "Yes. I don't like it, but Officer Gage says you have a warrant."

"Not me. The police have it. It's only to help them solve these thefts that have been taking place. They want to find your bracelet and a few other things that have gone missing."

Her mind was spinning. Something must have happened, or Rick and Craig wouldn't be huddled in the dining room. She wanted desperately to call Kate but made herself carry on as if nothing was wrong.

"I understand," Dr. Rowan said.

Craig returned, and Rick headed down the hallway for the elevator.

"Doctor, it seems another valuable item is missing," Craig said to Eliza Rowan. "If I could just take a quick peek at your luggage? And then I'll escort you out to your car."

With a sigh, Dr. Rowan stood back, and Craig hoisted her suitcase onto the desk. He quickly removed her neatly folded clothing and felt the top and sides of the luggage, then did a minute survey of the area where the handle retracted into the bag.

"All done," he said. "I can repack for you, or if you'd prefer, you may do it yourself."

"I'll do it."

As she stepped closer to the desk, the elevator opened again. Instead of Rick, Max Pelletier appeared in the archway to the hall.

"I've been waiting for hours. Are you going to let me leave today?"

"We appreciate your patience, Mr. Pelletier," Craig said

without a trace of irony in his voice. "We're systematically checking the rooms and luggage, now that we have a warrant. We started on the third floor, but we'll get to you as soon as we can."

The desk phone rang again, and Jillian snatched it up.

"It's me," Kate said. "Did they tell you?"

"No." Jillian tried to infuse her voice with cordiality. "How may I help you?"

"The old map of Prince Edward Island is missing."

"I see." Jillian kept her gaze on the computer screen and didn't look toward Dr. Rowan. "Thank you for calling." She hung up and pulled the receipt from the printer. "Here you go, Dr. Rowan. I hope you can visit us again under more pleasant circumstances."

She felt like a robot, but she didn't know what else to say. That antique, hand-drawn map had been in the Anne Shirley Room before her parents bought the inn. A local dealer had appraised it at six hundred dollars, possibly more at auction.

Geordie stepped forward. "May I take your suitcase for you, ma'am?"

"Well, I ... suppose so." Dr. Rowan surrendered the handle to him.

Were they just going to let her go? Geordie wheeled the suitcase onto the porch, chatting pleasantly about the favorable change in the weather.

Craig whispered quickly. "Map's missing."

"Kate just told me. But it wouldn't fit in her suitcase."

"Not without me finding it. We'll check her car, but I doubt it's there."

He hurried outside, and Jillian called Kate's cell phone.

"What is going on?" she demanded.

"I don't know. When I did the checklist, the old map was missing, but it was there yesterday. Rick said the only way she could have it is if she sneaked it out somehow while we weren't looking. He's positive it's not in her luggage."

"Craig is too." Jillian sat down behind the desk.

"Rick thinks someone's playing games with us," Kate said.

"What do you mean?"

"Distracting us with these small thefts while the murderer gets away."

Jillian frowned. "Well, these 'small thefts' could easily add up to a couple thousand dollars."

A few minutes later, Geordie and Craig came inside.

"Well, she's off to Massachusetts," Craig said.

"You're certain the map isn't in her car?" Jillian asked.

"As sure as we can be."

Jillian lowered her voice. "Are you going to let Pelletier go?"

"I don't want to. But he can't keep objecting to a search, since we have the warrants."

"Who else is left?" Geordie asked.

"Luke Brantley and Roger Cowper," Jillian said readily. "They're both willing to stay another night. And my neighbor, Zeb. But he's not a problem. He'll probably move back home tomorrow."

"Does agreeing to stay over mean they're innocent?" Geordie looked to Craig.

"Not necessarily. It may mean they need more time to figure out their next step."

Kate came quickly down the stairway. "Craig!"

"What?" He turned to face her.

"I finished the checklist on all the rooms, and you'll never believe it."

18

"I almost didn't believe it myself," Kate said.

Craig raised his eyebrows.

"I found the missing map in the Scout Finch Room."

"What?" Jillian stared at her.

Kate nodded. "It's just leaning up against the wall by the TV stand."

"You saw it there?" Craig asked.

"Yes."

"But Jillian and I were in there about an hour ago. It certainly wasn't there then."

"Unbelievable," Jillian muttered.

Kate shrugged. "Rick said we'd better check all the rooms up there fast, and we found it just now."

Craig shook his head slowly. "When we were checking Dr. Rowan's car, I mentioned the map to her. She claimed it was there this morning when she came down for breakfast. She didn't notice it missing while she was getting packed. I think Rick may be right—someone swiped it and stashed it in the empty room to distract us all while they sneak the other things out."

"But that someone must have a master key," Jillian said. "How else could they do this? I know we talked about rooms where the old keys hadn't been deactivated, but the two adjoining rooms haven't been used for more than a week. There's no way any of our keys in the drawer would open them. Only the master keys."

"Unless someone knew how to code key cards," Kate said, her eyes shining.

"That's a thought," Craig said. "You can code an extra master key any time you want to, correct?"

"Yes, now that the Internet is back up." Jillian met his pensive gaze.

Craig turned to Geordie. "Can you get on those background checks again? Look for anyone on the guest list who's worked in a hotel in the past."

"I'm on it, Sarge. Should I go back to the station?"

"You can use my computer in the office," Jillian said.

"Right through here." Kate opened the office door and beckoned to Geordie.

As Geordie followed her, Jillian heard him say quietly, "Are we still on for tomorrow night, Kate?"

"Planning on it," Kate said.

Geordie grinned. "A lot of places are still closed."

The office door swung shut as Kate said something like "... a quiet evening here."

Jillian swung around as her brother came down the stairs. "How do we stand on the list of valuables belonging to the inn?"

"The compass and the map are all I knew about so far that's missing," Rick said. "Well, and the bracelet. Dr. Rowan filled out a form for that, so we can contact her if it turns up."

"The books," Jillian added. "From Phileas Fogg and Rip Van Winkle."

"Oh, right."

Craig pulled the list from his pocket. "What about these movie posters?"

"Most of them aren't worth much," Jillian told him. "I paid fifteen dollars for the *Around the World in Eighty Days* one."

"The Lord of the Rings one is signed," Rick reminded her.

Jillian winced. "That's right. Roger Cowper is in that room."

"What about *Gone with the Wind*?" Craig asked.

She considered that for a moment. "The poster in that room is a reproduction. There are some small antique items and a few vintage clothes in there, but none of them is worth two hundred dollars."

Craig nodded, studying the list. "Okay. Well, we'll check these all again as people leave. Rick, you should go home."

"Yeah, I probably should. We've got a guy coming to fix the bedroom window, and I really should be there for Diana."

"Hey! You got someone to come work on the window that fast, and we still can't get the plumber here?" Jillian scowled at him.

"You'd better give your plumber another call," Rick said.

She sighed. "What about Max Pelletier? Are you going to let him go?"

Rick's lips tightened. "Let's check him out before I leave. Cowper and Brantley can wait until morning."

Kate stayed at the front desk and let Jillian go with them up to Max's room.

"Well, it's about time," he said angrily as he opened the door.

"Relax, Mr. Pelletier," Rick said. "We'll get you out of here as quick as we can."

"Well, it's almost lunchtime. I wanted to be home by now."

Jillian looked at the alarm clock on the bedside stand. He was right about lunch. She and Kate should be starting that by now. She zipped through the checklist for David Copperfield.

"All of the decorations are in place," she told Rick. "I'd better go to the kitchen."

"Okay, thanks."

She went down the elevator and stopped to speak to Kate, but she wasn't at the front desk. Geordie was still working at her computer in the office, but he had the door open so he could see anyone who entered the lobby.

"Oh, Kate went to start lunch," he told Jillian. Nobody's come in or gone out since you all went upstairs to check Mr. Pelletier's luggage."

"Thanks." Jillian hurried to the kitchen.

"Under control," Kate assured her as she burst through the door. I figure we're feeding at least eight people, maybe a couple more. Have they let Max go yet?"

"He's just about ready to check out. Want me to do it?"

"Sure, go ahead. Thanks to the market, I've got spaghetti and meatballs, chicken rosemary, corn chowder, and biscuits."

"Wow, look at you!"

"Well, it won't be ready for another thirty minutes or so, but I'm getting there. Go see Max off, and then come help me get everything out to the buffet. I'll have apple strudel, ice cream, and the pie we bought for dessert."

Jillian gave her a thumbs-up. The men were just coming off the elevator as she reached the lobby.

"Mr. Pelletier, we have lunch almost ready, if you'd like to stay," she said with a smile.

"No, thank you. I've been here long enough."

"I'm afraid you didn't get much research done." Jillian accepted the key card he handed her.

"That's an understatement."

"Well, in view of the circumstances, we're not charging you for the extra meals. I hope you'll visit us again sometime." She quickly performed the checkout routine and sent the receipt to the printer.

"Yeah, right." His sarcasm was impossible to miss.

"There you go." She handed him the receipt, and he picked up his suitcase.

"Let me help you," Craig said, reaching for a drab duffel bag.

"Oh, how could I forget? You're searching my car now." Max shook his head in disgust and flounced out the door with his suitcase.

Craig arched his eyebrows at Jillian but said nothing. He and Rick both followed Max out to the parking lot.

Jillian went to help Kate, and about ten minutes later, Craig and Rick both came into the dining room. The front of Rick's pants and jacket were wet.

"Is it raining again?" Jillian asked.

"Drizzling. And the pavement's still wet."

"Oh, so you crawled under the car. I'm sorry you had to do that."

Rick shrugged. "Can't ask my sergeant to do it. I'll head home and change."

"You don't want to eat here?"

"Diana just called me, and I told her I'd be there for lunch. The repairman's there."

"Go," Jillian told him.

"Well, I'm staying," Craig said with a grin. "Can't wait to see what you've come up with today."

"Give all the credit to Kate," Jillian said. "I take it Max's car passed inspection?"

"It did." Craig frowned. "We're almost out of options."

"Do you want to check Zeb's room and luggage?" she asked. "I'm sure he'll let you. He doesn't have a car here."

"We could take a look around the room, but I think we can leave his luggage until he's ready to leave. But you know as well as I do, he didn't take anything."

"No, but someone could have conveniently 'misplaced' something in his stuff."

"Well, I'm heading home," Rick said. "You want me to come back tonight?"

Craig stretched his arms. "I think we'll be all right. And isn't the night clerk coming in later?"

"Yes," Jillian replied. "Don Reece should be here by ten o'clock."

"Maybe you and Kate can sleep tonight," Craig said.

Jillian smiled. "I'd love to be back in my own bed, but I'm not sure we want to leave the inn until this bunch has cleared out. And Zeb's still here."

"When are you taking him home?" Rick asked.

"Maybe tomorrow. I might call Lee and see when he plans to come up."

"Okay. Well, I'll see you. Craig, I'll talk to you later. Geordie's staying this afternoon, unless they call him out for an emergency."

"Good. Take care, Rick."

Her brother walked out, and Jillian looked at Kate. "Ready for lunch? I can tell the guests it's ready."

"Yeah, go ahead."

Jillian called Luke's room and Roger's to tell them lunch was ready, then she went to tell Zeb. She was only halfway there when her cell rang.

"Lee," she said in surprise. "I was just heading for your uncle's room."

"Is he okay?"

"He's fine. He's still with us here at the inn."

"Well, I'm about halfway up there," Lee said. "Maybe he'll want to go home tonight. I thought I'd stay with him a couple of nights."

"I'm sure he'll love that and being back in his own home."

"Is he still sick?"

"He's well on the way to recovery. Maybe I should run over there this afternoon and make sure his heat's on and make up the bed with fresh linen."

"If you have time, that's great. I can stop in there first and make sure everything's ready, and then I'll come get him. How does that sound?"

"Perfect. You can both have supper with us." Jillian stopped outside Zeb's door. "Do you want me to tell him you're coming?"

"Yeah, thanks. Then he'll be prepared to make the transition. I really appreciate everything you've done for him."

"No problem," Jillian said with a smile. "He's been a model guest, and he'll have some stories to tell you when you arrive."

She signed off and tapped on Zeb's door.

"If you're Jillian, come in."

She grinned and reached for the door handle. Zeb was sitting in the chair in front of the desk, wearing the pants he'd arrived in and a flannel shirt.

"Hey, Zeb! Lee's on his way up here. He'll be here for supper."

The old man blinked and then smiled. "Terrific. Is he going to stay here?"

"He thought the two of you could stay at your house."

Zeb nodded with satisfaction. "Aye, that'll be good."

"Now, how about some lunch? Most of the other guests are gone."

"Who's left?" He stood slowly.

"Just you and Luke and Roger. Well, and Craig and Geordie."

"Hmm, small group."

Jillian frowned. "Yes. I hope the police don't regret letting the others go so soon."

"Is Rick gone?"

"He went home to eat with his family."

They ambled down the hallway toward the dining room. When they came to the lobby, Jillian was surprised to find both Craig and Geordie there.

Craig smiled at her. "Geordie says he'll watch the front desk so I can eat lunch with you and Kate." He glanced at Zeb. "And Mr. Wilding, of course. Then I thought I'd run home and check on how things are at my place and maybe pick up a few more clothes and my razor."

"Don Reece will be here tonight," Jillian said. "You don't need to stay over." The thought of the inn without him left her a bit bleak.

"Well, I want to be here at least until Don's installed behind that desk."

"Okay. Well, are we ready to eat?"

"Yeah, it looks good."

Geordie said, "You all go ahead. I'll sit here and mind the phone and the door, and I'll eat when you're done."

Jillian thanked him warmly.

Luke and Roger had already filled their plates and were eating at a corner table. Jillian went through the line with Zeb, pleased to see him take normal-sized portions of chowder and the chicken dish, along with two biscuits. He was definitely feeling better.

Kate grabbed the seat beside Zeb, and Jillian sat with Craig on the other side of the table. After they offered thanks, Zeb started on his corn chowder.

"Mm-mm-mm!" He waved his spoon at Kate. "Did you make this, young lady?"

"I did," Kate confessed.

"Well, any time you want to cook in my galley, just come on over."

Kate laughed. "I'll keep it in mind."

They ate for a few minutes, and then Zeb cocked an eye at Craig.

"Now, Sergeant, would you say the person who killed that Dryer man is someone who's still here at the inn?"

Craig threw a quick glance across the room at Luke and Roger. "Not necessarily."

"So, someone else could have come in here, done the deed, and sneaked out again?" Zeb's blue eyes were wide in innocence.

Craig hesitated. "I suppose that's remotely possible. But with so many people here all week, I don't think it happened that way."

Zeb took on a stubborn air. "Jillian tells me they can't watch the front door every single minute."

"No, but remember the storm that day," Craig said. "Anyone coming in would have left wet tracks on the floor, for one thing."

"And opening the front door sets off a chime in the kitchen," Kate said. "That way, if we're both out there, we know someone's gone in or out."

"Fancy that." Zeb turned back to his meal.

A few minutes later, Jillian asked, "Would you like some dessert, Zeb? There's apple strudel, pecan pie, and brownies, all with or without ice cream."

"Oh!" He eyed her sharply. "Did you make the pie?"

Kate answered for her. "No, Zeb, it's from the store. We

didn't have a lot of baking time this morning. Sorry. But I did make the apple strudel."

"Okay, then I'll have the strudel."

"Coming right up." Jillian pushed back her chair.

19

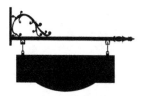

After lunch, Craig left to square things away at his house, and Mindy Nelson arrived to clean the rooms of the guests who had left.

Jillian gave her a big hug when she walked through the door.

"I'm so glad you could make it today."

"Me too!" Mindy grinned at her. "Which rooms need me first?"

"The ones where guests have checked out—Scarlett, Copperfield, and Anne Shirley. But let me check with Geordie real quick. I think it's okay for you to clean them now. I'm not sure about the Poirot Room."

Mindy eyed her suspiciously. "Is that the one where ..."

"It is." Jillian made a quick decision. "Actually, we're not supposed to do anything to that one until Craig or Rick says we can. We don't want to destroy evidence. And we may have to replace the carpet before we put anyone in there again—or at least have it professionally cleaned."

That satisfied Mindy, and she headed happily up to the second-floor linen closet.

Jillian made sure Kate could hold the fort, and then she grabbed a tote bag and hurried along the path to Zeb's house. Inside, it seemed a little cluttered, but she couldn't remember exactly how she'd left things. She'd shifted a few things around when she raised the shutters in his bedroom, and those dishes were probably in the kitchen sink at the time. She picked up a throw pillow from the living room floor and tossed it onto the couch.

She'd asked Zeb about clean sheets, and she found them in the closet where he'd told her to look. The towels and other items on the shelves were somewhat rumpled. Standing still, she stared at them. Zeb was such a neatnik. He always insisted everything be left shipshape. She frowned and closed the door.

As she made the bed, she took sharper notice of the bedroom. Zeb's slippers were askew on the floor at the edge of the bed, but that was understandable. She remembered helping him with his shoes before they left the house. Nothing else seemed out of place.

Quickly, she changed the sheets and took another change of clean clothes from his dresser. She bundled the dirty linens into the tote bag and laid the fresh items carefully on top. She cast one last glance over the living room. The telescope stood in its usual spot, and everything looked neat in there. After locking the front door, she hurried home.

"Nothing was really wrong," she told Kate a few minutes later, "but something didn't feel right."

"Well, he was sick for a day or two before you moved him," Kate said. "Maybe he just wasn't up to his usual standard."

"Maybe, but I think ..."

"What?" Kate eyed her keenly.

"After I start his sheets washing, I think I'll run down to the carriage house and make sure everything's okay down there."

"You think somebody's been sneaking into the houses around here?"

"I don't know. But everyone staying here knew our house was empty, and Zeb's too. I'd just like to have a look."

"Let me go."

Jillian nodded. "Okay. Is Geordie still in the office?"

"Yes. He took his lunch in there. I can't believe how hard he's working on those background checks." Kate looked pointedly at Zeb's clothes peeking out of Jillian's tote. "Take Zeb his things and give Mindy the dirty sheets. I'll go make a quick appraisal at our house."

"Maybe we should both go."

Kate hesitated. "I'll be careful."

Jillian gave in, but she didn't feel easy until her sister returned twenty minutes later and made her report.

"Everything's locked up tight. I couldn't see that anything was the least bit off."

"Thanks."

"And I brought you some extra undies and a clean T-shirt, in case we end up staying here again tonight." As Jillian started to protest, Kate added, "Just trying to be prepared."

Since both Luke and Roger planned to check out the next morning, Kate and Jillian didn't have to worry about meals for the next day beyond breakfast. They spent some time in the kitchen, preparing a substantial supper for that night, though.

The sun came out in the late afternoon, and Lee arrived as its low rays touched the inn's back windows. Kate was in the lobby, and she ushered him through to the kitchen and left him with her sister.

"Hi," Jillian said with a big smile, untying her apron. "How were the roads?"

"Not too bad. I stuck to the main routes. Had to go around on a detour for the bridge, though." He moved in for a quick hug.

"Have you seen Zeb yet?" Jillian pulled away quickly, not wanting to prolong the greeting.

"Not yet. I thought I'd say hello to him, then maybe go over and take a look at his place. Or maybe I should go there first and avoid surprises when I take him over. What do you think?"

"I went over after lunch and changed the bed." Jillian wasn't sure she should voice the uneasiness she'd felt in the house on the bluff. "Might be a good idea." She glanced at the clock. "Have you eaten supper?"

"No, I pushed on through."

"We've got a small buffet set up. Pork chops tonight, with mashed potatoes and veggies."

"Sounds good, but I think I'll run next door before it's full dark." When Jillian nodded, he added, "Want to come?"

She hovered between refusing and accepting. Would going along with him encourage Lee too strongly? She wouldn't mind taking another look, and having a man beside her should calm her fears.

"Yeah, I guess so. Let me fill Kate in."

As they passed through the dining room, Kate and Geordie, still in his patrolman's uniform, were fixing their plates.

Jillian said, "Geordie, this is Zeb's nephew, Lee Wilding." The two men shook hands. "We're going to pop next door and see how his house looks before Lee takes Zeb home."

"Good idea," Kate said. "Does Zeb know you're here, Lee?"

"Not yet. We won't be gone long. Thought it would be good to know everything's okay over there."

Jillian pulled on a jacket and walked with Lee out to his pickup in the parking area.

"I wasn't sure what I'd run into," he explained as he

opened the passenger door for her. "Sometimes it's nice to have the four-wheel drive."

"I can think of a couple of times I wished I had it," she admitted.

Lee got in on the driver's side and started the engine. "So, is Geordie your sister's boyfriend?"

"Not yet." Jillian smiled. "Tomorrow night's supposed to be their first date. But Geordie's on duty until another officer relieves him."

"On duty at the inn?" Lee frowned as he maneuvered out onto the road.

Jillian's chest squeezed. Lee didn't know about the murder yet. "Yeah. We ... had an incident at the inn. One of our guests was killed."

He jerked around to look at her, then returned his attention to the road. "Killed how? Was it an accident?"

"No. The police are investigating it."

It wasn't far to the Wilding driveway, and he flipped on the turn signal.

"I was going to let Zeb tell you about it," Jillian said. "I guess what you said about surprises applies, though. Somebody killed the guest in his room. He appeared to have been stabbed. They haven't got the autopsy report yet."

Lee's jaw tightened as he eased his truck into his uncle's drive. "Was Uncle Zeb there when it happened?"

"Yes. The body was discovered not long after I moved him in. But he was so sick, I didn't tell him about it until the next day."

"He's better now, though."

"A lot better. He'll be glad to see you."

Lee braked and brought the truck to a halt in front of the porch steps. Jillian didn't wait for him to come around. She opened her door and climbed out.

For a moment, Lee stood appraising the front part of the house.

"It looks like that pine branch came down on the edge of the porch." He pointed to where something had gouged the asphalt shingles on the edge of the eave.

Jillian nodded. "I don't remember noticing that before." She looked at the large branch lying nearby. "That's probably the culprit, all right."

"Let's go in." Lee approached the door with his keys in his hand.

They stepped inside, and he flipped a light switch. The overhead light came on.

"Well, his electricity's working," Lee said. "That's a good sign."

"Yeah, it was on when I came over earlier." Jillian stepped into the kitchen, and everything seemed in order, as neat as Zeb customarily kept it except for the few dishes in the sink. Maybe she could wash those up quickly. She opened the refrigerator and peered inside, wrinkling her nose. Several dishes would need to be discarded.

"Jillian?" Lee called from the living room.

She shut the fridge and turned to join him. When she reached the doorway, she stopped short. "Where's his telescope?"

"I was just going to ask you if he took it to the inn," Lee replied.

"No." She stepped forward, frowning. Zeb's wonderful telescope usually stood by the bay window in his living room, where he could scan the bay and the opposite shore with it. It was a very nice instrument, better than the one in the inn's Horatio Hornblower room, and more expensive too, she was sure.

"It was right there this afternoon, when I came to change

the bed and get him some fresh clothes. I took particular notice."

They gazed at each other for a moment. Jillian tried to think of an explanation. Only one came to mind.

"Do you think someone stole it?" Lee asked.

"They must have. We've had a few items stolen at the inn, but whenever a guest checked out this morning, the police checked their luggage and car."

"Really? They checked people's cars?"

"Because of the murder. And a couple of other things. One of the guests reported a bracelet missing, and Kate thought yesterday that someone had been in her room. And the man who was killed was wearing a ring that the police didn't find later. And several decorative items were missing from the rooms, one of them in Kate's room. It was there yesterday, but not today. So, the officers got a warrant to check everyone leaving the inn. So far, nothing's turned up."

"Well, Uncle Zeb's telescope was too big to carry out in a suitcase, wasn't it?"

She let out a slow breath, thinking. "It had the stand too."

"But that folds up."

"I don't know. But it is fairly large, and it's heavy." She met Lee's gaze. "I don't see how someone could have taken it in the last three or four hours."

"How many guests checked out today?"

"Four. A couple and two singles. We only have two guests left, other than Zeb."

Lee bit his lip for a moment. "I'll have to tell him," he said reluctantly.

"Let's get Geordie over here to look around."

"Okay. Would you call him?

While she made the call, Lee walked from room to room. When he came back, she was putting her phone away.

"Geordie is putting in a call to the sergeant. One of them will be here soon."

"Well, I didn't find any broken windows," Lee said. "The back door is locked, so I'd say that if someone came in here, they picked a lock."

"They must have, because I made sure the front door was securely locked when I left."

Lee frowned. "It's someone local, maybe, who knew that scope was in here."

"Look around and see if anything else is missing."

"I'm not sure I'd know. It looks pretty neat in here."

"I straightened up a little," Jillian said. She hadn't entered the bedroom yet on this visit. "Come on, let's take a look."

A couple of Zeb's dresser drawers were open.

"I don't think I'd have left those like that," she said. "I was kind of hurrying, though, just trying to get him enough clothes to change into so he'd be nice and clean when you got here."

Lee went into the small bathroom, and she heard the medicine cabinet open. "Do you know if he had any prescriptions?" he called.

"We took them with us." She peered into the cabinet. "I can't say for certain, but it looks to me the same as it did a couple of days ago, when I moved him to the inn."

They walked back into the living room, and Jillian turned toward the kitchen. "It isn't possible to inventory his kitchen, but ..." She stood in the doorway looking around. "Hold on."

Something glinted on the floor, down low where the counters were recessed at the bottom, below the lower cabinets. She hurried across the room and knelt down, reaching for the small item. A diamond set in a circle of eight small rubies twinkled in the light from the overhead fixture. Frowning, she held it out to Lee.

"I wouldn't think that belonged to Zeb."

Lee took the sparkling ring from her carefully. "Neither would I. A woman's ring. Not yours, I take it."

"Definitely not."

"I wonder if Uncle Zeb had any female visitors lately."

"The stones in that ring look real, though I'm not sure," Jillian said. "But surely if someone lost a piece of jewelry like that here, they'd have asked Zeb about it."

"Let's take it over to the inn. If he can't explain it, we'll tell the police contingent."

"Fair enough."

Lee tucked the ring into his pocket, and they went out.

20

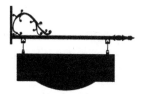

Geordie studied the ring with interest. "It's pretty, but I don't know anything about jewelry. Your brother called a few minutes ago, and he's coming back for the evening. He should probably look at it—I mean, he's the detective, so to speak."

He started to hold it out to Lee, but Kate stuck out her hand. "May I see it?"

Geordie dropped it into her palm. She held it up close and studied it.

"Do you recognize it?" Jillian asked.

Kate shook her head. "Afraid not. But it does look expensive. If it's fake, it's very good." She handed it back to Lee. "Has Zeb seen it?"

"Not yet. Lee and I were going to show it to him," Jillian said.

"He's in the living room, sitting by the fireplace." Kate turned to Geordie. "Do you mind staying out here for a couple of minutes?"

"No, I figure I'm here until either Rick or the sergeant gets here—or at least, your night clerk. I'm not sure if the chief wants an officer here all night or not."

Not wanting to miss out on whatever they learned, Kate led the way eagerly through the dining room to the comfortable living room beyond. Luke Brantley and Roger Cowper sat in armchairs with coffee mugs in their hands, while Zeb had the fireside wing chair, an afghan spread over his knees.

"Hey, Zeb, you've got company," Kate called.

The old man looked up with a hesitant smile, then gazed past her and spotted his nephew. "Well, Lee!" He didn't rise but extended his hand.

Lee shook it heartily. "Hey, Uncle Zeb. Sorry I couldn't get here sooner. How are you feeling?"

"Fit as a fiddle. How about you? Everything okay at your place?"

"Yeah, I decided to take the boat out of the water. It was a pain, but I'm glad now that I did. A lot of boats were run up on shore in the storm and damaged." As he spoke, Lee pulled another chair over and sat down close to Zeb. "So, Jillian and I just went over to your place to make sure the power was on and that everything was okay."

"Oh." Zeb looked from him to Jillian in apparent confusion.

Jillian stepped close to his chair and patted his shoulder. "Lee wants to stay at your place with you tonight, but we wanted to make sure it was ready for you to go home."

"Okay."

"Uncle Zeb, it's not okay," Lee said quietly.

"What? What's wrong? Did the windows break? We should have—"

"Nothing like that," Lee said. "But your telescope isn't where you usually have it, by the bay window."

"Huh?" Zeb craned his neck around to meet Jillian's gaze. "It was there when we left to come over here."

"Yes, it was," she said.

"Somebody took it?"

"We don't know yet," Lee said.

Kate cleared her throat. "We thought when Rick gets here, we'd ask him to go over with Lee and check it out."

Zeb nodded slowly.

Kate noticed that Luke and Roger appeared to be listening in on the conversation.

"There's one other thing," Lee said. His back was to the two guests, and Kate wondered if he should be discussing this in their presence.

"Excuse me." She leaned in and said, "Maybe you should step down to Zeb's room, or into the office?" She rolled her eyes toward where Luke and Roger sat.

Lee seemed oblivious, but Jillian understood.

"Yes, Lee. It might be a good idea to continue this in private."

"Oh. Okay." Lee stood uncertainly.

"Come on, Zeb." Jillian helped him stand. As they left the living room, nobody looked over at Luke and Roger.

The front door swung open as they passed the lobby. To Kate's surprise, a man and a woman entered.

"Are you open?" the middle-aged man asked with a smile. "We sure hope so."

Geordie, who sat behind the front desk, swiveled his head to throw a questioning look at the sisters.

Before Kate could react, Jillian swung toward the front desk. "Yes, we are. Would you like to check in?"

"We sure would," the man replied.

"We don't have a reservation," the woman said apologetically.

Thankful Mindy had made it in to clean that day, Kate continued on to the office's hallway door and ushered Lee and

Zeb inside.

Geordie sidled up to her and whispered, "I thought that was Rick coming in just now. Those people surprised me, 'cause I really thought I caught a glimpse of his SUV."

"Go check," Kate said. "If he's arrived, show him right in here."

She went into the office and shut the door. Before she sat down behind the desk, she made sure there was an extra chair for her brother.

"Let's hold off a second," she told Lee. "Geordie thinks Officer Gage is here."

"Meaning Rick," Zeb said.

"Yes." Kate flushed a little. Zeb and Lee both knew Rick, so she needn't be so formal. Still, this was official business.

She went to the door that opened directly behind the front desk. Jillian was handing the newcomers a keycard.

"The Scarlett O'Hara Room is on the third floor. Let me take you up in the elevator."

Kate wished Jillian had given them another room, not the one next to her. Immediately she felt guilty. She was being selfish, and besides, she didn't really have to sleep at the inn tonight if she didn't want to. Maybe the police would think it was a bad idea for her to stay in a room that had been burglarized.

As Jillian and the guests moved into the hall, the front door opened, and Rick came in. He spotted Kate peeking out from the office. She waved and beckoned to him.

He entered the small room and looked around, nodding to Geordie and taking in the presence of Lee and Zeb.

"Mr. Wilding. Lee. What's happening?"

Lee cleared his throat. "Jillian and I went over to my uncle's house to see if everything was ready for him to move home. We discovered two things that alarmed us."

"Oh?" Rick focused soberly on Lee.

"His telescope is missing, for one."

"The big one in his living room?"

Lee nodded.

"I saved up a long time for that," Zeb said.

"Okay. What else?"

"Jillian spotted this on the floor in the kitchen." Lee took a ring from his shirt pocket and handed it to Rick.

"What is it?" Zeb asked.

"A ring," Lee said. "It looks like a lady's ring." To his uncle, he said apologetically, "That's why we came in here. So we could show it to you without the other hotel guests seeing it."

Rick studied the ring for a moment, then handed it to Zeb. "Ever seen it before?"

Zeb held it up in toward the light. "Sparkly. But no, I don't think so."

"No ladies have lost jewelry at your house lately?" Rick's lips quirked in a smile.

"If they have, they didn't tell me."

"Where's Jillian, anyhow?" Rick asked.

"A new couple checked in, and she's taking them up to the Scarlett O'Hara Room," Kate said. "That's okay, isn't it?"

"Sure. You've got to make a living. Just don't put anyone in Hercule Poirot yet."

She nodded. "Do you know if Craig's coming back? He went home for a while, but ..."

"Not for sure," Rick said. "I think he went to help on a domestic call." He smiled at Geordie. "The chief said to tell you that you're officially off duty."

Geordie glanced at Kate. "Is it okay if I stay here for a little while?"

"I don't mind," Rick said. "Just don't put in for overtime."

Kate smiled at Geordie. "I need to do some work in the kitchen."

"Need any help?"

"Another pair of hands is always welcome."

He smiled. "Glad to do it."

"And after that, I suppose you should head home and get some sleep," Kate said.

"We'll see." Geordie had the air of a man willing to stick around as long as the innkeepers would tolerate his presence.

"Did you eat, Uncle Zeb?" Lee asked.

"No, I was hoping you'd get here in time for us to sit down together. Kate told me there's plenty."

"That sounds good to me," Lee said.

"Okay, you folks who haven't eaten, go do it," Rick said. "I'll touch base with Jillian. Oh, Kate, the telescope in Hornblower is still there, right?"

Kate opened her mouth to affirm that, but hesitated. "It was last time I was up there."

"Let's check again, just to make sure. If you loan me your key, I'll go up."

"All right." She handed him her room card. "And I did go check the carriage house. Nothing seemed disturbed there."

As they moved into the hallway, Jillian stepped off the elevator.

"Anything I should know?" she asked.

Kate shook her head. "Zeb doesn't recognize the—the thing you found."

"Gotcha." Jillian turned her attention to Rick. "Glad you're here."

"Lee and Zeb are going to eat," he said. "If you haven't, then I suggest you do too. I'm going to run up and check the decorative items in Hornblower again, for peace of mind."

"Good idea," Jillian said. "And after we eat, I'll run the dishwasher and clean up."

"Geordie said he'd help," Kate put in as she moved with him toward the dining room. She looked into his eyes. "How do you feel about busing dishes?"

———

Jillian went with Lee and Zeb into the dining room. They'd just picked up their silverware and napkins when Kate breezed out of the kitchen with a covered plate.

"I zapped your pork chops, so they'd be nice and hot for you." She uncovered the plate and slid the meat into the warming tray.

"Thank you, young lady." Zeb grinned and stepped up to select a chop.

Kate retreated to the kitchen, and Jillian was soon seated with Lee and Zeb, their dishes brimming with food.

When he'd eaten a few bites and complimented the cooks, Zeb said, "I thought the storm might do some damage at my house, but I didn't expect a burglary."

Rick came into the dining room, fixed himself a cup of coffee, and came to sit in the unoccupied chair at their table. "Your telescope is right where it should be, Jillian." He held out the diamond ring. "Okay, what about this ring, Zeb? Lee?"

"I have no idea where it came from," Lee said. "Like I said, your sister saw it when we were looking around Uncle Zeb's house. We were trying to see if we could find the telescope in some unexpected place, or if anything else was missing." He looked at Zeb. "You'll have to take a look to be sure. Jillian and I couldn't think of anything else, but we might not notice something not being there."

"Is my ship in a bottle still there?"

Jillian pictured it mentally, safe and sound as usual on the mantelpiece.

"Yeah, right where it always is," Lee said.

Zeb nodded. "I don't keep cash and valuables around my house, Rick."

"Okay. I'd like to go over and look around myself. I'm starting to think it might be best if you stay here one more night. I plan to stick around at least until midnight. Another officer will relieve me later."

"What about Lee?" Zeb looked anxiously at his nephew.

"We'll find Lee a room too," Jillian said. "In fact, Lee can take the room I've been using, right across from yours. I'm sure Kate won't mind if I sleep with her upstairs. Her room has two queen beds." She set aside all thoughts of moving back to the carriage house tonight. She knew Kate wanted some answers before she gave up the Horatio Hornblower Room, and she did too.

"Okay," Zeb said. "If Lee's all right with it?" He arched his eyebrows.

"Sure," Lee said. "I hate to impose on you, but it might be best, until this is cleared up. And I'd like to be under the same roof with Uncle Zeb."

"Let me just double-check with Kate, and I'll move my things out of the Jeeves Room," Jillian said.

Lee chuckled. "Jeeves, eh? I guess I'll be your butler for the time being, Uncle Zeb."

Jillian stepped into the kitchen, where Kate and Geordie were laughing together as Kate put away food and Geordie scrubbed the meat pan in the sink. Kate was agreeable to letting Lee stay.

"And I want to go over to Zeb's with Rick for a few minutes, so could you and Geordie watch the front desk while we're gone? I'll tell you when we're ready."

"Sure," Geordie said, and Jillian again got the impression he'd agree to do anything for half an hour, so long as it involved Kate.

Jillian hurried back to the table. "It's fine. We've got plenty of room now. No charge for you, Lee."

"Nonsense."

She shook her head and reached for her water glass. "No, I'm serious. Zeb is here as a friend, and I expect you to stay tonight on the same basis. Kate might not admit it, but she and I will feel more secure with one more man in the house too."

Rick pushed back his chair. "One of you gents want to give me a house key?"

"I want to go over to Zeb's with you, Rick," Jillian said.

"What for?"

"To go through his fridge real quick and point out things for you. Kate and Geordie can watch the front desk for a little while, and Lee can get settled."

"You've got to move your stuff out for him," Rick protested.

"That won't take me five minutes. Wait here—I mean it." She fixed him with her sternest teacher glare. "Don't you go without me."

Rick held up both hands in surrender.

She dashed down the hall to Jeeves, and by the time she'd thrown her few personal items into her overnight bag, Kate was at the door.

"Hey, I thought I could make up the bed for Lee, so you can go with Rick," Kate said. "He's pacing the lobby and muttering to himself."

Jillian laughed. "Thanks. I'll stash my bag in the office for now."

When she got to the lobby, Rick was alone. Jillian tipped her head and cased the dining room.

"Where's Zeb?"

"Lee took him down to his room," Rick said. "He'll keep him occupied until we get back."

"Good. I was afraid Zeb would insist on going."

"Nope. I think he's quite comfortable here—but he is concerned about his telescope."

"I don't blame him," Jillian said. "It's a nice one."

She got her coat and gloves, and they stepped out onto the porch in the twilight. "Want to walk?" she asked.

"Might be kind of soggy after all the rain."

Jillian shrugged.

"Okay, let's go." Rick led her around to the side porch and down the steps. The turf did squelch a little, but Jillian was wearing rugged shoes. She kept pace with Rick, wondering when would be the next time she saw Zeb's signal flags flying above the trees.

They took the path through the woods, to the bridge their father had built. Rick stopped and peered over the railing, down into the stream that took runoff into the bay. Tonight it gushed noisily full.

"I've never seen it this high," Jillian said.

"All that rain. But this bridge isn't in any danger. Dad built it high and solid."

They walked the few additional yards into Zeb's yard. Jillian squinted at the driveway. "Hey, look. Is that a car parked out by the road?"

Rick swung around and looked where she pointed. It was getting dark, and she wasn't sure, but there seemed to be a darker blob down low, beyond the trees that edged Zeb's property.

"Maybe." Rick eyed the driveway, which was surfaced in coarse gravel, then swung his gaze up to the house. He shot out a hand to rest on Jillian's arm. "Wait."

"What?" she whispered.

"Thought I saw a flicker of light inside."

She froze, and they stood staring at Zeb's windows, barely breathing.

After a bit, she whispered, "Could have been a light off the bay. His shutters aren't up. Maybe sometimes you can see lights from across the harbor, or from boats out on the water."

Rick frowned, and she could almost read his thoughts. Honestly, they were too low to see any stray lights shining in through the windows on the back of the house.

"You got the key?" He held out his hand.

Jillian gave him the key Zeb had entrusted to her a year earlier.

Rick put a finger to his lips and tiptoed onto the porch. Jillian followed as quietly as she could. Her brother put out his hand and tried the doorknob. It turned, and he pushed the door open an inch or two then stared into her eyes.

Her heart pounding, Jillian shrugged. "Lee locked it when we left earlier."

"You're sure?" he hissed.

She nodded.

Rick waved her back a step then removed his pistol from his holster. He held up his left fist and stuck out one finger, then two, then three. On three, he shoved the door open and stepped inside.

21

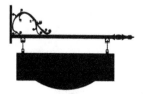

At the inn, Kate and Geordie had a lively game of Flinch going on the surface of the check-in desk. In the middle of a rapid-fire dispersion of cards, Kate felt someone watching her. She tossed her final card and looked up. Luke stood in the opening between the lobby and the dining room, a mournful expression on his face.

"Hello," Geordie said. "Brantley, isn't it?"

Luke nodded.

"Would you like to join us?"

"Uh, no thanks." He turned away and headed toward the living room.

Kate wondered how much Geordie knew about her past with Luke. She hadn't brought it up. Had Jillian or Rick taken the initiative to explain? Craig knew too. She gazed across the desk at Geordie, but he seemed as carefree as ever.

"Another round?" He scooped up the cards.

"Haven't had enough yet?" She managed a smile. She liked Geordie. True, he was just about her height, but she'd quit noticing that. In fact, sometimes it seemed pleasant to look eye-to-eye with a man. And he'd proven himself as an officer, through his diligence and quick wits.

Should she tell him? If he already knew, he wasn't letting Luke's presence bother him. And he was polite enough not to mention it to her. If he didn't know, well, what did it matter? Luke would soon be gone.

Geordie dealt the cards quickly, and she dove for her pile. The front door opened, and Craig stepped in.

"Hi, Sarge," Geordie said, pushing to his feet. It seemed an automatic reaction to his superior's entry, even though he was off duty.

"Thought you were done for the day," Craig said.

"I am. We're just playing a game."

Craig smiled at his opponent. "How's it going, Kate?"

"Okay. Lee Wilding is here, and he was going to take Zeb home for the night, but—"

"They think someone broke in over at the Wilding house," Geordie said.

Craig's brow furrowed. "Where's Officer Gage?"

"He and Jillian went over there," Kate said. "Rick wanted to look around, and Jillian's cleaning out the refrigerator."

"Hmm. Well, I have a little news for Rick. None of the guests who left earlier today has come back, have they?"

"No," Kate said. "We did get a new couple this afternoon. Hold on." She jotted numbers on the score sheet, stood, and poked a few buttons on the computer keyboard. "The Hallidays."

"First-timers?"

She nodded, reading the information Jillian had put in. "From Madison. They're up on the third floor, next to me."

"So, you've got them and Cowper and Brantley?"

"Yes," Kate said. "And Zeb and his nephew are down the hall in Zeb's room. They're both going to stay here tonight, too, because of the goings-on over at Zeb's house. We're putting Lee across the hall, where Jillian was staying, and she's moving up with me tonight."

Craig hesitated. "I guess I'll let Rick fill me in on what he's found over there when they get back."

"Make yourself at home. Have some coffee if you like." Kate waved toward the dining room. "They should be back soon."

———

Jillian's heart raced. She wanted to follow Rick inside, but she knew he'd be angry if she did. She hesitated only a couple of seconds, but it was enough.

"Hold it," Rick barked.

Footsteps pounded inside the house, followed by a couple of thumps. Unable to stand it any longer, Jillian stepped through the front door. The noises were coming from the kitchen.

She dashed to the doorway. The window behind the small dining table was open, and a chair lay on its side. Rick was hurrying around the table, and he leaned out the open window. Whirling, he caught sight of Jillian.

"Get back!"

She ducked to one side, and he ran past her, to the entry and out onto the porch. She could hear his footfalls, and others farther away.

"Police! Stop!"

By the time she reached the porch, Rick was halfway down the driveway. She couldn't see the person he pursued, but a few seconds later, a car's engine roared to life out at the road, and a dark vehicle tore past the end of Zeb's driveway, gathering speed as it fled.

Rick's shoulders slumped and he headed back toward her, talking into his radio as he walked.

"Okay," he said as he came close. "'Cause I'm on foot, and I can't do a thing. Thanks, Sarge." He signed off and looked up at her bleakly. "We shoulda drove over."

"I'm sorry."

"Nah, not your fault."

"Did you get a look at him?" Jillian said.

"Not really. Just his legs and feet going out the window. Then I saw him from behind, running, but it's nearly dark, and he was already out of my reach."

"But you're sure it was a he—a man?"

Rick scowled.

"Sorry," Jillian said. "I know this is what you do all the time. I just thought—"

"No, that's good. I needed a reminder to focus on the details. And yes, I'm about ninety percent sure it was a man. He ran like a man."

"What else?" she prompted.

"Sneakers. He was wearing sneakers."

"There might be prints under the window."

"Yeah, there might."

Rick pulled his regulation flashlight from his belt, and they went carefully back via the intruder's route, around the side of the house to the kitchen window. Jillian didn't need to be told to stay back. Rick bent over, studying the ground. A couple of skid marks showed, where Jillian assumed the man hit the ground.

"I don't know. Forensics might be able to make something of that." Rick straightened with a tight smile. "Come on. Geordie and Craig are going after him. Let's take a look in that kitchen."

As they reentered the room, Jillian registered that the door to Zeb's pantry closet stood wide open. She hadn't thought about it before, only about the escaping intruder.

Rick walked over to it and stared into the gaping interior. "Did you and Lee look in here when you came over earlier?"

She shook her head. "I don't think so. We both realized we couldn't thoroughly search the kitchen cupboards for missing items and sort of skipped over it. We'd noticed that the telescope was gone, of course, and I think we were concentrating more on Zeb's nautical art and knickknacks."

"Well, it looks like we got here just in time." Rick tugged a zippered cloth bag out onto the kitchen floor.

"What's that?" Jillian asked.

"Some sort of duffel bag. Could be Zeb's." Rick eyed her speculatively.

"No, he has one he calls his seabag, but it's over at the inn."

"Here goes." Rick reached for the zipper pull, grasped just the tip end, and gingerly slid it along the track. A smile spread across his face. "What do you know?"

Jillian stepped closer. "What have you got, brother mine?"

He fumbled in his jacket pocket for a moment and came out with a pair of latex gloves, which he pulled on. Stooping over the bag, he drew out a long brass tube.

"Zeb's telescope," Jillian whispered.

"Not only that. The stand's in here, and so's your compass and a bag of baubles."

"What kind of baubles?"

He hefted a plastic bag full of glittering jewelry and held it out to her. She reached toward it but pulled her hands back, conscious that she might destroy evidence. She leaned closer and stared in amazement at the jumble of enamel, metal, and gems inside.

"Do you think that diamond and ruby ring was in this bag?

How did it get—" She glanced across the room toward where she'd found it.

Rick shrugged. "Maybe when he was stuffing the telescope into the duffel bag?"

"That's what I'm thinking," she said.

"The plastic bag is open just a little, and that ring was so small, maybe he didn't notice it when it fell out and rolled under the kickboard."

Jillian lifted her chin. "Is there a book in there?"

"Like, an early edition of *Around the World in Eighty Days*?"

"Yeah, exactly like that."

Rick knelt next to the duffel bag. "Here you go." He lifted out the book she'd bought when she redecorated the Phileas Fogg Room. "There's a few more things in the bottom. We'll have to go through it all carefully at the police station."

"Well, some of it's not from the inn," Jillian said with certainty. She peered at the bag of jewelry. "That turquoise bracelet looks like the one Dr. Rowan described."

"Yeah, it does."

"Hey, wait a sec." Jillian squinted at the jumbled contents of the bag.

"What you got?"

"That ring." She pointed at the top section, without touching the plastic.

Rick separated the man's ring she indicated from the other items within the bag.

"I'm not positive," she said, "but I think that's the ring Alan Dryer was wearing when he checked in."

Rick peered at it intently. "We'll check it out, believe me. I don't see any initials engraved inside."

Jillian sighed. "I suppose DNA could tell if it's really Alan's ring."

"Probably, but last I knew, the lab was way backed up. Last

time we asked for that kind of information, it took weeks to get a response."

"I'm glad we live in the modern world, but sometimes it's frustrating—when you know what *could* be done, but you don't have the means to do it."

"Yeah."

"Hey, Rick?"

"Hmm?"

"Do you think that jewelry could be from the store in Bangor?"

"You read my mind. The report said it was almost all bracelets and rings with precious stones. This is what, a gallon bag? It looks small, but that could easily be fifty or a hundred thousand bucks' worth of gems in there."

Jillian met his gaze. "So, what do we do now?"

"I'll stay here until more officers arrive. Craig will compare what's here to what was listed as missing in Bangor. If it seems like a match, or even a partial match, we'll contact the department up there. And since we suspect one item might belong to the murder victim, we'll contact the state police again. I'll be really surprised if they don't send one of their detectives down here now."

———

At eight o'clock, Kate wearily closed the dishwasher and started it.

"Tired?" Jillian asked.

"Yes. But that's the last meal we serve for guests, other than breakfast, right?"

"Right." Jillian's warm hand rested on her shoulder. "Go to bed early, Kate."

"Tomorrow night I'm going out with Geordie. Or not. We

decided to see what's open. If it's like it was today, and the restaurants in town are shut down, we'll stay here and play games again, I guess."

"Do you like him?"

Kate considered that seriously for a moment. "Yeah. I've gotten to know him a little better the last couple of days. He's fun. And he's pretty sharp mentally too. But I'm not making any quick commitments."

Jillian smiled. "You'll have fun tomorrow, whatever you decide to do for the evening." She sighed and collapsed on a stool. "I shouldn't have abandoned you when I went over to Zeb's with Rick."

Kate shrugged. "We had no idea what was going on over there."

The kitchen door opened, and Craig and Rick walked in, with Geordie trailing behind. Kate smiled at him, and Geordie came to stand beside her.

Craig went straight to Jillian and grasped her hand. "How are you gals holding up?"

"I'm fine," Jillian said. "We're tired, but we've decided to stay here one more night—in the Hornblower Room."

"We checked your house," Rick said. "I don't think anyone's been poking around there."

"Good." Kate sank down on a stool. "We were afraid they might be, after we found out someone had been in Zeb's house, but when I looked, I didn't see anything wrong."

"Your place is secure," Craig's gaze flitted around the big kitchen. "I'd like to sit down with you all and the Wildings, but the office is a little small. What do you think about meeting in here?"

"What about the living room?" Kate said. "It's not as private as the office, but if we make sure nobody's in the dining room, it should be okay."

"Yeah, we can see anyone who comes in there from the lobby." Jillian looked inquiringly at Rick.

"Sounds good to me," her brother said.

"Do you want me back out front?" Geordie asked.

His relief was evident when Craig said, "No, you can stay with us, Geordie. Maybe keep an eye on the doorway, though."

Kate settled in on the sofa near the fireplace with Geordie. He made sure the angle of the couch allowed him to view the entry from the dining room, and beyond, into the lobby. While Rick built up the fire, Jillian went down the hall to ask Zeb and Lee to join them. Craig ambled toward an armchair, but his cell rang. He turned back into the dining room to take the call.

Kate gave Geordie a rueful smile. "Not how we'd planned tonight."

"No, it's not, but it's okay."

"Thanks for understanding. I'm not sure someone who wasn't a police officer or related to one would feel that way. And I hope tomorrow night we have a chance to get away for a little while and do something together."

"I'd like that."

Lee, Zeb, and Jillian came in, and Craig followed them.

"Everybody get comfortable," Craig said. "I have a little news."

Rick set the poker in its rack. When everyone was settled, Craig said, "As you know, we couldn't find the person who ran out of Zeb's house when Rick and Jillian arrived. The state police have set up alerts for him.

Rick scowled. "Fat lot of good that will do. I didn't get a plate number—not even a good description of the vehicle."

"Well, now we know how witnesses feel when they can't give us a precise description," Craig said.

"Thanks, but no thanks. I shoulda come up with more. You said they've got a traffic stop at the only open bridge, right?"

"Yes, but it's possible he got off the peninsula before that was in place." Craig spread his hands. "The alternative is that he's still in the area and lying low." He looked around at all of them. "The good news is that one of the robbers from the jewelry heist in Bangor on Tuesday has been apprehended."

Kate sat up straighter. "Really?"

"Yes. It appears there were two of them, and they split up when they left the scene. One of them was arrested this morning in Dover-Foxcroft."

"Wow," Kate said.

Jillian nodded with satisfaction.

"What about the loot?" Rick asked.

"He had some of it. And get this—he was carrying it in a zippered duffel bag."

"Just like our guy had." Rick didn't look happy. Kate knew he would continue to blame himself until the thief was behind bars.

"The jewelry you and Jillian found at the Wilding house matches the store owner's description for approximately half the pieces that were stolen from the store. And there's something else," Craig said. "Dave Hall called me just now from the station. He's been working on the background checks Geordie started on your guests earlier this week."

Geordie perked up. "This afternoon, I gave him everything I had so far."

Craig nodded. "And he found some more bits and pieces. I think you'll find one item in particular very interesting." His gaze met Jillian's. "It seems one of your guests used to work in a hotel in the Boston area."

Jillian's jaw dropped, and Kate's mind raced.

"The room keys," she blurted.

Craig cracked a smile. "Somehow, Kate, I knew you and your sister would pick up on that. Yes, this person would be very well-versed in coding room keys. Once he picked the lock on the drawer and could get at the blanks, he could use your computer to code a key for any room he wanted to enter."

"Until the power went out," Jillian said.

"That's right."

Kate looked over at Jillian. "But all he needed was one master key. If he made that the day he checked in—"

"I think that's what he did," Craig said. "He probably waited until you were both in the kitchen or were otherwise distracted."

Jillian sat back, staring at Craig. "Okay, who was it?"

"Better yet," Kate said, "Is he still here?"

22

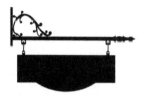

"I don't know," Jillian said half an hour later. She looked around at Rick, Craig, Kate, and the Wildings, all seated in the living room. "I'm not sure this is a good plan."

Rick glared at her. "If you girls will just stay out of the way and let us do our job, it's a terrific plan."

"Girls?" Kate shoved her hands to her hips. "We're women."

"Oh, pardon me." Rick rolled his eyes. "You are my little sister, and to me, you'll always be a girl."

"Fine, *boy*," Kate replied. "Then maybe you'll listen to your *big* sister. Tell him, Jillian."

"Well, I'm not crazy about it." Jillian turned tentatively to Craig.

"Since the state police can't get a detective here tonight, I think it may be the best plan," he said.

Jillian's mind darted from one possibility to another. "But we don't want to put our guests in danger."

"I know. We've removed all the police vehicles except

Rick's, and we hope he'll think it's business as usual here—your brother hanging around, but not a legion of cops."

"But why would Max come back here?" Kate asked. "It seems stupid to me."

"Or at least counterproductive." Jillian ran a hand through her short hair, wishing she could come up with a better solution.

"We have his loot," Craig said. "He's already invested a lot of time and risk in this. He doesn't want to walk away from it, and since he can't get off the peninsula immediately, I'm betting he'll try to get it. He and his partner thought the heist would be quick and fairly easy, and they'd drive away into oblivion. But the storm caught up with them."

"But still ..."

Craig cocked his head to one side. "The other reason is that if he's still in Skirmish Cove, he can't get off the peninsula without being arrested. He knows that. We've still got an active roadblock at the only bridge open right now. So, if he has to be here, why not try to get his loot back?"

"What if he's not still here?" Lee asked.

"We've got to count on the state police and departments in other towns to help us there. If he's out of our jurisdiction, there's a lot smaller chance of him being caught. But we can't assume he got clean away. We have to act like he's still close by."

"Why would he come here, not to Zeb's house?" Kate asked.

Rick sighed. "He may not have seen Jillian and me at Zeb's house, but I think he did. He knew who we were when we walked in on him. He might go over to Zeb's first, on the off chance we didn't find his stash, but once he sees it's not there, he'll come here."

"But all of the jewelry is over at the police station now,"

Kate said. Geordie and Dave had left twenty minutes earlier to take the pieces stolen from the jewelry store to the station and secure it in the evidence locker.

"He can't know that for sure," Craig said. "Unless he eluded the officers looking for him and sneaked back here to keep watch. And even if he was watching the inn, which I doubt, he wouldn't have seen the bag of jewelry when Dave and Geordie went out. We've kept his duffel bag and the larger items here. In fact, I'm hoping you can have your compass back immediately, and Zeb can have his telescope."

"Yeah," Rick said. "If he does come here and sees the bag and feels the weight of those things in it, it may be enough to convince him you've kept all his loot here overnight."

Lee spoke for the first time. "I'm not sure I'd believe it."

"We put out a false radio call in case he's monitoring that somehow," Craig said. "We sent out the fact that the state police couldn't come tonight, and an officer will stay here. But you'll have two, and Rick and I will be on the alert all night."

The doorbell rang, and Jillian peered toward the lobby. "That's Don Reece. Maybe we should have told him not to come."

"We don't want Don in danger," Kate said.

"We'll loop him in," Craig assured them. When Jillian had installed Don on the front desk and returned to the living room, Craig was saying, "If Max Pelletier is as clever as we think he is, he won't try to come in the front door."

"How will he get in?" Lee asked.

"The master key card he stole will open the side door as well," Craig said. "Jillian and Kate could have recoded those so that no one could use an old one. But we decided not to, to give Pelletier a false sense of security. If he tries to sneak in either door, we'll be waiting for him."

Zeb shook his head. "Isn't he the marine biologist?"

"So he said," Rick told him. "He was lying about that."

"Why am I not surprised?" Kate asked bitterly. "It was too fancy. He should have said he was a plumber or something."

"Then you'd have asked him to fix the pipes in the Scout Finch Room," Rick said with a bit of a sneer on his lips.

Kate scowled. "Okay, then, an accountant. Something plain."

"Well, he didn't, so that's that," Rick said with a firm nod.

Craig gave her a tight smile. "We can't know what he's thinking, Kate. I'm guessing he pulled that occupation out of thin air as he was checking in. Maybe it's a longtime interest of his."

"How do we know for sure he's the jewelry store thief?" Lee asked.

"The man they caught in Dover-Foxcroft gave up his name and a description of his vehicle. He said Pelletier was heading toward Bucksport. He has contacts there, apparently.

"But in the storm ..." Jillian said.

"Yeah. He ended up here, and he used his real name. I guess he didn't have time to come up with phony I.D." Rick shrugged. "This is a pretty good place to lie low, when you think about it."

"If he'd just done that." Craig frowned. "But he couldn't resist sneaking into other guests' rooms and checking out their belongings. And apparently, he couldn't keep his hands off that antique compass in Kate's room and a few of your other antiques."

"Why did he steal the map and hide it in a different room?" Kate asked.

"Just to throw us off and keep us busy." Rick's tone expressed his remorse at not catching on to Max's ways earlier.

"Or maybe he couldn't sneak it out," Jillian said. "The frame's too big to fit in his duffel bag."

Lee nodded soberly. "Be thankful he didn't take it out of the frame. He might have damaged it."

"I suppose he got the idea of hiding the stuff at my place when I came over here to stay," Zeb said mournfully.

"Maybe so." Jillian patted his shoulder. "All the guests knew I was bringing my neighbor over here, and you were too sick for a couple of days to go check on things at your house. It was a handy place, and if they hid stuff off the premises, we wouldn't see anything in their luggage when we checked them out. He could just drive over there and pick it up."

"Plus, he found the bonus—Zeb's telescope." Kate shook her head. "He must have sneaked the loot out of the inn while we were away from the desk. Or else he went out the side door with it when no one was in the kitchen."

"He probably heard me and Luke talking about the generator being out there and using that door," Rick said. "I guess we were a little sloppy."

"Don't blame yourself. All of us were focusing on the guests and keeping them safe and well fed. I didn't see any harm in updating them on progress toward getting the water and heat back, and we told everyone about the generator."

"Jillian and I spent a lot of time in the kitchen while he was here," Kate said. "We didn't figure anyone else would arrive during the power outage, and it never occurred to us that someone would sneak out and then creep back in."

Craig folded his arms, frowning. "I suppose he could have dropped the duffel out a window."

"The shutters were up," Kate pointed out.

"But the upstairs ones are easy to open."

"Another thing," Jillian said slowly. "We haven't found the book of Washington Irving stories from the Rip Van Winkle Room yet."

"No, but I think it will turn up." Craig nodded reluctantly. "It may be in one of the other rooms now."

"That wasn't worth anything," Rick scoffed.

"How do we know?" Kate turned on him. "It was in the house when Mom and Dad bought it. It could be two hundred years old."

"I guess it's possible," Jillian said. "That collection first appeared around 1820."

"Yeah, and she would know." Kate's chin jutted out stubbornly. "She's been to Washington Irving's house."

Jillian couldn't help smiling. One of the last big projects she'd done as an English teacher was to take a dozen seniors on a two-day field trip to Tarrytown, New York, to visit Sunnyside, Irving's old estate. She and the other chaperones, as well as the students, had enjoyed the trip tremendously, and she'd had a soft spot for Rip Van Winkle and Ichabod Crane ever since.

"Well, it may just be a worthless old, beat-up volume someone had in their attic for decades and decided to sell at a yard sale," Rick said.

Kate scowled. "I bet it's special, and that nasty Max Pelletier knew it. If we get that book back, we're getting it appraised."

Jillian patted her shoulder. "Agreed. But what now? What are we supposed to do? Should we alert Luke and Roger and the Hallidays?"

"That might be best," Craig said.

Rick shook his head vehemently. "Why? If we keep the duffel bag in the office beside the safe, where he's likely to look for it, he won't go upstairs."

"But still," Jillian said. "If we think it's likely a murderer will come back here ... I'm just sayin', if I were a guest, I'd want to know."

"I think you're right," Zeb said. You could give them the option of moving to the hotel downtown."

Jillian eyed him with concern. "Do *you* want to go somewhere else, Zeb? I certainly don't want to put you and Lee in danger."

"Me? No. I want to be where the action is." Zeb winked at her.

"Even if you stay," Craig said quickly, "you need to keep to your rooms tonight and not get mixed up in this."

Jillian could tell Craig was worried. It would go against his nature to put civilians in a precarious position. She drew him aside and asked quietly, "Did your chief approve this plan?"

"He's gone home for the night. He told us to use our own discretion."

"But does he know you're hoping to lure Max here, with civilians on the premises?"

"Not exactly. He knows we put the stolen jewelry in the evidence room, and that we hope to draw Pelletier out if he's still on the peninsula. But he doesn't know the details." Craig sighed.

"It was Rick's idea, wasn't it? To keep the duffel bag here." She studied his face intently.

"Yes, but—"

"But Rick is smart, and you don't like to show any disloyalty."

Craig's lips pressed into a thin line.

"Don't you think the others should at least know?" she asked.

"Do you think they're more likely to get in the way if they know, or if they don't know and just blunder into it when they go down to get coffee or something?"

Jillian rested her hand on his arm. "I'm not sure. But safety first."

His eyes shifted away for a second, then back to her. "You're right. And thank you." Craig turned to the others. "Look, Jillian has a good point. I think we should tell the other guests and let them decide whether or not they want to stay here. It isn't really fair to leave them in the dark when we think there's a strong possibility Pelletier will come back for his loot."

His cell phone whirred, and he answered it. "Yeah, Geordie. Okay. Yeah. Thanks." He put the phone away. "One of our EMTs found Pelletier's car. It seems he abandoned it a block from the marina. At least, he's not in it now."

"Isn't the road flooded at the marina?" Kate asked.

"The water's gone down. It's possible to drive through there now," Craig replied.

Jillian looked from him to Rick. "So ... he'll steal another car?"

"Maybe he has, or will, but I think he's still in town," Rick said.

Craig nodded. "Dispatch has alerted the roadblock personnel that he may be driving another rig now."

"But if he's trapped in Skirmish Cove, how could he possibly think he could retrieve that bag and then get away with it?" Lee asked.

"By boat," Rick said grimly. "He can't get past the roadblock, so I think he'd steal a boat, not a car, and escape that way."

"And just abandon his vehicle?" Lee frowned.

"If you were trapped, and keeping your car meant a stiff jail sentence, what would you do?" Rick stared Lee down.

Jillian was uncomfortable with the tension in the air. She touched Craig's sleeve. "So, the other guests ...?"

"Yes, let's get them together and lay this out for them. If

they want to leave, we'll get an officer to escort them to the hotel downtown."

Rick opened his mouth then closed it and nodded. "Whatever you say, Sarge. But let's talk to them up in the lounge on the third floor. Just in case Pelletier's already hanging around and watching this place."

"All right," Craig said, "I'll go up and gather them in the lounge. Will you stay down here and keep an eye on things?"

"Sure." Rick got to his feet. "Zeb, Lee, how about we get you into your rooms now? You can take along some snacks and beverages if you like. And I'll double-check your windows."

"Kate and I will check all the downstairs windows that open besides Zeb and Lee's," Jillian said.

Kate nodded, and they tested the living room windows as Craig went out toward the stairway.

Ten minutes later, they were satisfied that the side door was locked, though a master key could open it, and the windows of the storage room, kitchen, dining room, and office were locked up tight. They paused in the lobby to bring Don up to speed, and Rick came along the hallway.

"Zeb and Lee are set for the night," he said. "Lee's going to stay in with Zeb for a while and play some cards, but he'll be okay. I cautioned him to look carefully before he crosses the hall to his room, and to make sure Zeb's door locks when he leaves him."

Even so, Jillian didn't feel completely easy. "I don't know what else we can do, but now I'm wondering if they would have been safer over at Zeb's."

"Nah." Rick shook his head. "Pelletier will look there. And besides, does Zeb even have a guest room?"

"No, I think Lee sleeps on the sofa when he visits."

"Ugh. Trust me, he'll sleep better over here. They both will."

"You could be right," Jillian said. "I know Zeb wants to get back into his own home, but he seems to realize he should wait."

"He's a sharp old bird." Rick's phone rang, and he pulled it from his pocket. "Diana."

He turned away and stepped inside the dining room. Jillian could hear his half of the conversation, and her heart went out to Diana.

"Yeah, I'm afraid so, honey. Okay. You sure? I'll call you as soon as we're done with this mess. Yeah, I love you too."

Jillian met Kate's eyes. Her sister regretted as much as she did that they were keeping Rick away from his family. But they both knew, as much as Rick loved Diana, they wouldn't be able to make him go home.

Rick came back to the lobby and said to the desk clerk, "Don, are you sure you want to be here tonight?"

"Yes. I figure you want things to look as normal as possible," Don replied. "I've got you and Sergeant Watkins both on speed dial if I need you."

"Good. Okay, I'll see you later." Rick set off up the stairway.

"I guess Kate and I should go upstairs and stay there," Jillian said.

"Yeah, let's go," Kate said. "You took your stuff up, right?"

"Yes, I managed that right after we ate dinner. Stairs or elevator?"

"Let's live a little and take the elevator. G'night, Don." Kate walked down the hall.

"Good night, ladies," Don sang with a twinkle in his eye.

Jillian smiled. "See you in the morning." She didn't like thinking that they might have reason to meet up again before it was time to start breakfast prep.

When they reached the third floor and stepped off the elevator, Luke and Roger were leaving the landing for the stairs. Jillian and Kate held back until they'd descended and then strode to the lounge, where they found Rick and Craig. The door to the Scarlett O'Hara Room was closed.

"What did they say?" Kate demanded.

"The Hallidays were a little apprehensive, but they talked it over and decided to stay," Craig replied. "I assured them the murder took place down below, and there was no reason for the thief to come up here if he turns up at all. So, they're keeping to their room. If all goes well, I'm sure they'll talk up the inn to all their friends and come back again another time. Now, Cowper was about at the end of his patience. He's going to the hotel."

"Did you call him an escort?" Jillian asked.

"No, he said he'd get himself there."

"Should I go down to check him out?"

"Let Don handle it," Rick said.

Jillian nodded slowly. "Okay. I'll just call down and alert Don that Mr. Cowper wants to leave." She turned away to make the quick call on her cell.

"What about Luke?" Kate asked.

"He's staying," Rick said. "That guy's got ice water in his veins."

Kate made a small, derisive sound in her throat.

"Well, we're off to bed," Jillian said. "Night-night."

"Good night," Craig said.

Rick gave them a languid wave. "Sleep tight."

When they were inside the Hornblower Room, Kate locked the door and put the safety chain in place. Jillian opened her bag on the unused bed, and Kate went to brush her teeth.

"I don't know about you, but I'm beat," Kate said when she

came out of the bathroom. She walked over to the window and made sure the curtains were completely closed.

"Yeah, me, too, but I want a shower." Jillian yawned. She pulled a few things from her bag and headed for the bathroom.

Kate undressed and put on her pajamas. This would be like sleeping in her big sister's room when she was a kid. Why didn't she feel pajama-party excited? Being exhausted might have something to do with it. She crawled into bed and reached for her electronic reader. No mysteries or family sagas tonight, though. She'd go straight for her nightly Bible reading. The streaming of water and the humming of the hair dryer lulled her, and she jerked awake twice.

Jillian came out of the bathroom just as she'd finally finished her chapter. Kate shut down her reader and laid it on the nightstand beside the clock.

"You ready to sleep?"

"Yeah." Jillian paused by the telescope. It looked much more modern than anything Horatio Hornblower would have used. "How much do we have this thing valued at?"

"I think two or three hundred dollars," Kate said.

"Is that all? Zeb's has got to be worth more than that."

Kate nodded. "It's old. And it's brass. It's also bigger than ours, and more powerful."

"I guess that explains why Max stole Zeb's and not ours."

Jillian climbed into bed, and Kate turned out her lamp. She closed her eyes, willing herself to sleep, but she kept thinking about the murder and the thefts, and Don, Craig, and Rick keeping watch. She rolled over and squinted at the digital clock. Nearly midnight. With a sigh, she wriggled down in the bed.

Instead of counting sheep, she counted eggs. They'd been able to stock up again, and there should be plenty for breakfast tomorrow. Should she have made more muffins?

She prayed silently, thanking God for keeping her family and the inn's guests safe since Dryer's murder. She listed off all the blessings she'd received that day. New guests to help make up their losses. Lee's safe arrival. Recovering the compass and Zeb's telescope. Finding a large part of the stolen jewelry. Don coming in to take the night shift on the desk. Geordie ... Her time with him was a bonus.

Her mind drifted hazily back to the breakfast menu, and she sat up with a catch in her breath. She hadn't taken the breakfast meats out of the freezer and put them in the refrigerator. With all the discussion about the thefts, she'd forgotten. Maybe Jillian had done it, but she didn't think so.

"Jillian?" she whispered.

No answer, but she could hear her sister's steady breathing.

With a sigh, Kate used her cell's flashlight app to locate her slippers and robe. She grabbed the master key from the desk, padded over to the door, and unlocked it quietly. Stepping into the lounge, she searched for Rick or Craig, but neither one was there now. They must be making rounds somewhere downstairs.

She shut the door and tiptoed to the stairs. If she used the elevator, its noise might wake up some people, and she'd have to explain her actions to the guys.

She started down the stairway, careful not to make any sound. As she descended into the well-lit lobby, goosebumps rose on her arms. Don wasn't at the desk. The front door was shut, as usual. Silly. *He probably went to the powder room.* She took the last three steps peering toward the closed office door, the dining room, and the hallway.

Don's feet, in his customary loafers, poked out from the hall end of the desk. Kate froze for a moment. A surge of adrenaline set her heart racing.

She ran the short distance and flung herself down on her knees in the cramped space between the counter and the wall behind. The folding camp chair he liked to use lay partly collapsed on its side beyond him.

"Don!" She whispered his name, instinct telling her not to cry out. She wriggled in by the wall and looked into his face. His eyes were shut, and his lips were slack. His shirt moved as he pulled in a breath, and she exhaled deeply.

God, what do I do? Maybe he'd had a heart attack. Should she call 911? Where were Rick and Craig?

"Don!"

He flinched and moved his head to the side, just enough so that Kate saw a smear of blood on the rug beneath his short-cropped hair.

She clenched her fists. *Think!*

On her knees, she crawled to the edge of the archway and shoved back her long hair. From her position, she could see much of the dining room and the length of the first-floor hall. Everything looked normal, and she heard nothing. She crawled back behind the desk and rose to her knees. Reaching over Don's feet and legs, she lifted the desk phone's receiver and keyed in #11 for the Hornblower Room.

It rang four times before Jillian said sleepily, "Yeah, Don?"

"It's Kate," she stage-whispered. "I'm in the lobby, and Don's unconscious."

23

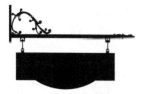

"What?" Jillian shrieked.

Kate yanked the receiver away from her ear for a second, then put it back.

"—happened? Where are the guys?"

"Hush," Kate whispered. "I don't know. It looks like someone clobbered him over the head. He's breathing, but I think we need an ambulance."

"I'll call one," Jillian said immediately.

Kate darted glances toward the stairs, the hall, and the dining room. "Okay, but call Craig or Rick first. Somebody's been here, and I need them." She hung up, wincing at the small clatter the receiver made in its cradle. Hunching down behind the desk, she listened. Were her brother and Craig in trouble too?

She swallowed hard and bent over Don once more. Taking his wrist, she felt his pulse. It seemed strong and steady. The wound wasn't bleeding much—at least, the stain on the rug hadn't spread.

Quiet footsteps approached down the stairs. Kate huddled

lower behind the desk. She couldn't see who was coming, but she didn't dare peek.

A moment later, someone leaned on the desk, sending a little creak from it. She held her breath.

"Kate, you okay?"

She looked up into Craig's taut face and nodded. "Thank God, you're here. I don't know who did this to him, but he's got a head wound. Where's Rick?"

"He's supposed to be keeping watch in the storage room behind the kitchen."

She hesitated. "You'd better check on him."

"Yeah." Instead of turning away, Craig took out his cell phone and punched a couple of buttons. Holding it to his ear, he waited.

Kate was about to speak when Craig said softly, "You okay, buddy?"

She shut her eyes for a moment in silent gratitude. Her brother had answered the call.

"Listen," Craig went on, "someone's attacked Don Reece. I'm guessing our suspect's in the building. Should I come out there? Okay. If I hear anything from out your way, I'll be there." He stuck the phone in his pocket and gazed down at Kate. "All quiet so far. Do you think Don will be all right?"

"I don't know for sure, but his pulse and respiration are steady. Jillian said she'd call an ambulance."

Craig nodded. "Let's hope they don't have to detour. Did you check the office?"

Kate caught her breath. She'd almost forgotten about the duffel bag in the office. "No." She swiveled and reached for the office door's handle, but it didn't budge.

"Still locked," she whispered.

"I'll try the hall door."

"Have you got the master key?"

He nodded and tiptoed around the corner. A few seconds later, she heard a click as the lock engaged, and he was back.

"It was locked, and I didn't see anyone down the hall. I looked inside, and the bag's still there."

"You told Jillian to stay put, right?" she asked.

"I sure did. I wish you were up there too."

Kate shook her head vigorously. "I can help here. You need my eyes and ears."

He sighed as though not sure he agreed with her. "Probably best if you don't go up those stairs alone."

"Craig, why would Max do this to Don? I mean, he didn't have to come in the front door, right? He could sneak in the side door."

"Well, that was the plan. Or it's what we expected. That's why Rick's out there in the storage room."

"Unless ..." Kate frowned.

"What are you thinking?"

"Unless he knew someone was watching that door. Otherwise, why would he have to get past Don?"

"Yes, but ... Kate, Don appears to have been hit from behind. Max couldn't come through the front door and do that to him."

She scowled. No matter how she imagined the scene, Craig was right. Somehow, the assailant had gotten behind Don while he was behind the desk.

"What if he was already inside?" she said slowly.

Craig's eyebrows morphed together. "What do you mean?"

"What if he knew about the secret rooms and hid in there? Or the attic?"

"We searched the secret rooms and the attic."

"But that was yesterday."

Craig wasn't buying it, she could tell from his expression.

"Ever since Rick and Jillian chased him out of Zeb's house, he's been on the run. They found his car ..."

Kate stood and held his gaze. "I'm talking about after he ditched his car. What if he hiked back here and sneaked in the side door while we were all elsewhere?"

"Most of us were in the living room for quite a while after supper. And no one was in the kitchen." Craig clenched his teeth.

"Yes, and he could have entered the storeroom then through the side door and hidden there until most of us went to bed. He's not there now, or Rick would've found him. Somehow, he got upstairs—Now, bear with me," she said quickly, as Craig seemed about to interrupt. "Imagine that he got in here with his master key and hid where you'd already searched. He waited till late, when things got quiet."

"There's still Rick, Don, and me to get by."

"Yes, and if he was upstairs or somewhere out here, other than the storeroom—"

"I know he wasn't in the storeroom tonight. Rick and I searched it thoroughly before he took up his post there."

"Okay," Kate said. "So, he was somewhere out here or upstairs. And he had to pass Don to get back to the kitchen to escape, either by coming down the stairs or by using the elevator or the hallway it's in. But the elevator's too risky. The noise. And someone might see the door open."

"I agree." Craig was listening to her now, thinking it out.

Kate nodded. "So, he sneaks downstairs. Maybe he waits until Don goes for a cup of coffee or to use the restroom. He hides, and when Don comes back to the desk, he whacks him."

"Then where is he now?" Craig asked.

"Someplace on this floor."

They gazed at each other for a moment.

"Stay here with Don," Craig said. He strode to the dining

room doorway, looked cautiously inside, and reached to flip a switch. Light flooded the large room. He peered around and then advanced, out of Kate's sight.

She looked down at Don. As soon as she knew he was safe, she'd call his wife.

He gave a faint moan, and she scurried in beside him.

"Don, it's okay. Help is coming."

He blinked, and his eyes opened in narrow slits. "Kate? Oh!" He reached a hand toward the gash on the back of his skull.

"Easy. Someone hit you on the head. We've called for an ambulance."

She listened for a siren but heard nothing.

"That robber guy?" Don's voice was scratchy.

"We don't—" She stopped as Don's eyes widened. He opened his mouth to speak, and she felt movement behind her —a stir of air, a faint rustling of cloth.

Kate twisted around to find herself face-to-face with Max Pelletier just as something heavy and metallic came down toward her head. She jerked away, and the tool landed hard on her shoulder.

In spite of the pain, she shoved herself toward him, lowering her head. There was little room for her to maneuver behind the desk, but Max flew backward. She fell with him, landing heavily on top of him. The tool flew from his hand and clattered on the floor.

Her left arm and shoulder hurt too badly to use them, but she pummeled him with her right fist. Aiming for his face, she punched repeatedly. Max yelped and pulled his head back. Her next blow hit his Adam's apple. He wheezed in a breath and gave a choking, hacking cough.

"Easy, Kate!"

She didn't know whose voice it was at first, but strong

hands lifted her off Max's body and Craig grabbed the sprawled man's shoulders.

"On your face!" Craig leaned over Max's form with handcuffs in his hand.

The person holding her away from Max pulled her a few steps farther toward the stairs. As Max slowly rolled over, Craig cuffed his hands behind his back.

She wiggled until she could see her brother's face next to hers.

"Rick!"

"Yeah. You okay?"

"My arm hurts."

"Did he hit you with that pipe wrench?"

"Yeah."

"Okay, let's sit you down." He guided her into the dining room and pulled out a chair at the nearest table. As Kate sank into it, the faint wail of a siren caught her attention.

"You'll need to unlock the door for the EMTs," she told Rick.

"Just sit still."

Other voices overlapped one another, and she lifted her chin. Lee and Zeb were in the lobby, peppering Don and Craig with questions as Rick marched to the front door. Flashing red lights gave the gathering in the lobby a festive look as two EMTs came inside.

"Hi, Linda," Rick said.

"Thank you, Lord," Kate whispered.

"Somebody's hurt here?"

Kate recognized Linda Niles, from the local fire department's rescue unit. The second EMT was a man she didn't know.

"Yes, our desk clerk, Don Reece," Rick said. "Head injury. Right over here. And then my sister, in there."

"I know Don," Linda said.

By then, Lee had righted Don's chair and helped him into it. Linda was smaller than her partner, and she squeezed in behind the desk, beside Don.

Rick came into the dining room with the other EMT.

"Kate, do you know Scott?"

She shook her head and winced as pain ran from her shoulder up the side of her neck.

"Let him take a look at you."

By the time she'd explained to Scott what happened to her and he'd gently probed her shoulder, arm, and neck, several more people had entered the room. Kate looked up at Jillian, Luke, and Zeb.

"Are you okay?" Jillian demanded.

"I ... I think so. I'm sore."

"I think you should go to the hospital and have a doctor check you out," Scott said.

"No, nothing's broken. I'm sure I'll have a big bruise, but I want to stay here." They'd be an hour getting to the hospital by the detour, and they would probably just tell her to rest and take painkillers. She reached out to Jillian. "Don't let them take me."

Jillian gave a grimace of indecision.

"She's a big girl," Zeb said. "Let her make her own choice."

"I guess so." Jillian met Scott's gaze. "I'm her sister, and we're staying in the same room tonight. I'll look after her."

Scott stood and drew Jillian aside. Kate figured he was either telling her why she should go to the hospital or telling her what to watch for throughout the rest of the night.

"You sure you're all right?" Luke was staring at her with the ultimate manly concern molding his face.

Somehow, his solicitous expression didn't move Kate. She wished Geordie was here.

From the lobby, she heard Craig's voice clearly as he asked his prisoner, "Why did you do it, Max? Why did you stab Alan Dryer?"

"I ... I didn't mean to kill him. It happened so fast. I was in his room ..." His voice was scratchy, and Kate hoped his throat still hurt.

"Yeah," Craig said. "You were ransacking it, and he walked in on you, right?"

Jillian strode to the opening and stood listening in the archway between the dining room and the lobby.

"I reacted without thinking about it," Max said.

Jillian stirred and stepped forward. "If you weren't thinking, why did you put towels on the bed and lift him up there?"

"I ... I thought he'd live. I wasn't sure what to do, but ... by the time I put him up there, it was too late to do anything else to help him. Honest, I didn't mean to kill him."

"No, just steal his ring and let him bleed out," Jillian said bitterly.

"I need a lawyer," Max croaked out.

"There'll be plenty of time for that once we get you to the police station," Craig told him. "You're under arrest for the murder of Alan Dryer." He recited the Miranda rights and asked if Max understood. "I'm sure you'll be charged with a second count of murder in the Bangor jewelry store robbery, not to mention several counts of theft, armed robbery, breaking and entering, and the attempted murder of Mr. Reece and Miss Gage."

"All right, your ride's here. Let's go." Rick spoke from near the front door, his voice crisp and authoritative.

Lee entered the dining room, and Jillian turned back and came to her sister's side.

"What's happening?" Kate asked.

Lee gave her a wan smile. "They're taking Pelletier to the police station."

"Good," Kate said vehemently, and those gathered around her chuckled.

Craig came in and crouched beside her chair. "Kate, I'm so sorry this happened to you."

"I'll be okay. Thanks for coming to my rescue, though."

"You were holding your own."

"I hope I hurt him as bad as he hurt me." She immediately felt guilty at the ferocity of her tone.

"You gave him a good one in the throat. Linda checked him over, and she says he'll recover just fine. I'm sorry Rick and I didn't get out there faster."

Forgiveness, she thought. *I really should forgive him.* But it went against her instincts. "Where was he before he hit me?" Kate looked around, her head swimming, and she sucked in a breath.

"We're not sure, but he may have been down the hall in the closet past the elevator.

"No, that's locked."

"Don't forget, Max made himself a key to everything. It's also possible he lurked in the alcove down by Lee's room, waiting for a chance to get in the office. But personally, I'm betting on the closet."

Jillian bent toward her, resting a hand on Craig's shoulder. "Can I get you anything, Kate?"

"Just get me to my bed. Oh, and I think I'll use the elevator this time."

Scott stepped forward. "If you're sure you don't want to come with us ..."

"I don't, but thanks anyhow." Kate lumbered to her feet, and Jillian caught her arm.

"I'll catch up with you tomorrow for a complete statement," Craig said.

Kate groaned. As they came into the lobby, the front door was closing on Max and two police officers. Rick came and blocked her way, looking her up and down.

"Was that Geordie?" Kate asked.

"Yes, and Dave Hall. Don't worry, I told Geordie he can call on my sister tomorrow, after you've had a rest."

"Since when do I need your permission—"

"Since you started jumping on murderers." Rick's face softened. "Nice job, sis."

"Thanks. For everything."

"Well, I thought you'd like to know, he had the knife on him."

Kate blinked up at him. "The one that killed Alan Dryer?"

Rick nodded. "We assume so. It's now in an evidence bag, going with Dave and Geordie to the station, along with that wrench he used on you and Don. Be glad he didn't come at you with the knife."

"I'll say."

"Now, go to bed."

"Wait." Kate waved feebly toward the front desk. "Who's going to ..."

"I am," Rick said firmly. "Now, get out of here. I need to call my wife."

"Come on," Jillian said softly in her ear, and Kate let her sister lead her to the elevator.

24

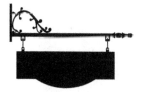

The next morning, Jillian manned the front desk after breakfast. When Luke showed up in the lobby with his roller bag, she stood and smiled at him.

"Checking out, Luke?"

"Yeah. I've got to say, you have a really nice place here. I know this week was challenging, but you came through for us guests in every way."

"Thanks. Tell all your friends and send them here."

"Don't worry, I will."

He laid his room key on the counter, and Jillian handed him his receipt. Luke glanced at it.

"Doesn't seem like you've charged me enough."

"You did help us out with the shutters and the generator, and ... well, I know you're having some problems at work. Kate and I agreed not to charge you for any of the extra meals."

"That's generous of you."

"Just don't tell your friends *that.*"

He laughed and then sobered, sending a plaintive look toward the dining room. Jillian expected him to ask where Kate was, or at least to tell her to say goodbye to Kate for him, but he did neither.

Taking the handle of his bag, he said, "I expect we'll see each other at Max's trial."

Jillian grimaced. "Yeah. That could be a while, though."

"Yeah. It will take them a while just to sort through all the charges. Well, goodbye, Jillian."

"Goodbye, Luke."

The Hallidays had checked out earlier, so Jillian left her post. Two guests who had been booked for that night had canceled. They expected three others to come in later, but not for several hours. She headed down the hallway and arrived at Zeb's door at the same time Lee left his room across the hall.

"Well, hi," he said. "I was just going to help Uncle Zeb get ready to move home."

She chuckled. "I was thinking the same thing. You don't want to stay for lunch?"

"No, I think we've been here long enough. And Zeb wants to get his telescope back where it belongs and make sure it wasn't damaged."

"If it was, he should tell Craig or Rick, and they'll add it to the list of damages Max carried out."

"Did he do any damage to the hotel?"

"You mean besides the carpet, the mattress, and the linens in Alan Dryer's room? We haven't found a missing antique book yet. I guess scratches on doors and drawers he picked don't count."

Lee gave a low whistle. "Will you have to sue him to get satisfaction for those things?"

"I'm not sure we want to bother. Yes, he owes us, but it could take more time and effort than we want to put into it. We'll probably just make replacements and try to forget it."

"I know I'll never forget this adventure." Lee eyed her soberly. "Jillian, Uncle Zeb showed me his will this morning."

She nodded. Zeb had asked her for the document at breakfast, and she'd taken it to him. "I hope you're okay with it."

"Sure." He hesitated.

"Not upset that he's leaving me his flags?"

Lee laughed. "No, not a bit. But ..."

"There's something else, isn't there?" Jillian frowned. "I knew it! He added something after I left the room to find witnesses, and he wouldn't let me see it afterward."

Lee let out a sigh. "I'm not sure I should tell you. He obviously didn't want you to know. But still, I think you should be prepared."

"Prepared? For what?"

"If I ... predecease Uncle Zeb ..."

"Hold it right there." She held up both hands to stop him. "That is not going to happen, Lee."

"Agreed. But, if it should ... well, I'll just say that you've been a wonderful friend and neighbor to him. I can't think of another person whose name should be in there instead of yours."

A lump was growing in Jillian's throat, and she swallowed hard. "I think I understand, and I don't like it."

"Hey." He smiled down at her. "It's not going to happen, so let's just let him have his way."

"We always do."

"Right." Lee turned and knocked on the door.

Zeb called, "Come in."

Jillian followed Lee inside, but her unsettled feeling wouldn't leave her.

Half an hour later, she went out on the porch with Kate and the Wildings. While Lee loaded their luggage and Zeb's telescope into his car's trunk, Jillian wrapped her arms around his uncle.

"Bye-bye, Zeb. I'll be over to see you and Lee tomorrow."

"All righty." Zeb planted a kiss on her cheek and turned to Kate.

Kate gave him a hug. "Come back soon."

"I will, you can be sure."

"We'll be watching for your flag signal tomorrow morning," Jillian told him.

"Aye. We'll run it up. In fact, I'll have Lee put one up as soon as we're in the house and settled."

"Wonderful," Jillian said.

Lee came back and mounted the steps. "All set, Uncle Zeb?"

"I am if you are."

Lee grinned and shook hands with Kate, then Jillian. "I can't thank you enough for the wonderful care you gave Zeb, and for taking care of me, too, when the need arose."

A moment later, they were off and out the driveway.

"Geordie called me," Kate said as they entered the lobby.

"Oh? Is this about your plans for tonight?"

Kate nodded, smiling. "Sheldon's Seafood is reopening today. We're going there for supper."

"Sounds good." Jillian went behind the desk and started clicking away on the computer keyboard.

"What are you doing?" Kate asked.

"Deactivating Zeb and Lee's room keys and issuing new master cards. I don't want any chance anybody can get in when we're not looking."

"Good idea."

Jillian looked up as Craig came down the stairs two at a time.

"What's up?" she asked.

Craig held up a large brown book. "Guess what I found in the attic."

Kate's jaw dropped.

"Aha," Jillian said. "Washington Irving tales, I presume."

He nodded. "Looks like you were right. Max hid out in the attic for a while. I found this on the floor, along with an empty soda can and a couple of food wrappers. Somehow he sneaked out of there and down into the closet by the elevator."

"Does that account for all the loot?" Kate asked.

"We think so. We've photographed the turquoise bracelet for evidence and will return it to Dr. Rowan. It matches the pictures she sent us exactly. And you've got your compass and your map already, and now this book. Dryer's ring will be kept in evidence for the murder trial."

Shaking her head, Jillian closed the computer program. "You had to mention the trial. We'll have a reunion then."

"Yeah, several of your guests will have to come back for that, but it won't be for months."

Kate eyed his jeans and jersey. "You're not on duty, are you?"

"Nope. I'm here on my own time. I couldn't sleep well last night, wondering where Pelletier hid out. I apologize to both of you."

"For what?" Jillian asked.

"I never should have had you leave the master key the way it was so he could get in. I see now how foolish that was."

"We all agreed last night that it seemed the best way to catch him."

"It also put you and all your guests in danger. Next time, I'll know better."

Jillian studied his sober face. "Will you get in trouble over that?"

"It was Rick's idea," Kate said quickly.

Craig frowned, considering for a moment. "Because the state police never got involved, probably not. If they'd been here, I doubt they'd have allowed it."

"And they might not have caught him," Jillian said.

Kate frowned. "It was scary, and I'm sorry Don was hurt, but I still think it was the right way to go."

"Oh, speaking of Don," Jillian said, "his daughter, Hannah, called me a little while ago. She said the doctor let him come home early this morning. He's supposed to take it easy for a few days, but otherwise he's okay."

"What about tonight?" Kate asked.

"Don't worry. I called Wayne Johnson, and he'll come in tonight. He's our weekend night clerk," she explained to Craig.

"Well, good. Now I'm going home and catch up on a whole bunch of stuff." He smiled beguilingly at Jillian. "I hope we can do something together tomorrow night."

She grinned. "I hear Sheldon's is open."

"Terrific."

"Geordie and I are going there tonight. We'll give you a review." Kate glanced at her sister, then at Craig. Jillian didn't take her eyes off Craig's face. "Well, I think I have stuff to catch up on in the kitchen." Kate slipped out of the lobby.

Craig placed both hands on the check-in counter and leaned toward Jillian. "I'll pick you up around six?"

"Sounds good."

They met halfway over the desk for a kiss, and Craig left smiling.

The end

ABOUT THE AUTHOR

Susan Page Davis is the author of more than one hundred books. Her books include Christian novels and novellas in the historical romance, mystery, and romantic suspense genres. Her work has won several awards, including the Carol Award, three Will Rogers Medallions, and two Faith, Hope, & Love Reader's Choice Awards. She has also been a finalist in the WILLA Literary Awards and Selah Awards, and a multi-time finalist in the Carol Awards. A Maine native, Susan has lived in Oregon and now resides in western Kentucky with her husband Jim, a retired news editor. They are the parents of six and grandparents of eleven.

Visit her website at: https://susanpagedavis.com.

MORE SKIRMISH COVE MYSTERIES

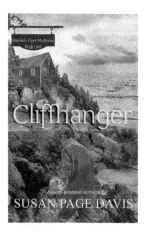

Cliffhanger—Book One

A charming themed inn, breaking waves, and a missing guest. What more could one ask?

The Novel Inn's reopening goes smoothly until a guest vanishes. The new owners prepare for their first large group—a former squad of cheerleaders meeting for a reunion. Things go awry when the head cheerleader fails to show up. Sisters Kate and Jillian, the innkeepers, enlist the help of their brother Rick, a local police officer. They're confident the missing woman will be found, but they soon learn to expect the unexpected, even during a walk on the beach.

Get your copy here:

https://scrivenings.link/cliffhanger

———

The Plot Thickens—Book Two

Jillian only wants to redecorate one room at the Novel Inn—but first, she has to deal with murder.

Murder strikes Skirmish Cove during the coastal town's winter carnival. Jillian Tunney, part owner of the nearby Novel Inn, discovers the body of a clerk at her favorite bookstore. With her sister Kate and brother, Officer Rick Gage, she tries to find out who killed him.

Meanwhile, Jillian is immersed in redecorating one of the themed rooms, but Kate is annoyed when a mysterious guest at the inn doesn't want to leave his room. The innkeepers find they have way too many secrets to solve.

Get your copy here:

https://scrivenings.link/theplotthickens

TRUE BLUE MYSTERIES BY SUSAN PAGE DAVIS

Blue Plate Special—Book One

Campbell McBride drives to her father's house in Murray, Kentucky, dreading telling him she's lost her job as an English professor. Her father, private investigator Bill McBride, isn't there or at his office in town. His brash young employee, Nick Emerson, says Bill hasn't come in this morning, but he did call the night before with news that he had a new case.

When her dad doesn't show up by late afternoon, Campbell and Nick decide to follow up on a phone number he'd jotted on a memo sheet. They learn who last spoke to her father, but they also find a dead body. The next day, Campbell files a missing persons report. When Bill's car is found, locked and empty in a secluded spot, she and Nick must get past their differences and work together to find him.

Get your copy here:

https://scrivenings.link/blueplatespecial

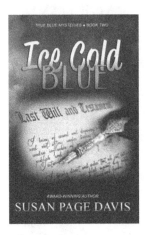

Ice Cold Blue—Book Two

Campbell McBride is now working for her father Bill as a private investigator in Murray, Kentucky. Xina Harrison wants them to find out what is going on with her aunt, Katherine Tyler.

Katherine is a rich, reclusive author, and she has resisted letting Xina visit her for several years. Xina arrived unannounced, and Katherine was upset and didn't want to let her in. When Xina did gain entry, she learned Katherine fired her longtime housekeeper. She noticed that a few family heirlooms previously on display have disappeared. Xina is afraid someone is stealing from her aunt or influencing her to give them her money and valuables. True Blue accepts the case, and the investigators follow a twisting path to the truth.

Get your copy here:

https://scrivenings.link/icecoldblue

Persian Blue Puzzle—Book Three

An antisocial cat, an elusive investment broker, and a hope-selling psychic raise suspicions in a western Kentucky community.

Someone's broken into Miss Louanne's house. Campbell McBride and her father Bill have moved their home and detective business into an old Victorian house. Their new neighbors bring in unexpected cases for True Blue Investigations to unravel.

While helping Miss Louanne look for her missing cat, Campbell learns of other suspicious activities in Murray. Another neighbor tells the detectives about a stranger in town who's peddling an investment plan. They aren't sure any crimes have been committed, but they're intrigued enough for Campbell to visit a psychic along with police detective Keith Fuller's mom and to start checking up on the financier.

Things heat up when a customer threatens the psychic and then she vanishes.

Get your copy here:

https://scrivenings.link/persianbluepuzzle

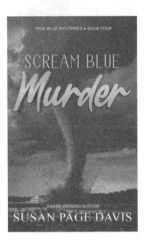

Scream Blue Murder

by Susan Page Davis

True Blue Mysteries—Book Four

An old photo, a twister, and a friend being stalked ...

A tornado rips through town, and Campbell McBride and her dad take shelter. Afterward, they try to help others who were hard hit, and a body is discovered in the debris of a cottage near their friends' home. Was the man dead before the twister struck? The owners of the ruined cottage hire True Blue Investigations to help identify the victim and find out how he got on their property. Meanwhile, among the volunteers, Campbell meets her mother's old school friend, Jackie. It seems Jackie married her mom's former boyfriend—and now she has eyes on Campbell's widowed father.

Get your copy here:

https://scrivenings.link/screambluemurder

THE HOMEWARD TRAILS SERIES BY SUSAN PAGE DAVIS

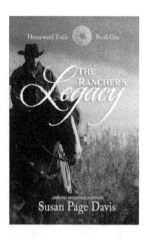

The Rancher's Legacy—Book One

Will Rogers Medallion—Copper Award Winner

Matthew Anderson and his father try to help neighbor Bill Maxwell when his ranch is attacked. On the day his daughter Rachel is to return from school back East, outlaws target the Maxwell ranch. After Rachel's world is shattered, she won't even consider the plan her father and Matt's cooked up—to see their two children marry and combine the ranches.

Meanwhile in Maine, sea captain's widow Edith Rose hires a private investigator to locate her three missing grandchildren. The children were abandoned by their father nearly twenty years ago. They've been adopted into very different families, and they're scattered across the country. Can investigator Ryland Atkins find them all while the elderly woman still lives? His first attempt is to find the boy now called Matthew Anderson. Can Ryland survive his trip into the wild Colorado Territory and find Matt before the outlaws finish destroying a legacy?

Get your copy here:

https://scrivenings.link/therancherslegacy

———

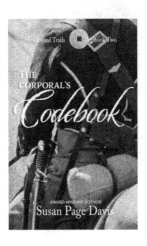

The Corporal's Codebook—Book Two

Jack Miller stumbles through the Civil War, winding up a telegrapher and cryptographer for the army. In the field with General Sherman in Georgia, he is captured along with his precious cipher key.

His captor, Hamilton Buckley, thinks he should have been president of the Confederacy, not Jefferson Davis. Jack doubts Buckley's sanity and longs to escape. Buckley's kindhearted niece, Marilla, might help him—but only if Jack helps her achieve her own goal.

Meanwhile, a private investigator, stymied by the difficulty of travel and communication in wartime, is trying his best to locate Jack for the grandmother he longs to see again but can barely remember.

Get your copy here:

https://scrivenings.link/thecorporalscodebook

———

The Sister's Search—**Book Three**

A young woman searches for her missing brother and finds much more awaits her—if she can escape war-torn Texas.

Molly Weaver and her widowed mother embark on an arduous journey at the end of the Civil War. They hope to join Molly's brother Andrew on his ranch in Texas. When they arrive, Andrew is missing and squatters threaten the ranch.

Can they trust Joe, the stranger who claims to be Andrew's friend? Joe's offer to help may be a godsend—or a snare. And who is the man claiming to be Molly's father? If he's telling the truth, Molly's past is a sham, and she must learn where she really belongs.

Get your copy here:

https://scrivenings.link/thesisterssearch

Scrivenings
PRESS
Quench your thirst for story.
www.ScriveningsPress.com

Stay up-to-date on your favorite books and authors with our free e-newsletters.

ScriveningsPress.com

CPSIA information can be obtained
at www.ICGtesting.com
Printed in the USA
LVHW081223310523
748422LV00009B/125